Everyone was naked.

From where Jamie Parker stood next to the bright aqua-colored swimming pool of the Paradise Lost Resort, a hundred-plus people were sunning, splashing, or surveying each other, all in the nude. And here she was, a part of it, showing her boobs, buns, and more, and so was her pretend boyfriend, Jim McKenna, who was definitely showing more. The two undercover cops were definitely "uncovered" for the whole resort to see.

A tall, busty, attractive blonde wearing only high heels passed by, giving them a very enticing smile. McKenna awkwardly smiled back.

"Actually, I think she smiled at you," he said softly to Jamie. And he was probably right; this place wasn't just for getting a tan.

A soft mid-afternoon Florida breeze touched both their naked bodies. It actually felt good. Jamie's long hair blew softly across her face. They looked at each other and laughed. She thought about what a different world they were now in, and a part of—a world hidden from the outside reality of routine jobs and routine lives. She smiled to herself.

For Jamie, Paradise Lost might just actually be her "Paradise Found."

As they walked to the pool, not looking like a "pretend" couple, but like a real couple, neither knew a mysterious set of eyes had been watching them the whole time and now continued to follow them.

For Jamie, her "Paradise Found" was soon to become "Paradise Hell."

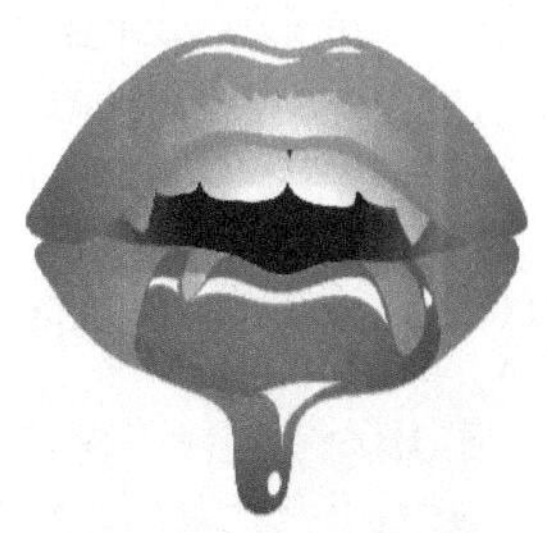

THE NAKED DEAD

by Joe Janowicz

This is a work of fiction. Names, characters, places, and incidents either are the product of the author's imagination or are used fictitiously. Any resemblance to actual persons, living or dead, names, events, or locales is entirely coincidental.

Copyright ©2019 by Joe Janowicz

Editor: Elly Stevens
Cover Design and Formatting: Megan J. Parker

Printed in the United States of America
by NewField Publications

All rights reserved. No part of this book may be reproduced or transmitted in any form or by any means, electronic or mechanical, including photocopying, recording or by any information storage and retrieval system, without the written permission of the Publisher, except where permitted by law.

For additional information on Joe's books and comic books, go to **JoeJanowiczAuthor.com**

*When the clothes come off,
the killing begins.*

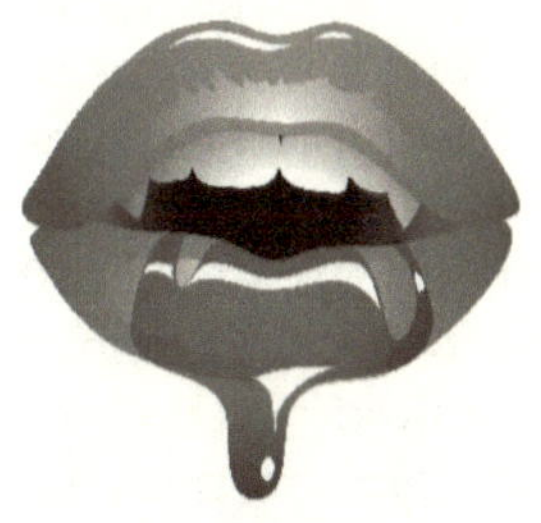

CHAPTER 1

Johnny Rains had a nice ass. A real nice ass. It had that round, extraordinary tight bubble shape, and it always drew a lot of looks from both women and men of all ages. There was even a rumor that it was so tight you could bounce quarters off of it. But not today. Today it was soggy, very discolored, and somewhat wrinkled as it bobbed in the early morning pool water waiting for someone to discover it. It was a "dead" ass. So was Johnny Rains. Face down, floating with arms outstretched, almost forming the shape of a human cross. Not that Johnny was religious in his life. He may have been, but it didn't matter. He was the No. 1 box-office male porn star in both adult movies and internet sex photos. Handsome, personable, wealthy, long blonde hair and a hot-looking killer "bod," as his fans and multiple lovers would say. He had it all, and, he "had" it all.

He was nicknamed "Long Dong Johnny," and deservedly so. Longer than a ruler and thicker than a...but that's another story. And here he was in his prime—youthful, early 30s, dead naked in the breaking dawn in the overly large heart-shaped main pool at the Paradise Lost Naturist Resort, after what was an amazing night of hundreds of nudists, swingers, and porn stars who gathered together to celebrate this year's first night of the week-long, annual Nude-a-Rama Convention, dancing the night away to one of the hippest naked DJs on the planet. Johnny was the life of the party, kissing, hugging, and mugging for pictures and autographs.

With a bottle of Don Perignon champagne in one hand, and two naked, busty young babes on either side of his golden tanned muscular body, he was last seen on his way to a resort bungalow to bed them both as the clock struck midnight. Rock hard, Long Dong John. Oh, what a night he was to have! Sex, sex, and more sex. And for dessert? Death. His.

It would be six hours before a wandering drunk came to the edge of the resort main pool to relieve himself when he looked down into the aqua blue water and found Johnny floating by under his arced pee. And when they finally pulled Johnny out of the water, it was a sight to behold, or a sight to be retold.

"Oh, my God," exclaimed a young female onlooker, who was quite a looker herself, totally naked, while pointing at him as they pulled him out of the water.

"He has a teenie..."

Yes, freshly dead Johnny had a "teenie" weenie. His legendary extra-long manhood, his money-making "tool" of the trade, had suffered an embarrassing turn of the events, "shrinkage." That's what cold water does to fingers and...a legendary penis. Shrinkage, man's worst friend. And, certainly, no friend to a major porn star named Johnny.

But that was the least of his dead worries; he was also completely drained of all his blood. All.

At least he had died with a frozen smile on his sunken, bloodless face.

CHAPTER 2

Jamie Parker enjoyed her morning run. It had become a part of her routine, and she looked forward to it each and every day as she ran along the Tampa, Florida, tree-lined jogging trails and flowery gardens in a nearby park. It was a great way to start a new day, especially when the morning sun accompanied her every stride. It was also necessary for her to stay fit for her job.

Running was a metaphor for where her life was leading. All was good, or mostly good, from a single woman's perspective in the crazy world that surrounded her day-to-day in a job as a police detective. Her promotion from street police work to the criminal detective unit had just happened and, while it came with a pay raise, it also required her to be on call at anytime, anywhere.

She had just purchased her own first little house—no more apartments for her—and lived alone without the baggage of previous roommates or former boyfriends who always wanted to move in to "play house" and save themselves some money. Then there was Bentley, a Labrador she recently rescued from an animal shelter and who became her "home-time" companion. Brown and gold with that still growing look, Bentley was more than a dog, he was her best friend. She always talked to him after a hard day's work, and he listened attentively and never talked back. Maybe a bark or two, or a few fond licks to show his interest and love. And today it was like most mornings, Bentley running alongside her, as she carried a long leash only because the law demanded it. The "law," she smiled to herself. A lot of rules. The good ones protected the community; the other ones were just a pain in the butt but had to be enforced. As a police officer, she knew rules kept order and were needed to stop the bad guys. And so, she smiled even more as she dropped the leash and let Bentley, named after her favorite uncle Ben who passed away a few years back, run for a short distance on his own.

"What are they gonna do, arrest me?" she laughed to herself.

As the park trail came to an end, so did her morning jog. Twenty minutes. That's all she could fit in before a nice cold shower and big, hearty breakfast to prepare herself for another day of unknowns. In her business, that was part of the what made the job so interesting. The "unknowns." And today, a lot of unknowns were waiting for her.

Picking up the dog leash, she crossed over Millbrook Road and back to her modest-size starter home, a one-story ranch, with two same-size small bedrooms. Jamie only really needed one, as Bentley slept with her. It had a nice living room with a small unused fireplace, an updated kitchen, a bathroom with a big tiled shower—also updated, and the typical "Florida room." Not bad for a fifty-some-year-old house built when her home state was growing with retirees. It was modestly furnished with just a little bit of this and a little bit of that, as she waited for the next paycheck before additional living items could be purchased.

Jamie lived all of her life in the "Sunshine State," and even went to a mid-state, growing, top college, the University of Central Florida, "UCF," where she studied criminal justice, criminal law, and police leadership. At the top of her class, she was recruited by the Orlando Police department, and just over a year ago was offered a promotion and relocated to Tampa. She loved it there, as she was close enough to the beaches, parks, and jogging trails for her and Bentley to enjoy.

Her shower was too quick, and the breakfast was eaten too fast, but there was enough time for a few more kisses and licks from Bentley before she left to drive to her office. Her kindly neighbor, Mrs. Little, looked after Bentley if Jamie had to put in extra hours. She loved dogs and had two herself—both Pugs, Toby and Miss Pru, who followed her everywhere.

Police headquarters was about a 20-minute drive if enough green lights were in her favor, and not far from the main section of New Tampa, a growing suburb that was taking the place of an overcrowded downtown Tampa with new shops, restaurants, and lots and lots of people—retirees, snow birds, those "here-they-come-again" folks who came down south for the winter every year to get away from the snow and, of course, lots of tourists. A popular theme park wasn't far, and plenty of newly built and being built recreational areas and resorts dotted the coast and everywhere in between.

Hurriedly dressing while listening to the morning news and weather report, she reached for her holster and gun, attaching it to her side.

"A high of 90 degrees today with no chance of rain in sight for the next five days. Time to enjoy the sun and have fun in the days ahead!" a cheerful millennial weather reporter blurted out.

"Sun and fun," she thought to herself. That would have to wait for the weekend. It was Wednesday morning, middle of the week, "hump day" as the newscaster called it for the average 40-hour worker. Really not applicable to her, what with the double hours a detective puts in, both on and off the job. But she smiled knowing that this is what she wanted to do, and every day was a new day with different challenges. In the town of New Tampa, Florida, where the crime rate was lower than the rest of the state, and the last big case was solving the missing car stolen from a local dealership by the owner who drunkenly forgot where he put it, one could only hope for something a bit more exciting and a bit more challenging today. And that's when a police text notification buzzed on her cell phone and caught her attention.

Reading the text, her eyes widened, and she let out an interesting sigh.

"Oh my."

She texted back the words, "On my way," and called Mrs. Little to enlist her help. She patted Bentley goodbye, leaving him to protect the house while she started her day by protecting the world, and finding a killer in a nudist resort.

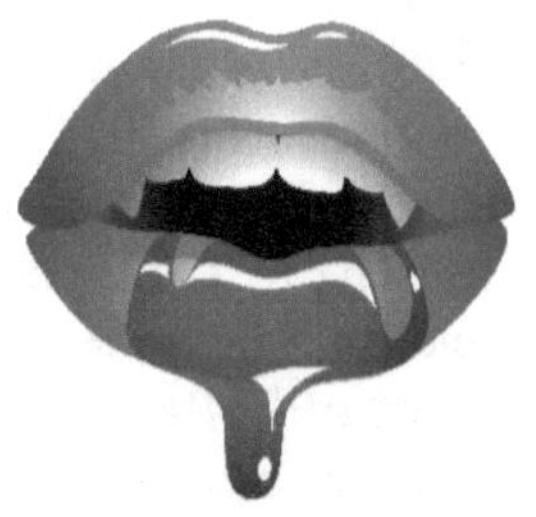

CHAPTER 3

"**H**oly shit! The mannequin has testicles!" a shocked woman's voice exclaimed.

And so, the 2nd naked victim was found.

As the coroner's crew and police were carting off the bagged body of Long Dong John, aka Johnny Rains, a cry came out from a nearby group of naked nosey onlookers. Just past the heart-shaped pool and next to its towering palm-tree-lined two-story waterfall, a series of resort shops led the way to the grand three-story entrance and clubhouse: A shop to buy food and beverages and some blow-up toys, the regular pool kind, not the sex kind. A shop with sex toys and sexy other things, the regular kind with batteries and hand cranks, not the pool kind. And a unisex clothing shop, minus swimwear but with all the many different naughty nighties and thongs for dongs with sequins and lace. And there, in the shop window, were three naked mannequins, each wearing next to nothing, to entice the inquisitive customer in purchasing the latest sexual fashions.

The first mannequin was dressed in a red see-through bra and panty set. "Hot." The second mannequin had bare plastic breasts with large metal nipple clamps and a leather peek-a-boo thong. "Hot and Painful." The third mannequin wasn't a mannequin at all. It was a bare-naked man attached to a large metal display rack holding him up. His face was discolored and sunken in. His head was held up with a gold-sequined belt wrapped around his forehead and attached to the rack. A similar one was attached to his waist. He was naked. He was dead. And he had a big set of balls.

"Jesus Christ, there's a dead man in the window!" shouted a naked woman carrying a towel over her shoulder on the way to the pool, her voice immediately drawing the attention of the police on scene.

"And look at his neck... There's blood dripping from two large punctures...two holes!" a naked male guest exclaimed while pointing at the man.

Two distinct, equal holes, as if bitten by some sort of creature. Holes that when looked at closely by the medical examiner appeared to have been dragged downward leaving a scratch, a mark, a slight tear in the skin leading to the openings in the neck. Two holes that looked like they were made by the fangs of a bat or maybe a vampire. Two fang marks on a body also drained of blood. Similar to the marks that would be found on the equally dead and drained Johnny Rains.

Being early morning, the shop was still closed, but apparently the horrific murder happened sometime in the middle of the night.

So, did the other.

When the local police first received the call about the body in the pool an hour earlier, two separate police cars drove hurriedly through the surrounding streets. At that point, there was a report of only one dead body. But after they got there, they found two.

New Tampa was a growing community. Lots of money coming into an area of Florida that used to be swampland with alligators and a lot of trailer parks in between. Today, it's a growing 24-square-mile region north of Tampa that has grown from a population of 7,000 residents in 1990 to nearly 50,000 today. There are gated communities with expensive homes and condos, malls, restaurants, mini-malls, more restaurants, and a state-of-the-art multi-million-dollar clothing-optional, make that "no clothing permitted" nudist resort. Why here and how? First, year-round, exceptionally good, if not great, weather to be butt naked in the sun. Secondly, a government grandfathered clause given to what was once a small 1930 nudist resort, built in mostly undeveloped Pasco County next to a small pond in a wooded area far away from downtown Tampa, with no sign of any suburb within miles. Until now. Over the years, suburbs sprawled, this way and that way, with more snowbirds moving south every year. The once small nudist resort grew, expanded, and grew even more, as wealthy investors saw this as a potential money-making machine. And it was.

In the first police car on the scene, Officer James McKenna, mid-thirties, tall, handsome, once a star quarterback for the Florida State Gators football team, a 4-year military man with several accommodations of heroic deeds from tours in Afghanistan, and a single guy married to his work, stopped at the gated front security entrance to gain permission to enter. In his car was his partner, Officer Bobby Dozier, totally opposite of McKenna, closing in on retirement, with a tired, bored look and a box of "just bought" donuts fighting for space on his overly large belly.

"We've been called here for a possible homicide," McKenna hurriedly shouted out to the entrance guard, waiting for the large metal swing gate to open.

Paradise Lost was a private resort, walled off from the outside world, with a world of its own on the inside. Clean, spacious, and well-maintained, it had resort-style accommodations with a quarter-acre tropical lagoon pool with large palm trees and a 30-foot waterfall grotto. There were multiple outdoor hot tubs for two, three, or a half dozen people, in between additional waist-deep pools for water volleyball, socializing, relaxing, or drinking at one of the many outdoor bars. Constant tropical music played to chase your cares away and there were a bevy of beautiful barmaids and hunky bartenders, all naked, to take your drink order and feast your eyes upon. The 40,000-square-foot clubhouse had two very large party rooms inside, sprawling to the outside, with veranda sports bars. Additionally, there was a giant-sized sauna, a gym with every piece of workout equipment imaginable, a relaxing massage-therapy spa, and a neon-lit spacious nightclub to dance the night way. And, a six-lane, just added, bowling alley to toss your balls, bowling balls, while bare naked. Who would have thought, naked bowling?

Paradise Lost was a nudist enthusiast's dream come true. And a destination place for swingers to come and "swing" the night away. They even had a special "swing set for two" in the middle of the dance floor. It swung "both ways." It was the No. 1 "no-clothing" resort in the world. You were either a yearly member, or a daily paying visitor. Everyone who was allowed in had to be of age, and background checks were required, but were minimal at best. And it was expensive. Very expensive. It kept the riffraff and gawkers out, and allowed the rich and famous to go in, undisturbed. Celebrities came by special invitation; they were treated like royalty. Resort rules permitted couples only, with single guys allowed entrance for weekend dances, or something more called a "threesome." Didn't matter to McKenna. He wasn't a part of any those categories, and he didn't like to dance. He was there to do his job.

"Follow the road; main clubhouse ahead. Philip Winston, one of the new resort owners is waiting for you," the security guard stated and indicated with a pointing hand.

"Winston, Philip Winston. Hey, I heard of him. He's one of the owners of the area's pro-basketball team," Officer Dozier blurted out as McKenna's car entered the walled-off resort.

It was a short drive, a nice winding road lined with beautiful flowering plants and freshly planted palm trees. There were clusters of two-story condo buildings and some jogging paths in between and around them. Being close to 8 a.m., the on-site live-ins and the guests were just waking up, sobering up, and starting to venture outside.

"Naked people!" Dozier stopped munching on his donut and stared out the police cruiser's open window. "And look at the boobs on those babes!"

Two 20-something, naked, attractive women jogged passed them while turning their heads to see what an approaching police car with its flashing lights was doing there. Dozier simultaneously turned his head as far as it would go watching them outside the open window.

"Don't hurt yourself," McKenna laughed out loud.

"I heard of this place! My wife would kill me if she knew I was here," Dozier added excitedly.

"Let's hope that doesn't happen." McKenna's laugh changed to a more serious tone. "There's already one dead body in the pool. We don't need anymore."

"Naked people." Dozier shook his head in disbelief and smiled to himself almost as if he were happy someone had died here, so he could get this once-in-a-lifetime assignment to see bare breasts and naked buns while eating his favorite donuts.

A quick, short drive led to a large half-circle driveway that ended at the entrance to the three-story main resort clubhouse, or "Funhouse," as it was called. It was huge, ornate, brand new, and very impressive looking. It even had life-size statues, naked statues, of course, adorning both sides of the driveway, making it look and feel like something out of Las Vegas, but placed in a middle of a jungle setting. As McKenna's police cruiser approached the front of the open-aired large entrance, there were more and more palm trees, professionally manicured shrubbery, and two very large enclosed metal cages on either side, each with several exotic-looking parrots.

A trio of businessmen waited for them at the entrance. They were casually but nicely dressed. Behind them, several early morning guests or residents weren't. They were naked as jaybirds.

One of the parrots called out loud, "Here come the cops! Here come the cops!"

McKenna and Dozier got out of the vehicle. A young naked man wearing a valet cap approached them, but then stopped and backed away. Another police car hurriedly pulled in behind them.

Officer Randall Williams, newly relocated from somewhere in New York that he didn't want to remember, stepped out, leaving his car running and his bubble red lights flashing. The rotating red light cast a strange feeling to an otherwise warm and sunny typical day in an adult fantasy world such as this. Williams was black, early forties, with a muscular build, but a bit rougher looking, probably from his difficult time growing up in New York. He was also well respected on the force and known as a good father and a good husband. Had three teenage sons and a 10-year-old daughter. A wife, his age, was a Tampa schoolteacher and the love of his life. His front dashboard displayed taped photos of them. He was proud of his family. Maybe the photos were also a way to remind him to be safe, not stupid, 'cause he had a family to go home to.

"Not exactly Disney World," he greeted McKenna with a nod. They were friends from the very first day he had moved here.

From the three businessmen who waited for them, one in particular stood out. Philip Winston. Early 40s, very professional in appearance and demeanor. Businessman, Co-Owner of the new Tampa Bay Buckaroos Pro Basketball team, Realtor, Builder, Investor, Entrepreneur, respected local community leader, multi-millionaire, and one of the Co-Owners of this resort. Now recently single, three times previously married, and known as quite a womanizer. Although some of this was either rumored or real, he was a man who stayed away from the press, didn't like his picture taken, and of recent, kept to himself. Also said to have money in the porn industry. Probably why the annual "Nude-a-Rama" Porn-star and Swingers Convention was held here.

Extending his hand, he didn't smile, didn't frown, and had the face of a gambling man—you just didn't know what he was thinking or what cards he held or didn't hold. He was all business, but underneath it all, he carried secrets only he knew. And secrets you wouldn't want to know.

"I'm Philip Winston, this is Harold Davis, day manager, and Chris Perkins night manager. If you follow me, I'll show you the body."

Without another word he turned, and everyone followed.

One of the parrots cawed out again, "Copper! Copper! Copper!" as the red flashing light illuminated the bird's metal cage. Smart parrot—there were three of them.

The open-air, two-story lobby was huge and impressive, with two ornate 15-foot-in-circumference connecting brick fountains that sprayed colored water into the air and splashed gently on the multiple breeds of unique fish swimming in them. They observed the marble tile floors, several extra-large-sized cushiony love couches and chairs, perfectly spaced stone pillars with growing green vines that reached upwards into a glass ceiling sky, and a large grand piano in the center with a naked 40-year-old man playing soothing classical music. But most eye catching were the three attractive, very attractive young women, naked young women, except for their high heels, very high heels, serving morning mimosas, or whatever else one cared to order from a half-moon-shaped bar at the far end of the entrance. It was enough to take one's breath away.

"Paradise Lost, and found," Officer Dozier thought to himself as he unknowingly rubbed his protruding big belly while taking in all the "delicious" sights to behold. Especially the two young female nude joggers who entered the spacious lobby room from behind and smiled at him as they passed on their way for a morning cooling-off naked dip in the main pool.

A large and impressive ornate registration entrance desk was at the right side of the entrance, and two muscular, tough-looking, but not too tough-looking men stood nearby. Everyone was naked. So were their muscles.

A free-standing sign stood in their path at the front of the lobby.

"NO clothing permitted beyond this point."

Dozier looked at McKenna and Williams with a look of horror. Everyone here was well built and looked like they belonged naked, even his partners, but him? If only he hadn't eaten the donuts!

McKenna caught the look and quickly replied, "Don't worry, you can keep your badge on if you want."

Williams broke a smile of brilliant white teeth. One of the few times he ever was seen smiling while on duty. And they all entered wearing their clothes.

CHAPTER 4

Johnny Rains slowly opened his eyes. And he was startled at what he saw. Everything appeared to be upside down. And it was. The bare wooden floor was on the ceiling, and the ceiling which had become the floor, was both white and dark, and seemed to have no finite ending. But he could make out a beam, a wooden beam, which seemed to run parallel to the floor and was suspended by apparent nothingness. A small open doorway far off in the distance was also upside down, and a very bright light shone through it, giving a halo effect as if it were the doorway to heaven, but of course it wasn't, or then again, maybe it really was. From his awakening perspective, his whole life was now upside down, as he himself hung upside down. He could finally see that his bare legs were tied together, and he was swinging from that large wooden ceiling beam.

He was naked, his mouth had a thick, gooey, black tape over it that made him gag, and his hands swung freely inches away from a clean and somewhat freshly polished wooden floor. From what he could see, it was mostly dark in the room. Dim lighting surrounded him and cast eerie shadows in the silence. He was alone, upside down, and hung like a slab of meat swinging back and forth in an empty butcher's room.

His brain struggled to become more conscious, and he tried to remember what happened and how he got there. And, most importantly, how he got into this predicament, if one could politely call it that. All he knew was that his head felt ready to explode, whether from the blood that rushed to his head in this topsy-turvy position, or that he was still drunk and drugged from one hell of a night's partying.

"Maybe this is hell," he thought to himself. *"This can't be real. This is a dream, or maybe I'm in another bondage movie... Where the fuck am I?"*

As he tried to make some sense with his jumbled thoughts, his body swayed, turned and twisted. There was no way his free hands could reach up and untie himself, even though he was somewhat athletic—that just happens in books and movies. This was neither. This was real, too real. He was finally becoming lucid and realizing that he was in a situation that was making him more apprehensive by the moment. This wasn't a dream, this wasn't a scene from one of his many adult-themed movies, this was a nightmare. A living nightmare.

His thoughts quickly raced to last night. *"Last night? The partying, the dancing, the adoring fans, the wannabe porn stars, and, of course, the two busty babes who enticed me to go back to their room. But this isn't their room. This is some sort of dark place with no windows, just black-draped walls, and an endless darkness that leads to nowhere, except that strange door in the distance with an empty bright white light. Where the hell am I?"*

With one free hand he was able to find an edge on the tape across his mouth and face and he was able to pull it free. Some of his skin and two-day-old facial hair came off with it, and a few drops of his blood rolled down his sore lips. He let the tape fall to the floor below, as he also did with his hand.

The room was quiet, too quiet. He twisted his head around, looking for anything or something to help him.

"Hello! Help me! Anyone? Help me!" he shouted into the all-embracing abyss of darkness.

He hung for a long time, or maybe a short time. It didn't matter how long. Time didn't matter at all. What mattered was what he could or couldn't do, and what was going to happen next. And then "next" came quickly.

Suddenly and slowly, somehow out of that surrounding darkness, something stepped forward, something very shadow-like, something or someone shrouded in what looked like an all-black long-flowing robe. Something or someone who was wearing very high spiked heels. Heels that made a resonating, loud, and unnerving noise with each step on the wooden floor.

"Where the fuck am I?" he shouted out as if he were in control, but of course he wasn't. It was more of his macho movie porno persona than that of a real-life hero, which he wasn't.

"Who are you? Get me down. Get...me...down," he commanded in vain.

There was no reply, no answer, just a continuing silence. A long, strange silence as the shadowy figure kept coming forward and finally stopping several feet away from his upside-down naked body.

His mind raced with jumbled thoughts and graphic images. *"What happened last night? I was in bed with two hot women taking turns with each one, while they took turns with each other. One riding me, while the other was kissing me. Long, deep kisses, and I was ready to come and then..."*

A man's voice from somewhere else, somewhere unseen, somewhere hidden in the room interrupted his memory. It was a deep, piercing voice, empty of emotion, but filled with fearful and disturbing words.

"We've been waiting for you to wake up, Johnny Rains. We didn't want to start the party without you. After all, you do like to party, don't you?"

"Get me down! I don't know who the fuck you are, but if this is some sort of joke, fuck you and get me down, now!"

The silent, black-robed, shadowy figure paid no attention, nor seem bothered by Johnny's shouting. Quietly, she reached behind in the darkness and rolled out a waist-high, small metal, all-silver-looking cart. On top of it was a medium-sized ornate silver bucket, a short, or maybe long, thin plastic hose, and what looked like a large, make that very large, and very long metal needle attached to it.

From behind him, something unknown and remaining in the shadows, slithered across the floor and grabbed the back of his hands. Catching him by utter surprise and shock, he tried to break free. But the hands that held him were big and strong and held him tight. They were cold, very cold, and it sent a chill up his naked back. Since this had happened from behind, he had no way of knowing who or what was holding him. But his brain knew that whatever it was, he probably did not want to see what it looked like.

"Jesus Christ, let go of me. Let go of me!"

He struggled in vain. Although having a slightly muscled and chiseled-looking body that he was proud to show off in his photos and movies, he was tired from his evening "sexcapades" and whatever alcohol or exotic party favors remained in his system. The slight swaying of his body upside down also made him dizzy, and not knowing how long he had been hanging upside down, the blood rush to his head made him even weaker.

The out-of-sight and unknown man's voice continued, almost hypnotically, lulling him to stop struggling and become somewhat resigned to whatever was next.

"Johnny, Johnny, Johnny. No need to struggle. Relax and enjoy the rest of your life. It won't be much longer now."

"Much longer now?" Those frightening words startled his brain and brought his body back to some life as he began to struggle again. But the cold, large hands holding his wrists grew tighter.

"Oww!" He let out a cry of pain.

"It's time, Johnny. It's time." The man's voice was both comforting and chilling.

In his upside-down world, he could see that the shadowy high-heeled figure in black had come closer. Her long floor-length, silk-hooded black robe, which hid her face from him, was open in the front and he could see her fully naked body in the patches of the dim illuminating room light. She was absolutely magnificent. Flawless, youthful, tanned skin that revealed not a trace of hair where her long legs met her curved beckoning hips. And her breasts were perfect. Large, firm, yet soft looking with thick protruding pink nipples that looked aroused and ready to be touched and kissed. Her shape defined her as a goddess. But in reality, she was anything but. For all he knew, and all he imagined, she could be the devil. And he wasn't far from the truth.

He watched helplessly as she quietly and methodically took the ornate silver bucket off the cart and placed it on the floor close to his hanging body. It appeared to have some religious symbols on it: A cross. A sad man's face with a wreath of thorns on his head. A crying winged angel. And a smiling devil. He, himself, was not much of a religious man, but he knew these symbols were portraying some sort of ceremony. His eyes followed her every movement as she took the plastic hose from the cart and stretched it open. It was a clear vinyl hose, maybe an inch in thickness. But it was the needle, the long silver needle, that scared him the most. She attached it to one end of the hose with a clamp and made sure it was tightly attached. This wasn't going to be some weird sexual game where he was going to have a hose stuck up his bare ass. No, this was a long, sharp-looking needle to be inserted into him, but where, and why? And as he mulled on the "where," she didn't, jabbing it directly into his large free-hanging balls—a long, sharp, thin needle thrust deeply into his testicles and continuing into his heavy-breathing belly.

He screamed and struggled at the same time. But the cold hands that held him were too strong. His scream was too weak. And the pain was too horrible.

His eyes opened and closed a thousand times as tears rolled downward across his forehead and into his thick blonde hair. Blood immediately started to flow through the clear vinyl hose, his blood. The other end of the hose was open and was placed into the silver bucket. His eyes widened in complete terror. Shock resonated throughout his trembling body.

His only words were what one would expect one's only words to be:

"No...please...no...!"

This was not a sex game. This was not another woman in heat who wanted sex. No, this was not simple pain and pleasure enjoyed in a midnight sexual embrace. There was no enjoyment here. No pleasure here. Only pain. Only ungodly, unbearable pain.

The unknown man's words of "Let the party begin" echoed through his dizzy and exhausted mind. This was not a "party." From the looks of things, there would be no more of that, not now, not ever again. What was being played out in an endless moment of excruciating pain was a different party from all the parties he was accustomed to. This would definitely not be another notch in his sexual romper-room lifestyle. No "slam, bam, thank you, ma'am," no sexual climax tonight. No, this was a different orgasm. The ultimate orgasm. The final climax.

As the last of his blood drained from his body through the clear hose and into the almost-filled silver bucket, his last few moments of consciousness gave him the strength to finally see her face. She was the most beautiful, alluring, and haunting woman he had ever seen or would ever see again. Oh, very, very beautiful! And in that final moment, he recognized her, and yet he didn't. He knew her; and he didn't. But it must have been... or could have been... or maybe never had been. Her. Yes, it was her. Or maybe it wasn't. He didn't know the why, but he started to understand the how. Of all the many women he ever had, of all the many lovers he left behind, she was the culmination of his every fantasy. She was neither real nor unreal. She was a reflection of his life and a fitting end to what little life he had left. And in that upside-down loving face he looked at, he knew what would come next. He felt it throughout his body and all through his mind. Perhaps this was a rendezvous with Fate.

If he could have peed, he would have, but he was no longer frightened to do so. He was becoming at peace with himself, and he was so empty, so very empty, of his precious body fluids. All that remained were a few last drops.

This mysterious woman, this goddess of the unknown, bent forward slowly and quietly, her haunting face brightening with a sardonic smile as she savored the moment to come.

Her two dark eyes changed to red demonic eyes. Her eyes pierced his soul as she smiled wide and opened her mouth. Two big, perfectly white, sharp fangs were revealed with drops of her saliva glistening in what appeared to be a white light that surrounded them both. He knew it was time. Just like in the movies. Just as the mysterious voice had stated earlier.

Her long, sharp, protruding fangs sunk deep into his bare neck, seeking and savoring those last remaining drops, and he experienced one last, long orgasm. The best orgasm of his entire sex-filled, porno-driven life. The one final orgasm that lasts forever.

Death.

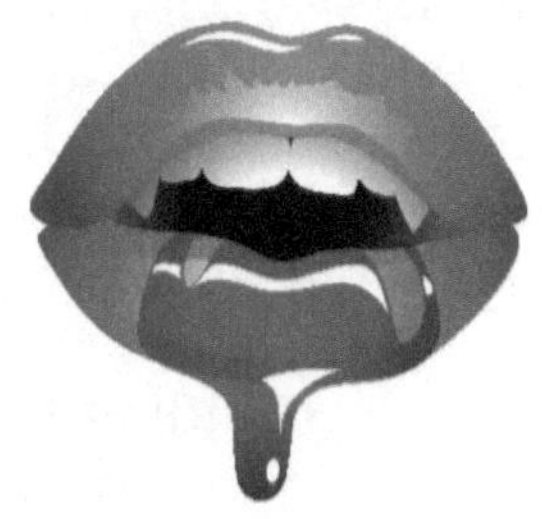

CHAPTER 5

The first thing Jamie noticed as her car approached the front-entrance security gates of Paradise Lost was that there was little or no activity. No additional police cruisers, fire trucks, ambulances, and no press corps—the expected things at a reported murder site.

"Maybe they are already inside?" she thought to herself. Then she got the call.

It was from her boss, New Tampa Police Chief Harold Johnson, a long-time police officer who worked his way up the ranks and now oversaw the thirty-person department she was a part of.

"Parker here," she answered, picking up her cell phone.

"Where are you?" a husky, strained, man's voice asked without a cheerful "good-morning-to-you" vibe. A voice that had chain smoked one too many cigarettes over a lifetime of dedicated and stress-filled police work.

"Outside the gate to the resort. Close to the Security Entrance. Seems quiet. Where is everyone?"

There was a pause.

"We got a problem. Return here. We can discuss it in person," Chief Johnson replied sounding extremely exhausted and emotionally bothered.

"A problem?"

"No discussion over the air; keep this silent."

"Okay. On my way home."

Home. She smiled to herself. She had two homes. Her home with Bentley. And her home with twenty-nine other officers and staff administration personnel. Sometimes they both blended as one.

Then her smile turned into a slight frown as she turned her car around. *"No over-the-phone discussion, silent communication. Something's up. Something big, something..."*

Her thoughts trailed off as she turned onto Highway 441 and headed back towards the office.

It was about a twenty-minute drive, depending on daily traffic patterns. With so many retirees and new families moving in, every day seemed like a Saturday. Lots of traffic, going this way and that. Like ants scurrying here and there. Either working or playing. The roads were always busy, and today was no different.

Jamie reached out of her driver's window and put on her attachable red bubble and activated her specially installed police siren. Not the typical ominous black, government-funded, police cruiser with all the fancy cop decals; this was a normal-looking, state-issued, Ford auxiliary vehicle with a souped-up motor and a locked gun box in her dashboard for any type of dangerous situation or unexpected emergencies. She wondered if she would need to use it today.

The station house building was a typical red-colored brick, two-story building, built a few years back, which blended in along with the rest of the growing community. Three large flag poles heralded its front entrance displaying the American flag, the

Florida state flag, and New Tampa Police flag, and certainly gave anyone looking for this place a form of reference. The flags all seemed to wave in unison in the soft morning Florida breezes. As the weatherman reported on local television, there was no rain in sight for this sunny July day in this part of the state. A good day to have fun in the sun. *"Hmm,"* she wondered to herself. *"What kind of fun went wrong in the nudist resort?"*

Chief Harold Johnson was not in his usual friendly mood, not that he was often friendly anyway. Approaching sixty, and with daily reminders that he was just a few months away from a planned retirement up North, which was a repeating joke in the office as most retirees moved South, he stood at the opened door of the conference room with paperwork in his hands, waiting for everyone to gather. Officers McKenna and Dozier were already there. Officer Williams was just entering, and Detective Parker was not far behind with a half cup of yesterday's coffee in her hand that she had hurriedly picked off her desk. *"Cold coffee is better than no coffee,"* she thought to herself, as she took a seat at the conference table after closing the door behind her.

Directly across from her was McKenna. She liked him in an interesting sort of way. He was single, married to his work, always had a nice smile for her, but that was all—not that she expected to be flirted with, even though she was probably, and without much doubt, the most attractive single woman in the New Tampa Police Department. She recalled that, when she first saw him, she thought he could have been a GQ model with his toned athletic body, and she liked the way he carried himself with confidence. He had "the look." He was "down-right handsome," as one of her college girlfriends from Georgia would say when she saw a hunky guy just like McKenna. Down-right handsome, and he was.

Basically, he intrigued her, as he was quiet, reserved, and kept to himself. No one knew much about his personal life, if he even had one. He was known as the "best on the squad" of nine officers, and when he looked at you with his piercing blue eyes, how could you not feel an extra heartbeat or two? Other than work talk, he didn't say much to her. Maybe he was gay, she once thought, but no, God forbid, not him. As for the other male officers and staff assistants in the office, they mostly minded their own business or chit-chatted about upcoming days off and weekends at the nearby beaches. She had been "hit" on by a few of the married older officers, but she just politely smiled and moved away from them as quickly as she could. She was all business, too. But McKenna, he still intrigued her. There was more to his story, she imagined with her detective antenna thinking of the possibilities.

Chief Johnson was tall and still kept his weight in check for his age. Probably trying to send a message to his team, especially Dozier, who had the nickname "Donut Dozier" or sometimes just "Donuts" around the office. But Dozier was one of the nicest and most sincere people she had met and come to like in her new role there. She remembered that on the first day she came to work there, he had put a box of donuts on her desk with a note "Welcome to the New Tampa Team." She recalled eating one to be friendly and polite, although she really didn't like donuts, and he ate most of the rest.

The chief sat on the edge of the conference table, facing them, while putting his paperwork down on the table.

"We have a problem, a big problem. When the Paradise Lost Resort was first built in the 1930s, it was actually just a campground with a bunch of trailers and tents and some real naturist-type people who liked to get suntans all over. It was in a sparse, mostly uninhabited county that the legislators voted to allow to continue without much concern, or interference from the police, politicians, and religious folks. Turns out this was for a reason: a lot of them were nudists, too. And so, they created and passed some type of 'grandfathered legislation clause' that basically meant they were their 'own community' and the local and state police had no jurisdiction there. After all, who is gonna cause problems when you got lots of naked people strolling around, worshipping the weather, and not exactly having pants pockets to carry guns or other weapons? So, it was just a 'unique place,' all to itself. As our state grew in population and the cities started to sprawl into the empty areas called the suburbs, some money got pumped into it and it grew to what we have today as a 40-acre walled resort, which attracts more than just the local naked people. It attracts celebrities, dignitaries, the rich and famous, porn stars, and even big-named politicians, both local and national. And it isn't just for the sun. The resort now has restaurants, nightclubs, gaming rooms, spas, hotel rooms, swimming pools, and swingers. Lots of swingers."

"Swingers?" Dozier asked while munching on a donut. "They got swings, like in a playground?"

The chief looked at Dozier not knowing if this was a legitimate question, a joke, or if he was just as stupid as he looked. He smiled to himself, knowing the answer, and continued.

"And since some of the swingers, especially the celebrities and politicians, like to show off their 'trophy wives' or 'boy toys,' it is a big, well-kept secret to the world outside their world. There are strict rules: no photography, no cell phones. All guests turn in their phones to the front desk when they arrive and don't get them back until they leave. Drinking, gambling, and drugs are allowed. But police are not. Neither are FBI, CIA, Homeland Security, or any type of Florida or national law agencies. They have their own security force."

"Why, then, were we notified and let in?" Officer Williams spoke first.

"Somehow, this Johnny Rains character who was found floating dead this morning in their swimming pool was a big figure in the porn industry. Someone called 911 and we responded. When we showed up, two cars were let in, then an ambulance. No one else. The body had been removed from the pool and they were waiting for us to take it out of there, no questions asked. Then a second body was found in the window of one of their on-premise lingerie shops. McKenna, Dozier, and Williams, you three were there when that happened. We know all hell broke loose when some of the early-morning risers witnessed the discovery. The owners had us remove that body as well. We had no choice but to comply. You guys attempted to call for back-up, look for evidence, and close off the area for further investigation by Major Crimes and the CSI team."

Johnson took a slight pause and looked to the conference door to make sure it had been locked.

McKenna took advantage of his pause and quickly added, "Strangely, our radio and phone signals were dead. We had no communication available. One of the owners, Philip Winston, told us that was a security precaution and their techies had designed an electronic signal to kill all outgoing calls."

"But then, how did 911 get a call in the first place?" Jamie asked politely but inquisitively.

No answer to that from anyone in the room.

"And the caller?" she continued.

The chief picked up from where he left off. "The person who called 911 left a simple and short message and said, 'There's a murder at Paradise Lost,' and hung up. It was a woman's voice. That's it. We have it recorded."

He continued, "I was notified by the 911 operator since they weren't sure if it was a prank call. I had Dispatch radio McKenna, Dozier, and Williams because you three were the closest to the resort. In the meantime, I tried to contact the resort directly and asked to speak with their management. When I told the person on the phone who I was, they abruptly hung up. I then personally called your vehicles, but you must have been on the premises already because your phones were dead. That's when I contacted Detective Parker."

Chief Johnson unfolded his arms and moved off the table he had been sitting on and toward the window facing the outside world where the morning light added brightness to the sterile white conference room. He wasn't quite done with his story, but nodded to McKenna to continue and fill in the blanks.

"When we were on site," McKenna explained, "their security guards kept guests and staff away from us and kept us away from them. They didn't allow us to have any interaction. One of the owners, Philip Winston, met us when we arrived with two of his managers. He basically told us that someone 'must have accidentally drowned' in the pool and that there was no indication of any foul play. So that's when we started to ask a lot of questions and we were told the answers would be forthcoming and to just follow him and his staff to where the body was. The body was already out of the pool and had been moved to a private area a short distance away. It had been covered up by a large resort blanket with two security guards next to it. When I went to uncover it, I was told to just have it removed from their premises, based on their rights as a self-governed community."

McKenna paused and nodded to Williams, who continued the story.

"I approached the guards and told them I wanted to look at the body and they stood silent, blocking my way. That's when someone nearby let out a scream and we all hurried over to some shops where we found a second body. And this one sure didn't look like an accidental drowning."

McKenna then continued.

"It was another man. The body was tied, standing up, attached to a clothing rack in a shop window, naked. Dead naked. Apparently, this caught Winston and his people by surprise, and they scurried to get the guests away from the scene."

Jamie looked up from her note-taking. McKenna paused, then resumed.

"We were let into the shop but were not allowed to touch the body. There was a heated exchange between us and their staff. It was turning confrontational, but I called in for backup and found that none of our communication devices worked. I was told by Winston that the resort had a private phone system and all other devices were electronically blocked. Just like you said, Chief. That's when another one of their staff arrived and I was handed a larger-looking cell phone. Apparently, you called while we were there, and I was able to receive the call on their device. Before I could explain the situation, you told me we had to leave the scene immediately. I tried to question you, but you said it was a command, and hung up."

"Why did you ask us to leave?" It was Officer Williams' turn to ask a question.

The chief returned to his spot where he had previously leaned on the conference table. He looked very solemn.

"I got a call while you were there."

"A call?" Williams queried.

"I got a call from the mayor."

"The mayor?" McKenna responded with a look of questioning shock.

"Yeah, the naked mayor. Apparently, he was somewhere on site. He is connected to the owners, who are connected to the local legislators, who are connected to the state senator, who is connected to the governor who is connected to who knows who else!"

"They're all nudists?" Officer Dozier excitedly blurted out.

"It's not my business, nor my job to know who wears clothes or doesn't. But apparently some of these folks I just mentioned don't, and some of these people go there to party and they don't want us to be involved, especially right now since this is some sort of big nudie celebration week."

The words sunk in to the three officers and Detective Parker.

"And especially when someone, and now two 'someones,' ended up dead. And they have the law on their side with the grandfather clause to keep us out," the chief concluded in a frustrated tone.

"That's crazy!" Williams broke the silence.

"No, unfortunately, it's the law, and this is their lifestyle. A crazy lifestyle or whatever you want to think of it as. But there are two unsolved murders, two very strange murders, right here in our backyard, and we're the ones with our hands tied."

"How were they killed?" Jamie asked in a professional voice as she looked up from writing on her notepad.

The chief looked nervously around the room, reassuring himself that no one else could hear him, not that there was anyone else there, but the five of them.

"From our guys at the city morgue and their preliminary look at the two bodies, they were both very discolored and very emaciated. It appears they were drained of their blood. Both have two large puncture wounds in their necks."

This caught everyone by surprise.

Dozier, who had been reaching for another bite of a donut he had snuck into the meeting, stopped, then pulled his hand back, rubbing his neck as if he were checking for his own set of puncture wounds.

"An animal?" Dozier asked.

"Maybe the guy found in the pool, but the guy strapped to a clothing display in a boutique window?" McKenna replied with both an answer and a question.

Chief Johnson continued.

"And, although we have no jurisdiction there, this is our community, and we are sworn to protect the people of this community. All people, with or without clothes. We have a protocol and it's our duty no matter what our mayor or some resort owner says. And besides, someone else may be in jeopardy there, especially since the killer is still running loose."

"Sounds like we have a naked killer," Jamie added.

"Whether naked or dressed, it's my decision not to turn our backs on this situation, especially if there is some sort of a cover up going on. And from what I know, from what you said, and what I feel, something is going on behind their closed resort walls and it's our job to find out what, and to stop it."

The chief paused again, looking at all of them one by one and then let out a long, thinking sigh.

"So, I have a plan. And it's going to need volunteers."

"Undercover work?" Jamie asked.

"Sort of. More like 'uncovered' work," Johnson replied without a smile, just a serious, very serious look.

Everyone sat back in their chairs in a form of disbelief of what he just said, not only about the victims, but about the police work to be done, and how it was to be done.

"I'll go," Dozier raised his hand while quickly volunteering.

"There aren't any donut shops there, and to be honest, you don't quite fit the physical appearance demographics," Chief Johnson replied.

"Besides, I can't send a single man in, 'cause it's not allowed. Strict resort rules, unless they are invited in by a guest. And I'm not sending in a single woman, alone. Even though that is allowed."

"You want someone to go in there undercover, uncovered, to blend in and to search for evidence?" McKenna asked.

"And catch the killer," the chief stipulated, "while I try to find a way through this 'grandfathered' legal clause stuff. I've already contacted our DA's office to meet with him. Everything has to be hush-hush. The New Tampa mayor made it very clear to me, no involvement. So, whatever is done behind the scenes has to be by the book, 'cause my job, 'my ass,' is on the line."

"While we show our ass in person," Williams quickly added.

A brief moment of silence weaved its way through the group. They all looked around at each other knowing how this was probably going to play out.

Johnson leaned forward away from the table. "I know this is an unusual assignment. But we're all professionals."

Dozier was starting to fall asleep. Johnson rolled his eyes and continued.

"As I said, we're all professionals. So, this is something I need your help on. We've only got a couple of officers in this post and honestly not everyone fits the description of being a candidate for this, nor can I ask around too much because of the sensitivity of the situation. Williams, McKenna, Dozier, you were there. And Jamie..."

Johnson paused again, knowing what he had to say, what he had to ask, something he never faced before in all his police years, and now, right before retirement.

"To not draw any attention, I need a couple. A man and a woman. In today's world, you don't have to play husband and wife; you're just a couple. You're there to enjoy the resort, to be part of the convention. Not take part. I'm not asking you to do anything you do not want to do or be uncomfortable doing. This isn't an easy assignment to ask you to do. But, we have two strange murders in our town, in our jurisdiction, and we need answers quickly, before there are no answers to be found. I need two volunteers to go in today. Detective Parker, Officer McKenna, I want you two to stay here. Officer Williams, Officer Dozier, you're dismissed. You can leave, resume your work, but not a word about this to anyone. Understood?"

As Dozier got up from his chair, he turned to the chief to ask one more question.

"But what about the puncture wounds? It has to be some sort of animal. Maybe an alligator?"

Johnson just stared with a silent look of, "Are there any other stupid questions he can ask?"

"Alligators don't leave puncture wounds, and don't drain blood from their victims," Williams added quickly to answer Dozier's question.

"Maybe it's a vampire? Maybe Count Dracula actually lives," Dozier jumped back into the conversation, actually believing what he was saying, without thinking what he was saying.

"And, he's a nudist in Florida," Dozier concluded, smiling like he just solved the case.

"Or maybe it was done by someone who wants us to believe that it was a vampire," McKenna added.

Jamie looked at McKenna and said, "Well, at least we get to pack light," trying to bring the conversation back to some semblance of reality, although this case was becoming far from that.

CHAPTER 6

Larry Miller always had a penchant for being in the wrong place at the wrong time. And there could be no worse place, nor any worse time than while he stood stone-cold naked drunk, looking at the sexy clothing in the window of the Paradise Lost Resort Boutique. Definitely the wrong place, and definitely the wrong time. Especially tonight while a dead Johnny Rains bobbed like an apple in a water-filled bucket a short distance away in the main pool. Not that Larry knew about this, or even cared, because at this time he was "dead drunk" on his feet and would be "dead naked" just like Johnny in a matter of minutes.

Larry even had a "special nickname" that his friends gave him, and which he came to accept, "Lucky Larry." Sort of a play on words for *not* being so lucky. For example, he was at his first-ever major league baseball game when star player Barry Bonds hit his record-breaking 70th home run, but just moments before, Larry went to the bathroom and the baseball landed in his empty seat where another fan picked it up and sold it for $60,000. And the time he went to buy his first-ever instant-winner state lottery ticket and let a woman with a crying baby go ahead of him, and she immediately scratched off the ticket numbers, which would have been his, and won $50,000. He cried even louder than the baby. Or the time he went to the dentist and his x-rays were mixed up with someone else's, and they pulled two of his good teeth by mistake. He also got a horrible infection from that dental work, which bloated his whole body and kept him bedridden for a week. As a result, he wasn't able to use his expensive front-row ticket to see his favorite musician and singer, Prince, perform his last concert before he unexpectedly died. "Lucky Larry" was appropriately named.

Lucky Larry was also an avid autograph collector, not a real naturist at heart, not a swinger per se. Just an average-looking, 30-year-old, slightly overweight and prematurely balding accountant who collected autographs of movie stars—actually porn movie stars. And that's what brought him to Florida from his hometown of Batavia, New York, to attend the Paradise Lost Nude-a-Rama Convention where all his favorite female X-rated stars were. This was his first time at a place like this, and with more than a few beers in him, he easily forgot his normal shyness, enabling him to have fun in the sun while letting it literally "all hang out."

At the earlier evening "Meet and Greet the Stars" in the main lounge, he anxiously held a handful of glossy 8×10 photos of the porn stars who were advertised to attend that night. And they were all there in the flesh, as promised. Lots of bare flesh, boobs and butts, with lots and lots of curves sprinkled in between. And as the rules of the resort stated, no clothing allowed, except for the tall spiked heels all the women were permitted (and sort of required) to wear. Wouldn't want to stub or ruin their manicured toes!

So, Larry stood patiently in line while drinking more beers and met all of his favorite stars: Naughty

Nicki Storm, a blonde, big-busted, 44-Double D, "leading lady" of the new wave of group porn. And what a leading lady! Her male co-stars on screen were all led into a whipped-cream-covered bed with her, three at a time, for the most amazing sexual romps filmed. All in glorious 3-D. Just imagine, Double Ds in 3-D. They jumped right out of the screen and "into your face." And, of course, his favorite, the tattooed-covered black beauty, Wicked Wanda, who sat on every photo she signed with her big bare butt, smudging the freshly inked words, "Kiss My Ass."

Yes, Larry was having a great time, by himself. But how did he get into a couples-only resort for this special convention? Actually, he did bring a date—a Christian girlfriend, who thought they were going to a "typical family" resort. Seems Larry didn't exactly tell her all the "naked" details. And after he checked in, she checked out, when seeing two fully nude male guests who looked like each one had a "third leg," if you can imagine.

Arriving alone at the Meet and Greet autograph session, he made the excuse to Security that his significant other was "sick" back in their room. Since she was a registered guest, although by now she was on her way back to New York, they let him in. And he had lots of "ogling fun" as he met all the porn stars and got all the autographs and saw all their boobs and butts up close and in person. But that wasn't all he would get that night. After the party ended, it was his turn to suddenly "check out" and have his life suddenly end.

"Are you enjoying the midnight full moon?" a sultry female voice asked him as he stood weaving back and forth while looking in the resort's outdoor boutique window.

Turning slowly as to not fall over in his inebriated state, Larry cocked his head and squinted his eyes to see who was speaking to him.

Unfortunately, in the shadows of the resort's outdoor lighting, mixed with the moonlight, which was being obstructed by a passing cloud, all he could make out was a tall female figure with an amazing body that seemingly belonged on the cover of every man's fantasy magazine.

"Hello... Hello!" he responded, in a bit of a slurred, but happy voice. "Did I get your autograph tonight?" he asked this unknown woman, while holding up several of his signed 8×10s to determine if this naked goddess matched any of the porn stars he had met earlier.

"Nope. Nope. Nope. Nope. Nope. Nope." He slowly repeated the same word as he let each signed photo fall to his feet, not realizing what he was doing in his current state of mind.

All he had left in his hand was his favorite marker pen which he used to get his autographs.

"Hmmm, I don't have any photos left. Maybe you could sign me?" he asked drunkenly, while holding out the pen in a far-from-steady-looking hand.

The mysterious woman took the marking pen, as her hand gently caressed his in a teasing and seductive manner. The shadows still hid her face from Larry, but it didn't matter because he was totally smitten, or should one say, "just about to be bitten."

"Where would you like me to leave my mark?" she coyly teased him.

"Hmmm. Well...how about on my heart?" he laughed in response, while pointing to his heart.

"That would be nice, but I have a better place in mind," she responded sexily as she began to slowly step out of the shadows. He could finally see how very, very, beautiful she truly was. More beautiful than his "favorites" who he had met earlier tonight, the Naughty Nicki and the very Wicked Wanda.

And his response to her soft, sultry words and exquisite, perfect body was "obvious" from what he hoped would happen. He smiled and turned his eyes downward to show her that his "thingy" had become "very aroused" below his nude and somewhat flabby waist.

And her response was "not as obvious" from what he expected would happen, as she smiled back at him. Smiled wide and showed him two large fangs. Two very large, sharp, white fangs that glistened in the full moonlight, and which she quickly sunk deep into his neck.

Lucky Larry was "lucky" after all. He died with a big smile and a very big boner.

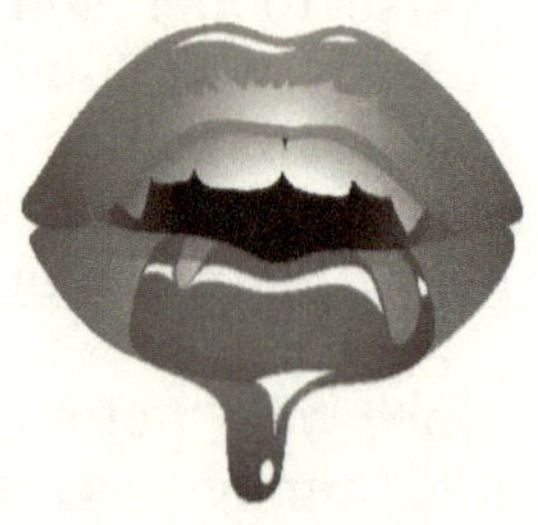

CHAPTER 7

Jamie's drive from police headquarters to her home was a conflicting one, to say the least, as she contemplated everything Chief Johnson said in both the conference room meeting and the following private discussion in his office. As a detective, she reviewed the facts he and the other officers shared regarding the two murders at Paradise Lost Resort. As a woman, she thought about the assignment in which she would have to "bare all" in front of many strangers—totally naked men and women and, of course, an equally nude Officer McKenna. Both sets of thoughts jumped back and forth in her mind. She wasn't sure which scenario gave her more of an adrenalin rush. And which scenario terrified her more.

The conclusion was simple and straightforward, this was going to be a most "unusual" case from the typical investigative work and resulting paperwork she was accustomed to in her New Tampa boundaries, as she would step out of those boundaries, unarmed, and into an unknown world, not governed by any laws, that awaited her in the nude. She half smiled, and also frowned to herself, as she thought about it.

Jamie recalled the meeting in the chief's office and how he had told her and McKenna that he needed them both for this assignment. It wasn't as if she or McKenna raised their hands and volunteered. Neither had come forward like fellow officer Dozier in the conference room meeting, but both were prepared to accept and face the situation as responsible and professional police officers. Neither she nor McKenna made jokes about going "undercover uncovered" either, but any awkwardness, or shyness, they may have thought about was immediately replaced with an attitude of mutual respect towards each other and, "Let's catch a killer."

Jamie thought about the chief's words, *"Find and discover all the facts and information, but do not put yourself in harm's way."*

Without any weapons or communication devices, they would be relying on their individual skill sets and working together as partners. Jamie's self-defense skills included two years of martial arts and police training. She had heard that McKenna was an amateur boxer in college and had also competed in a police academy boxing program, which he now taught to new recruits. So, she felt somewhat confident in handling most situations, but the whole "vampire-draining-blood scenario" was disturbing. But then again, murder is always disturbing. Committed by disturbed individuals who eventually make mistakes. And those mistakes leave evidence, which Jamie was relying on finding.

Chief Johnson had discussed the new identities they would be given to cover their police identities with newly made photo IDs, licenses, etc., which their department was already preparing. They would both keep their first names, so as not to complicate the situation and possibly draw any attention to themselves if they misspoke. She was now Jamie

Anderson, a marketing rep for a firm that was previously set up by Florida state troopers to use in similar undercover—but "covered up"—operations. McKenna was the "boyfriend," Jim Stanton, a physical therapist and personal trainer for another fictitious firm used by the police. Since Jamie never entered the resort, there was no concern about being recognized. As for McKenna, a quick dye job was necessary, turning his blonde hair into a dark shade of brown. Without his police uniform and with the awareness to avoid Winston, whom he met earlier today, they all agreed, as they discussed their investigative approach, that it could, should, and would work. "Meet, mingle, and memorize everything. Find out what other guests have heard, and if there are any connections between the two dead men. Coordinate and share, determine who is involved, and discover the motive," Chief Johnson outlined.

Jamie knew that the primary motives for murder are revenge, money, and sex. Then there's depravity, which involves psychopaths, sociopaths, and serial killers. She wondered what motive they'd find in paradise.

Williams and Dozier, and the rest of the back-up team would be called in when and if necessary. The "how" was still to be finalized. Basically, any guest could use the in-house phones in the lobby at the registration desk. However, Jamie and Jim were instructed to call a secured, non-police number, and use certain code words, especially since they didn't know if the phones were tapped or being recorded. Whatever else might happen while they were there, they would have to adapt to. And the biggest, most looming, "adapting" question was sharing a room and a bed in the nude with her assigned partner.

"In the nude." Jamie thought about that as she was now halfway home. She allowed herself to

daydream a bit. Was it something she secretly wanted, or was it happening all too fast?

She was pretty much a shy girl growing up, in a family dominated by men, two brothers, one older, one younger, and a father who worked two jobs to make ends meet. She lost her mom to cancer just as she became a teen. It was a traumatic time for Jamie. She had never seen death before, other than in a movie or reading about it in a book, but facing it in reality is a whole different feeling—one that stays with you a long, long time, and leaves a lot of invisible scars of pain and hurt. But her mother was strong to the end; maybe that's where she got some of her strengths. Jamie remembered that they stood by her bedside, saying their final goodbyes as her mother faded in and out of consciousness. That's when her mother spoke her final words, which came from the heart and in between the tears that gently rolled down her tired and pain-filled face. To this day, Jamie could still feel her mother weakly squeezing her hand and showing a fragile smile she would never forget. Nor would she forget the words she spoke.

"Be strong, for yourself, for your brothers, for your father. Be strong for me. I love you." And she slowly closed her eyes and died. They stood there in grief, hugging, and crying upon each other's shoulder.

Her teenage years that followed were mostly spent studying, studying, and studying. If she wanted to go to college and start a career, she needed the grades, and she got them and more. Top of her class, high school Valedictorian, and a scholarship to the University of Central Florida. Jamie wanted a career in law enforcement, to help people, to make a difference. Again, top of her class, and an immediate entrance to the Florida Law Enforcement Training Facility, then climbing the ladder quickly in the

Orlando Police Department, reaching the rank of Sergeant.

Jamie did have several boyfriends in college, and they were just that, friends. But in her last year she met, dated, and experienced her first love, and he became her first and only lover. He was also a senior, Jayson Burritt, a handsome law student who had told her "she made the stars twinkle in the sky" whenever he kissed her. She enjoyed the soft, sweet lips of his on hers, and she enjoyed their tender, yet passionate, lovemaking. He, too, was a virgin like her, and they learned to share their intimacy together, and she thought it would be an intimacy forever. They had both planned it in their minds, and especially in their hearts. Her world seemed perfect, until the night a drunk driver crossed the center line and collided with his car head-on as he was on his way to meet her, and maybe even to propose to her. He struggled to survive, going in and out of a coma for two days before he died, holding and squeezing her hand just like her mother had. He couldn't say the words, but she heard them in his eyes, "I love you." And he was gone. And she was alone, and her life felt empty again. An emptiness she had remembered from her mother's passing, but now deeper, and more painful than ever before. And she filled her void with her work ethic and his memory.

Jamie had a few more boy "friends" over the years that followed, up until now. The memory of her first and only love wouldn't permit another. Now she realized that, with this relocation to New Tampa and her promotion to Detective, a new life was about to begin and should begin, perhaps with the intriguing Jim McKenna?

Her thoughts were abruptly interrupted as she pulled into her driveway, and the past faded and the present loomed. How little did she know that she would find love again, in the most unusual and unexpected setting of all, a "nudist resort." Although, it wouldn't be with the person she expected.

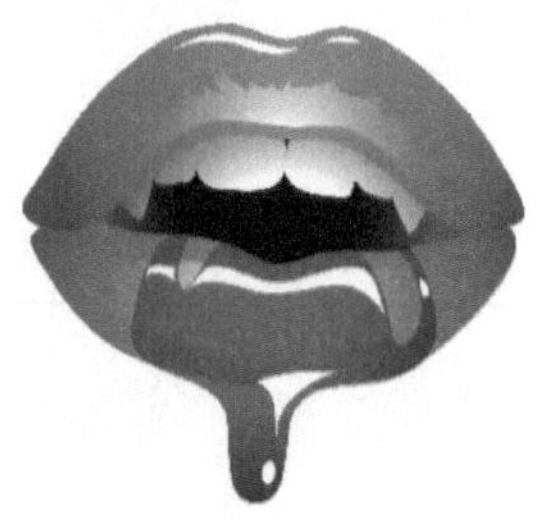

CHAPTER 8

As Jamie stood staring at her empty suitcase on the bed, Bentley sat on the carpet staring at her. She really had no clue what to pack for her stay at Paradise Lost Resort and Bentley had no clue as to where or why she was going. Dogs always seem to have a sixth sense whenever their "master" is going away. And, of course, it was very true for this dog. After all, she was a detective, so he had to be a "detective dog." But whatever was going on, hopefully, he would get a bone.

"Don't worry, boy." Jamie saw Bentley's sad eyes looking at her, and she knelt down to gently rub his head. "Mommy's just going on vacation for a few days and Mrs. Little will be coming over later to stay with you."

Bentley's dog expression seemed to change at the mention of Mrs. Little. He liked her; she always gave him a lot of extra dog treats when she came to visit.

"And don't worry, she'll bring you a big bone to chew." That made Bentley very happy. He wagged his tail and it made him forget about her empty suitcase. But, as for Jamie...

"Okay, won't need a bathing suit," she spoke out loud to herself, and to Bentley, who really had forgotten about the suitcase and could only think about a big, new bone.

"And, of course, no evening dress, or evening wear. Forget the shorts, and my brand-new halter top. Hmmm, won't need that. Okay, maybe just for the ride there," as she placed it next to the suitcase on her bed.

"Pajamas? Well, maybe I should bring those along as an insurance policy. After all, I will have a roommate." She half chuckled to herself, not knowing what she was really getting herself into, or what to really expect, personally or work wise. For a detective, the "not-knowing," always made her uncomfortable, until it became "a fact." Going into an investigation, you can't assume anything. You have to let the evidence speak for itself.

Jamie went to the top drawer on her nearby dresser, opened it, and took one look at her pajamas. They were what she wore most nights when she cuddled up in bed with a book and Bentley next to her. They had Disney cartoon characters all over them. She smiled, then laughed out loud.

"Really. On second thought..." She held them up in front of her and then quickly replaced them in the drawer.

Jamie opened the next drawer. Bras and panties. She shook her head and slowly closed the drawer. Pausing for a moment, she reopened the drawer and took out one of each and tossed them into her open suitcase.

"Rule No. 1, always have a clean pair of undies. Even in a nudist resort." She laughed out loud at what she said, as Bentley cocked his head looking at her.

Looking inside her bedroom closet, she spied her assortment of different shoes, and found a pair of sandals she recently bought, and a couple pairs of high heels that she hardly wore. Hadn't exactly been doing a lot of dating or nightclubbing since she moved here, but the resort had a nightclub and high heels were permitted, if not required. She would have preferred her jogging sneakers, just in case she needed to "run away." Again, she smiled to herself as she took the high heels and then added the jogging shoes.

And finally, lingerie.

She really hadn't many negligees, per se, just one or two leftovers from her college days that most likely still fit. There was a brand-new, never-worn-yet, see-through, black, full-length negligee that she bought recently when she saw it on display at the mall. Not imagining when or where she would wear it, but there it was in her closet, still in the box on the middle shelf next to her folded sweaters. She recalled from her quick internet research that the resort did have a themed lingerie dance advertised for one of the nights they would be there. Without much hesitation, Jamie took the nightgown out of the cardboard store box and kept it folded in its white tissue paper, while placing it on top of the few things in the mostly still-empty suitcase.

And, of course, cosmetics—the potions and lotions that were a staple to any woman. Not that she used a lot because of her natural beauty, but she needed all the necessary female vacation essentials. And then she saw it, tucked in with the rest—her one tube of deep red lipstick that she hadn't worn in years since her only true love, Jayson, had unexpectedly died. She recalled how he told her that he liked it on her for "special occasions," and that it made her look "extra sexy." There had been no need to wear it again, especially not as a police officer, nor in her role as a detective. But her undercover work at the resort would be different. It was definitely a "special occasion" and would be a "tool" for her to use, and attract men to talk with her, while she searched for clues.

"Well, it looks like I got everything," she proudly proclaimed to Bentley, after packing the final item—her toothbrush. "Fastest pack I ever did."

Before she closed the suitcase, she looked into it one last time, staring at the partially wrapped black negligee she had placed on top of everything. Jamie gently touched it, remembering something she had once "worn," a long time ago, something similar to it, though not so see-through.

As a sophomore in college, she had once posed "in her birthday suit" for an art class. She always had a nice, toned athletic body, and posing nude earned her $100 for one hour's work, and all you had to wear "was a smile." Although she did it mostly because it was a dare, she was trembling from head to foot when she disrobed. At 20, her body was flawless—tight, tanned, with round, firm breasts that were not too big, not too small, but just the right proportion and symmetrical, and long, toned legs that gave her a very, very appealing front and backside. She was proud of her body, and she was proud that she took care of it. Her shyness lasted about five minutes, and then she relaxed when she realized that the students were not ogling her nakedness but using their art skills to create lasting images. That moment gave her a sense of new-found confidence in herself and her body. Her only disappointment was looking at the finished art. There were naked depictions of her as a tall, or short, or thin, or fat, or pretty, or not so pretty woman; sometimes with big breasts, sometimes small breasts, sometimes three breasts; and even with a Picasso-like face with one giant eye. Enough to take your breath away, or at least make you laugh. Art certainly came in different flavors, and abstract art came in a rainbow of colors that made the imagination wonder out loud. After that day, Jamie was never ashamed to be seen nude again. How could she? A selected drawing of her hung in the art exhibit hall and she looked more like a naked flower than a beautiful, nude college student.

Bentley's sudden barking chased away her fond memories. Mrs. Little was at the door.

Jamie closed her suitcase and hurried out of her bedroom with Bentley running behind. After she greeted Mrs. Little and gave her some last-minute dog-watching instructions, Jamie looked at her watch and hurried back into her bedroom. Picking up the new pink halter top she had placed on the bed, she quickly slipped out of her conservative "look-at-me detective shirt and pants" and put on the halter top and matching tight, pink, contouring shorts. She quickly brushed her long blonde hair and, using hair-styling magic, put it into a "side" ponytail to the right of her face. She smiled at her image in the mirror. She looked really good. Then, she looked in the mirror again and made a quick, police-like decision. Off came the halter top, off came the bra. She donned the halter top by itself and felt that she looked much better now; so did her round, perky breasts. Now she felt satisfied with "her new look." The only thing missing was the red lipstick. It was packed, and it would have to wait. Besides, it would probably be the only thing she would be permitted to wear there, besides her high heels.

Outside her window she saw McKenna arrive in a sharp-looking sports car—a red Corvette convertible, no less. Not exactly the typical police car she was accustomed to seeing him in. She smiled and almost laughed out loud. Nope, nothing about this day was "typical" for her, so far, including the quickening "heartbeat" she felt, as she quickly left her house, her dog, and Mrs. Little behind to meet her pre-arranged, imagined, new "boyfriend" and go on a "totally not-so-typical naked vacation"...if one could call it that.

CHAPTER 9

She could smell blood. She liked its smell; it had a very special alluring aroma, which gave her a special euphoric feeling. And that feeling made her want it even more. Just like all the warm and wonderful blood she had last night. Not just one feeding, but two. But it still wasn't enough.

She needed more. And the sooner the better. The "craving" wasn't for her pleasure, the craving was for her survival. She knew it, and so did He.

She slowly forced herself to stand. She had been sleeping, or what she called "resting," in a large leather antique chair, more like a throne, with ornate marble arm rests, with two leather belt-buckle-type straps attached to it, one for each arm. They were not attached to her now; just hung from it. Holding the huge chair upright were four thick legs made out of dark cherry wood, with strange carvings of what appeared to be entwined and screaming naked people. The back of the chair was at least five feet tall, all plush leather, encased in a similarly carved, swirling wooden design that came to a point at the very top, as if it were leading the onlooker upwards to heaven. Although from the look of the chair, the environment it was in, and the occupant who had been on it, one would think hell was not below, but was possibly right there where she now stood.

The room was mostly dark, illuminated by equally placed metal standing fixtures, each holding small burning fires within an open crown. Cut into a gray stone slab floor, in a precisely cut half circle around the throne, a foot-wide trench was filled with dancing flames from a fire somewhere unseen below. It was apparent that this was all part of some type of long-lost ceremonial ritual setting.

There was a long, silent pause of deep thought by this mysterious woman, who was standing next to the chair. She stretched her neck, one way, then another, to slowly awaken her body and rid herself of any remnants of however long she had rested. Her "rest" was not like the rest one is accustomed to having. Her rest was dark, void, and empty of dreams, a time without time, with one continuous, all-encompassing, all-consuming thought—"blood."

The flames from the fiery pit illuminated her full-figure and revealed her goddess-like beauty, wearing only a long, full-length, black, see-through gown, open at the front and revealing her supple, totally nude, white flesh. She was the same woman who had earlier sunk her fangs into an upside-down, screaming Johnny Rains, and a drunken, aroused—very aroused—unlucky Larry Miller.

But that was then, and this was now.

A familiar man's voice broke the silence and seemed to resonate from out of nowhere. It was the same deep and haunting voice that spoke to the struggling and bound Johnny Rains.

"Ahh, you are finally awake. I hope you have rested well and feel alive from your meals?"

"Yes, Father. Thank you for the feeding. But I still hunger. I need more," she answered calmly into the darkness which surrounded her.

"And you shall, tonight, as we planned. We both know who is next. And your patience will lead to filling your lust as well as filling mine," the unseen voice replied.

"Yes. Our lust," she whispered with an eerie tone that would put fear into anyone who heard it; a voice that was both softly hypnotizing and dangerously menacing.

"Yes. I will be patient," she concluded, not with a sigh, but a wishful thought of what was to come.

The man's voice continued with a reassuring and meaningful comfort, "Relax now, Alexandria. Relax and let your hunger be our weapon."

As suddenly as the man's voice had surrounded her, and seemed to hold her, it disappeared into the darkness, as did she. Emotionless and without fear, she knew that, where she was going, there was no feeling of restriction. With every few steps she took, an avatar of her was reflected from the nearby, standing, dark-metal fixtures, which created for her a shadowy path forward. As she passed each one, the internal flames came to life and jumped higher and flickered brighter, as if responding to her very presence.

It wasn't long before she turned into a narrow, dark tunnel, which was illuminated by metal torches that appeared to be a living part of the corresponding black walls. She was oblivious to the haunting and repetitive sound of her stiletto high heels echoing within the tunnel. In the distance, she heard the familiar sound of falling water, which came from somewhere ahead. A cool wind from out of nowhere made her long black hair move as if it had a life of its own. The light at the end of the tunnel grew larger, closer, and more inviting as she approached it. Her destination was close at hand.

Emerging from the tunnel, she entered into a large circular, dimly lit chamber. It, too, was illuminated by equally spaced, mounted wall torches and similarly freestanding metal fixtures which all held same-sized flickering flames. The entire atmosphere was more surreal than real. The chamber was at least one hundred feet in diameter and half of that in height. Its walls and ceiling appeared to be made of the same dark rock but glittered in the light, as if it were alive with twinkling stars in a faraway universe. Whether the rock had pieces of quartz or actual diamonds, or just glistening drops of water, it blended as one, and looked more ancient than recent. But none of this mattered to her as she exuded a feeling of being at peace with herself, or at least being comfortable in this cold, unnatural setting.

However, inside her mind there was a strange emptiness. Her beauty was but a mask to hide something more. Perhaps a past tragedy or a present dilemma. Her eyes stared ahead, trance-like, lifeless, without expression. Maybe it was all a dream she was just a part of, but underneath it all was a calm, yet foreboding madness. In her mind she may have questioned who she really was; for all she knew, and for all we know, she may have been dead, or maybe wished she was.

She was more illuminated now from the many torches, making her elongated shadow seem to dance across the walls as she walked. The surrounding floor was also made from similar rock, but grounded and polished so one could easily walk across it. In the center of the chamber was a mid-sized pool of warm water, which gently bubbled as if being fed from an underground spring. A spout of water came straight out and upwards, and fell back in a fountain-like effect. She approached it and stood before it, looking at her reflection, which seemed to not only look back at her, but deep within her. As if looking for her soul. If she even had one.

Disrobing from her long black gown, and letting it fall to the floor beneath her, she stepped into the pool of water, still wearing her black stiletto high heels. The carved rock steps allowed her to go comfortably, and carefully, into the water, leading her to the center. She was waist deep as it bubbled around her, caressing her naked flesh. She cupped her hands and gently scooped the warm water, bringing both hands to the top of her large, perfectly shaped breasts. The water found its way around her long fingers and rolled down her skin and across her perfect, pink nipples, which quickly hardened from the touch of her fingers, creating a sensation, which made them even bigger. She closed her eyes and slowly rotated her head on her long, smooth-looking neck. Slowly, she brought her hands back, cupping her breasts, feeling each one gently, while arousing her innermost passions. She did this in silence; there were no moans from her personal touch. Only the repeating sound of the bubbling water, which lapped at her naked waist, broke whatever silence there was. Her only thought was of the taste that she needed and desired. The taste that was promised by her father and would soon be hers to enjoy. And in that moment, she drifted into a trance-like state. She slowly bared her long white fangs and let them scratch her perfectly shaped lips, letting a small trickle of her own substance roll into her slightly opened mouth.

Without hesitation, without shame, she slowly licked her lips, tasting herself. And with that taste, she finally let out a soft, almost silent-like moan. A very soft moan, which quickly grew into more of a primal scream. A frightening scream, which turned into a deafening scream. An endless scream, which contained one word that filled the chamber and echoed through the tunnel and across the walls for

what seemed like an eternity of time. One spoken
word.

"Blood!"

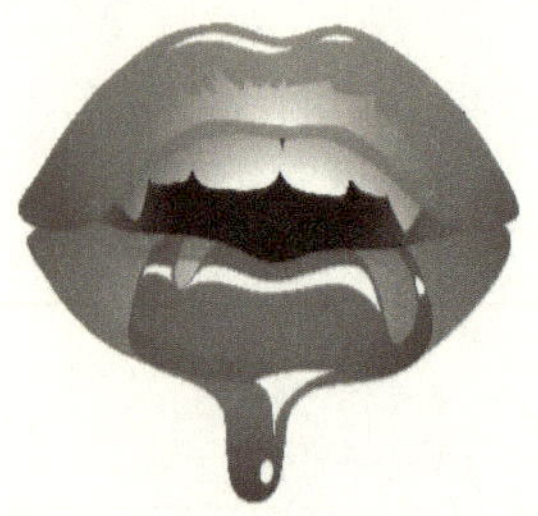

CHAPTER 10

The image on the TV security monitor was dark and somewhat blurry. Although most of the Paradise Lost Resort security cameras had been placed in well-lit areas or with a good viewing advantage, this one by the outdoor boutique shop was partially blocked by a recently grown palm tree frond. But they still could make out a partial figure, and then two, and then...?

"Jesus Christ, it looks like the woman is biting him on the neck!" exclaimed Perkins, the nighttime resort manager.

"That's sick sex," chimed in Davis, the daytime resort manager, shaking his head in both disbelief and a hint of being turned on by what he saw. Besides the typical naked sun worshippers, there were a lot of swingers here looking for sex. Was this woman one of them?

"Back it up and slow it down," demanded Philip Winston who stood next to both of them in the private security office located adjacent to the resort's main registration desk. There were no windows in the mid-sized office, just a lot of computers and a dozen security monitors showing ongoing live scenes of different areas of the resort.

They watched the recording again, frame by frame. The woman seen only from behind was tall, totally nude, in high stiletto heels, and had an attractive body with a very shapely backside.

"Jezuz, look at that ass!" Davis said out loud, mostly commenting to himself, but he was also heard by the two other men in the room. Neither of the them watching the TV monitor commented about his remark. The resort was always filled with nice-looking "ass."

The recording concluded with the man in the scene falling half out of the stationary camera frame and onto the pavement, and then being dragged completely out of the frame by another unseen person. The mysterious woman with her back to the camera walked out of the frame following the dragged body. At no moment in the recording could she be recognized. The man had been identified as a guest after he was found propped up dead in the boutique window that morning.

Perkins looked away from the security monitor screen and at Winston. It was apparent he was quite shocked at what he had just seen.

"We know who that man is. We identified him as Larry Miller from the guest registration photo we had on file. We've tried to match this woman in the recording with other guest IDs, but no luck so far, including Miller's guest who can't be located. All we can go on is the length and color of her hair, long and dark, and a damn hot-looking body. Sort of matches about half of the women here, which is about 200 and counting with the convention starting yesterday."

Winston stood silent, rubbing his chin with his right hand as if contemplating more than one thought. Finally, he spoke.

"Run a check on the day guests who come and go. Everyone shows a license with a photo or some form of photo ID at the main entrance gate; all of those are copied. Also check our staff files. She could be one of our people, and don't rule out that she could have been wearing a wig to hide her real identity."

"Shit, that takes us almost back to ground zero, checking all the guests and staff," Davis added.

"Put as many of our trusted people on it. This must be kept quiet. It was bad enough that we had police here this morning. And not only do we have this murder on our hands, but also that of the porn star," Winston replied in a voice of controlled displeasure.

"Could that have been a drowning?" Perkins questioned his boss.

"That's what we're telling anyone who asks—an 'accidental' drowning. We don't want to scare the guests or draw any more attention to the situation than we already have. There's too much at stake here with the special guests arriving later today and tomorrow, and their planned activities," Winston quickly replied while starting to pace the floor area around the monitor.

Davis and Perkins looked at each other without further comment. They knew him well enough to remain silent, as he obviously appeared to be stressed out and likely to snap at them.

As quickly as he started, Winston stopped his pacing and turned to address both of them.

"What baffles me most is how the main security camera was turned off at the main pool and by whom? We have no recording of what happened there. And at this point, the only tie-in between the two murders is that both victims were drained of all their blood. And on top of that, who the fuck called the police and on what phone? All our phones are tied into the computer system which records everything, and our records came up empty. All the guests' cell phones and computers are secured, and we have a specialized blocking signal for anyone who sneaks one in. Although these two guys don't appear connected, their deaths do."

"The marks on their necks?" Davis asked.

"Conners, our medical guy, examined the body when we pulled it from the pool and was perplexed at what could cause such bites," Perkins answered. It was obvious he was the smarter of the two managers, if it really mattered.

"Maybe an alligator got in the pool?" Davis responded while nodding his head, as if he just may have figured it out.

Winston gave him a look of disdain.

"I saw the exact same marks on the neck of this Miller guy when we pulled his body out of the boutique window. Two distinct bites, similar in size and both on the same side of their necks," Winston stated as an important fact that only he had previously picked up on and had been careful not to share with anyone, including the nosey police.

"That's creepy. I don't recall any bats flying around here," Perkins mentioned while slowly shaking his head trying to figure it out. Perhaps he wasn't that smart, after all.

Winston stood silent and then looked at both of his managers directly in their eyes.

"And both of them had all their blood drained."

Those words sent a deep chill through each of the two managers.

"Shit, that ain't no bat. That's Dracula!" Perkins exclaimed, probably having watched one too many vampire movies in his life.

Now it was Perkins' turn to get a look of disdain from Winston, but not quite the same look as Winston gave Davis.

Maybe there was something more to what his manager said that he had not previously thought of. Certainly, it was strange. Very strange.

"What about the police? Will they be back snooping around?" inquired Perkins.

"No. New Tampa Mayor Ellsworth was here last night partying, and not with his wife. When I told him of the situation, he got *real* nervous and called Police Chief Harold Johnson about his cops being here. The local police, who were already here onsite, were contacted and ordered to leave and they won't be allowed back." Winston started to rub his chin again, maybe it was a nervous habit of his, or maybe it was the fact that he had been awakened very early regarding this matter and didn't have time to shave. He always exuded an air of confidence along with his good looks and great business title. But now, he seemed not only irritated, but equally concerned.

"Right. We have that special waiver. We have our own legalized 'grandfathered jurisdiction' above and outside of the local law," Perkins reminded himself and Davis.

"And state law," Winston added to Davis's comment.

He quit rubbing his chin and looked at the monitor screen again. It remained in freeze frame on the last scene of the dead body being dragged away. He remained looking at the TV screen image with his back to the two managers as he spoke.

"We can't have another murder here, and we can't let rumors of what happened here spread. So, it's up to you both and your teams to keep all this quiet. Let's make our guests continue to feel comfortable, and don't let these murders affect any of the planned events."

He turned to face them both. Although he appeared calm on the outside, his inside was filled with a growing anger.

"If the killer is still here, we have to find him, or her, and stop them. There's too much at stake this week, and you both know what I mean. So just remember one thing: that mysterious woman's 'nice ass' you saw? Well, if you fuck any of this up, your 'not-so-nice asses' will never be seen here, or anywhere, again."

CHAPTER 11

"Officer McKenna, I mean Jim, Jim Stanton." Jamie extended her open hand into the convertible sports car. His newly dyed dark brown hair gave him a sexy look.

"Ms. Anderson." He nodded politely and shook her hand as if meeting for the first time.

"Nice car."

"Nice outfit."

"Nice assignment." They both laughed together having said the exact same thing at the exact same time. But maybe with different definitions of "nice" regarding this assignment.

"Your car?" Jamie inquired.

"Yes. Only drive it on special occasions. Most of the time I'm stuck in a police cruiser. But there's enough room for your luggage."

"I packed light. If you can call it that." She smiled as she placed her small, nearly empty travel suitcase behind his seat and noticed a similarly sized one for him. A brief passing thought of what little clothing he brought crossed her mind.

"What year?"

"Seventy-nine, one of the last Stingray models. My dad bought it and had it stored in his garage up North. When he passed, I brought it down."

"Sorry."

"Thanks. For his passing, or bringing the car to Florida?" McKenna responded in a joking tone.

"You're a cop; you figure it out."

"Touché!" she thought to herself as she smiled warmly while getting into his car. Apparently beneath his professional and tough-guy mannerisms that she had come to know, he actually had a sense of humor. So did she. This pleased her as she closed her car door and buckled herself in.

"Think we'll be noticed?" McKenna asked.

"No one would finger an undercover team in a car like this," Jamie replied.

"You're probably right," McKenna concurred. "That's why you're a detective. We'll know in about 20 minutes when we get there."

As the Corvette pulled away from her home, Jamie looked back and saw Mrs. Little and Bentley standing in the doorway. She smiled when she saw Bentley had a big bone in his mouth.

For the first few minutes, neither spoke. She enjoyed the warm afternoon Florida air that caressed her bare shoulders, as she sat back enjoying the ride. Jamie had never been in a car like this before, and she was savoring every moment. Other cars they passed looked at the classic car, and, of course, at them. *"We actually make an attractive couple,"* she thought to herself, as they passed a conservative-looking car with an elderly couple staring at them.

Jamie looked over at him as he comfortably shifted gears. His aviator sunglasses covered his blue eyes, which had caught her attention from the day they met. She remembered her mother once telling her as a young girl that you could tell the true depth of a man's heart by "looking directly into his eyes."

She liked what she saw the first time she looked at him. She also liked what she saw today. He wore a light blue short-sleeved polo shirt that hugged his athletic body. What caught her attention was that he had on a nice pair of black dress slacks and black leather shoes with no socks. At first, she wondered why, but then thought it was just one less item of clothing to take off. She also wondered if he was wearing underwear. She quickly turned her eyes away from his pants to look at the passing landscape.

"Come on, Jamie. Focus!" she said to herself with a personal and secretive grin as he changed gears and sped onto the highway that led to the resort.

She spoke first.

"Have you ever been to a naturist resort?"

"Well, yes and no," he replied with a short chuckle. "Yes, because I was there this morning, as you probably recall, and no, because I never have been to one before today."

"Are you nervous?" she discretely asked.

He smiled and looked at her quickly, while keeping his eye on the highway.

"Are you?"

"I posed nude once for an art class in college. I remember that my knees were shaking when I disrobed. They're kinda shaking now. But this is so far removed from anything I can imagine, hundreds of naked people, all strangers."

"Except one, me," he quickly added.

"Well, you don't count, sort of." She half-smiled in response. But Jamie knew that he did, in fact, count since they had to come across as a "couple," which meant some form of intimacy, whether it was touching or kissing, while naked. She didn't have that kind of issue when posing nude in an art class.

There was a slight pause between them, and then he looked quickly back to her.

"When I was a teenager our family used to go camping in the mountains. One afternoon my younger brother and I went hiking by ourselves. I was 15; he was 12. His name is Bobby, he still lives up North. Anyway, we came across a clearing with a nice pond and there were a group of young teenage girls—I remember five of them—and they were swimming, having a fun time. Maybe sisters, maybe school friends. I don't really know. They were all about my age or a little older and my brother and I were shocked to see that they had no clothes on as the water was only waist deep. But they weren't shocked to see us at all; they seemed comfortable with us there, and continued enjoying themselves, laughing, splashing, just having fun."

"They were all naked?"

"Yeah, and as Bobby and I stood there gawking, never having seen girls naked outside of a peek or two of our dad's *Playboy* magazines that he didn't hide very well under his bed, we were taking it all in when one of the older girls dared us to come in."

"And...?" Jamie asked with a definite interest in her voice.

"And we did. We took our clothes off and ran into the water to join them. Little did we know that one of the girls got out of the water behind our backs, took our clothes, and ran away. The others quickly followed, leaving us alone in the pond, totally naked while they all grabbed their clothes and ran off, laughing. After trying to figure out what to do, we had no choice but walk about a mile back to the family campgrounds."

"Nude?"

"Well, with one hand in front, and one hand behind," he admitted.

"That's funny!" She laughed at the thought of it.

"At the time, it wasn't funny, especially when we had to fess up to our mother. But now, when I think of it, yes, it was. So that's my 'naked experience' in front of strangers," he concluded with a half-smile to her, before returning his attention back to the road.

"So, the moral to your story is not to trust naked women because they might steal your clothes," Jamie laughed as she used her analytical detective skills to come up with a clever "punch line" to his story.

McKenna took his eyes off the road and turned and smiled warmly back at her.

"Actually, we won't have to worry about that where we're going, will we?" he concluded, smugly.

They both laughed, sort of, as McKenna's red Corvette turned off the main road and entered the private drive leading to the entrance of the Paradise Lost Naturist Resort. No matter what their past naked experience gave them, nothing would compare to, or prepare them for, the horrific experience that awaited them.

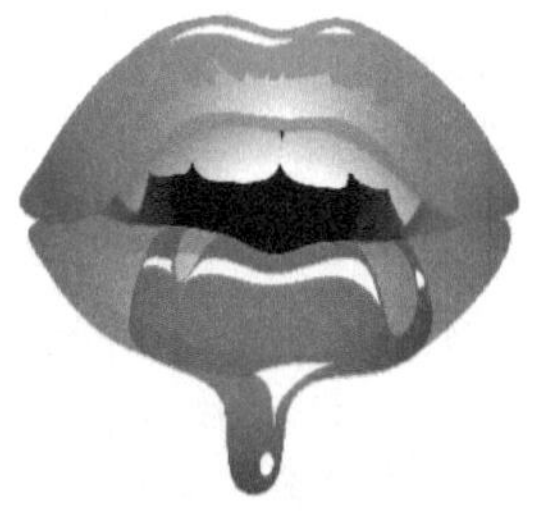

CHAPTER 12

"Here come the cops! Here come the cops!" the colorful blue Amazon parrot screamed loudly from its large metal cage as both McKenna and Parker got out of the Corvette at the entrance to the Paradise Lost Resort lobby.

A young naked man wearing a valet cap and sandals approached them. Jamie wasn't sure if it was the parrot's words or the naked young parking attendant that shocked her more.

"Don't worry, folks, the bird says that to everyone. His original owner loved police TV shows. How long's your stay?"

McKenna turned his attention from the bird to the attendant.

"Reservations for three nights. Be careful where you park the car, and..."

"Don't worry. I always sit on a clean towel." He quickly pulled one from the valet desk along curbside.

From this point on, they were known as Jim and Jamie. Jim grabbed the two small suitcases and walked into the lobby with Jamie. He had been here earlier today, but he acted like it was all brand new to him, so he stopped with her and pointed at the giant, ornate water fountain.

"Isn't that beautiful, Honey? This is better than the online photos we saw."

Jamie played along in case anyone was listening or watching. "This is going to be so much fun! I can't wait to start our vacation and get into the sun."

She grabbed him by the arm and held on warmly as they approached the front desk. Another couple was just finishing their check-in reservations. Both were in their early thirties and smiled at them, with smiles that were almost too friendly, as they left for their room.

"Welcome to Paradise!" The topless receptionist warmly greeted them. She was in her late 20s, an attractive blonde with large, artificial, cupcake-shaped breasts.

As Jim signed them in with their new identities and got the ground rules, both on paper and visually displayed on a large standing easel off to the right, Jamie did a casual observation of the place. She started to memorize the immediate layout, as a detective would instinctively do.

"Honey, we have to turn in our cell phones and computer. But we can use the phone here if you have to call your mom," Jim told her.

"Okay, who needs this stuff anyway? We're on vacation!" Jamie smiled to the receptionist, although she was already aware of the strict privacy rules and had already planned this out.

"The nightly Meet and Greet starts at 5 p.m. in the main lobby lounge off to the left of the piano bar. There will be complimentary champagne and appetizers." The desk clerk smiled as she handed them the code to their keyless room. After all, what naked guest would have a pocket to put their room key in?

A security guard immediately approached them and directed both through a free-standing metal-detection device to make certain they weren't sneaking in any other recording devices that were forbidden here.

"First timers?"

"Yes," they both smiled as they passed through. "We're here for the convention, too. And then later this week, off to Disney."

The guard politely smiled, although he probably cared less about their plans, having most likely heard it before from many of the guests.

"Enjoy the stay. Any questions, ask any of the resort security people. We all have blue armbands that indicate 'Security.'" He pointed at the band across his large, muscular arm. Jamie kept her eyes above his waist. He was naked. She was trying to adapt to it without appearing like a kid in a candy store.

Just follow the hallway to the left. You're near the end, Room 6913, poolside, with a patio exit to the grounds, unless you want to walk back through here and go nude through the lobby. Do you need help with your luggage?"

"Thanks, we packed light," Jim replied as Jamie held onto his arm, and they went towards the hallway leading to their room.

Jamie looked at the room numbers on the hotel doors they passed.

"6913, odd number for a first-floor room," then realizing the metaphor, she added, "Never mind," slightly laughing to both herself and to Jim.

Using a keyless touch pad outside their door, Jamie entered first, followed by Jim. It was a spacious room with a large heart-shaped king-sized bed and a floor-to-ceiling mirror behind it. The ceiling above the bed also had a corresponding same-sized heart-shaped mirror.

Jamie looked at their images in the wall mirror and the ceiling mirror, and then looked at Jim.

"Enough mirrors so we won't forget what we look like," Jamie said half-jokingly, half nervous.

Jim smiled. She liked his smile. It was comforting, and it made her feel somewhat relaxed. Somewhat.

"Well..." He surveyed the room, eyeing an all-glass-shelved bar area with assorted alcoholic bottles, several bouquets of fresh flowers throughout the room, a heart-shaped bowl of strawberries dipped in dark chocolate, and a single, long-stemmed red rose placed directly in the center of the red silk bedspread. "Sort of reminds me of home."

That made her laugh, and she quickly added. "Yeah, me, too, except no TV in the room to watch a show like Oprah, not that I can imagine anyone coming here to watch TV."

Jamie walked over to the large patio door that led to the immediate resort grounds outside. Sheer white curtains covered the windows, not that they really did. She took a moment to pause and look at the fantasy world outside. A row of huge, perfectly manicured tropical palm trees lined the pathway along all of the rooms and led directly to the nearby outdoor pool and grotto waterfall a short distance away. She could see several couples, totally nude, walking toward the pool. She had played this all out in her mind after she and McKenna left the Chief's office. Whatever she imagined couldn't match the reality that they were both now finally a part of. *"Paradise Lost. How appropriate,"* she thought to herself. *"And we're both still in our clothes."* She half smiled and nodded secretly to herself. She knew that wouldn't be the case for much longer.

When she turned back to Jim, he was standing next to the glass bar. He was very handsome. His piercing blue eyes met hers. She wondered if he probably was thinking the same thoughts.

"Drink?"

She moved closer to him. It was the first time in a long time that she been alone with a man, especially an attractive man like him, in a hotel room, and offered a drink.

"Not that I drink that much, but right about now, I think I need one," she replied in a tone that conveyed a mixture of honesty with slight apprehension.

"Yeah, me, too." His tone matched hers.

"Just some white wine. Chardonnay?"

He poured an open bottle of white wine into two decorative long-stemmed glasses, which awaited them on the glass bar top. He handed her one and then picked up the other.

"To Paradise."

"Yes, Paradise."

Clinking glasses, they both drank in silence, and then the tone changed to seriousness.

"So, we're really here." Jim spoke first.

"Yes, we are." Jamie nodded, wondering what he would say or do next, or even what she would say or do next.

"I'll sleep in the chair."

She only nodded, not sure of how to respond other than, "Of course," although that was not what she really wanted to say, but she did.

"Of course."

He took another sip from his glass.

"I know we haven't really socialized, or even spoken much at work, but I'll do everything I can do to make this assignment as comfortable as I can. I don't have any police training or a police manual on working procedures in the nude, but..."

"I know you will," she quickly added.

Jamie placed her wine glass on the glass bar top; it was half empty. Although she had enjoyed it, she felt maybe, just maybe, she shouldn't have any more, at least not now. She wanted to touch his arm in polite response to what he just said, but did not.

"And that goes for me, too. We're professionals, and, of course, adults, and we'll adjust to the place. I know it's just an assignment, but it just seems so..."

"...different?" It was his turn to quickly add to her sentence, with just a bit of sarcasm mixed somewhere within it.

She smiled, appreciating his comment. She knew it probably would be challenging for him, too. After all he was an attractive man, and there would be a lot of attractive women, nude women, even herself, and how would he be able to...?

"...and challenging. Don't forget challenging." He finished both her original thought and his own.

It was apparent that he knew of the "naked" challenges that would catch his eye and maybe arouse his...

"But we have a job to do, whether in clothes, or out of clothes," Jim said convincingly, or at least trying to convince himself.

"So..." she hesitated, as her hand touched her wine glass, but then left it alone. "I guess we should start."

"Yeah," he replied, taking a brief moment, and then continued. "As the Chief recommended, we'll make friendly with the guests and look for any clues that might help us figure this all out. Two murders, and weirdly done murders, with the all the victim's blood being sucked out, and the bodies left to be seen and found. It's almost as if the killer is leaving a message."

"Could be. We need to determine exactly where and when these murders were committed, as the bodies may have been purposely placed or moved. We may not have access to all areas."

It was McKenna's turn to put himself back into his policeman's role.

"So, let's start with a stop at the pool where they found the first body, and a stroll by the boutique shop where the other body was discovered."

"Yes. And..." Jamie paused for moment as if trying to find the right words to say next, even though she knew, and he knew, what those words were.

"Let's get changed, and fit right in," Jim added.

Again, Jamie laughed, "That's for sure—fit right in!"

"Interesting choice of words," she thought. "Yes, let's get changed." Her eyebrows lifted up and her smile widened even more as her mind filled with images of herself parading around without clothes in front of him.

"I've never done this before, the nude thing, with other naked people, so give me a minute to undress in the ladies room." She pointed to their bathroom.

"Sure. I'll just do the same in the men's room." He pointed to the patio door.

This time they both laughed. They both knew that, if this undercover assignment was going to work, they had to have some sense of humor wrapped around the serious work they had to do here, especially acting as a "couple."

Jamie picked up her still half-filled glass of wine and took it with her into the bathroom. Before she closed the door, she paused and slowly turned back to him.

"You promise you won't laugh?" she asked cutely.

"I can only promise I'll try not to stare," he responded coyly.

Jamie felt a slight blush come over her. She smiled, turned, and entered the bathroom, closing the door behind her.

Leaning her back against the closed door—not from fear or concern that he would suddenly enter—she knew she needed a moment to catch her breath from all that was going on in her mind and now in her heart. The first thing she did was to look at herself in the large bathroom mirror over the granite sink counter.

She let out a deep sigh and slowly shook her head, wondering if this was all a dream or if this was real. Here she was at thirty and neither famous nor wealthy, nor married like many of her girlfriends. She was a policewoman in a nudist resort with a hot-looking policeman she hardly knew and about to get naked with him to catch a killer who sucked blood out of the victims!

"Okay, Jamie, pull yourself together. It's not a dream; it's just a job," she said to the person in the mirror, who just happened to be her.

Jamie used one hand to untie her ponytail, allowing her blonde hair to fall playfully across her face. With both hands, she pushed it off to the sides, where it belonged, and stared in the mirror for a seemingly longer-than-long moment.

"It's showtime," she said out loud to herself, and then she laughed at her choice of words. "Showtime."

And then she began.

She removed her halter top first. Her breasts were quickly revealed since she had taken her bra off before she left the house. She was pleased with what she saw. They were perfect for her athletic body. Firm, very round, and they were real. Her nipples were a pleasing pink color with a nicely shaped areola around them. And they were starting to get aroused.

"Slow down, girl. Don't draw too much attention right away, especially from the guy on the other side of the door," she thought to herself, before continuing to undress.

She loosened the button on the waistband of her shorts and quickly pulled them downward. She had very nice-looking, long legs. She recalled how as a young teenager, before she started to develop her figure, she had the nickname "Legs" given to her from her close girlfriends. She was tall for her early teenage years, flat chested, thin, lanky, and all legs. And here she was years later admiring those legs in a nudist resort mirror with only a pair of pink-colored panties remaining on her body. But not for long. They came off quickly, as she stepped out of them and stood totally naked like the day she was born. She looked at herself, then turned her body, and then her head, back to look at herself again.

"No cellulite, thank God," she thought to herself. Mother Nature and her daily morning runs with Bentley kept her skin firm and tight.

Jamie tossed her head back slightly and, simultaneously, put her hands back into her long hair to give it a bit more fluffy-like style. She hadn't unpacked her cosmetics yet from her suitcase in the bedroom, so the red lipstick would have to wait. She slowly licked her supple lips to give them a moist look. She was as ready as she'd ever be.

One last look in the mirror. One more deep breath. One last sip of her wine. One more silently spoken word, *"Showtime."* And she exited the bathroom, leaving her empty glass behind.

Jim was standing with his back to her as she re-entered their bedroom. He was looking out the window at the pool nearby. He, too, was totally nude.

The first thing she saw was his "ass." His nice, tight ass. Forget the muscular shoulders and athletic- looking back, or even his narrow waist—it was all about his ass.

And then he turned to look at her.

Her eyes met his. His piercing blue eyes.

They both remained looking at each other. No words, no emotion.

He looked first.

Then she did.

He was like a Greek Adonis. Muscular, but not overly. A slight six-pack of abs, but not excessive. Tanned skin, toned, and tight. No fat around his waist and a very...

"Nice, very nice," she thought to herself as she admired his nude physique.

She quickly brought her eyes back upwards. His followed hers. And their eyes met again.

"You are very beautiful." He spoke softly, honestly, and respectfully.

"And you are very..."

"Don't make this any harder. I mean, it's hard enough. I mean..." Jim stumbled over his own words as he tried to find the right word.

"Difficult?"

He let out a deep breath. Yes, it was difficult for him to control his feelings and not be aroused by her nakedness, by her beauty, and by the way she looked at him.

"Well, from the looks of things..." she started to say, then paused briefly. *"Nice choice of words, Jamie,"* she chastised herself, as her mind raced with all sorts of thoughts that, if spoken out loud, she surely would need to have her mouth washed out with soap. "...you won't have to bring a gun," she concluded with a smile.

He knew what she meant, and she meant what she said.

And they both laughed together, sharing an awkward, yet special moment, like two teenagers seeing each other naked for the first time. And, of course, they were. Very naked.

He opened the patio door to the entrance of their adventure into Paradise, holding his hand out to hers. She gently took it, and tightly wrapped her fingers around his. The unknown was waiting for them just outside.

"Time to go to work." He looked at her as a detective, not a woman.

She squeezed his hand. Like a woman, not a detective.

"And time to catch a killer." She looked at him as a man, not a cop.

And he squeezed her hand.

Like Alice in Wonderland, unbeknownst to her, she was on the precipice of the rabbit hole.

CHAPTER 13

Rock Hard, aka Rock Harder, was the current big name in porn. Actually, he was the current "big dick." Measuring some 12-plus inches, he was also nicknamed "the ruler," not exactly like Queen Elizabeth, the Ruler, but sort of. He really was a "dick," because he was so rude and nasty to everyone, both on and off the movie sets. At age 50—even though he said he was only 40—he was the oldest actor in porn. Even at this age, he was still considered to be a "handsome and dapper-looking man" by some, including himself; it was the extra layers of daily pancake makeup and several facelifts that helped him keep the illusion of a youthful appearance. His movies made a lot of money—lots and lots of money—and he had a lot of fans—lots and lots of them, mostly guys—so he was able to be, and do, whatever he wanted to. And so, he was a dick. Rock Hard was also gay, not that it mattered.

Shortly after Parker and McKenna checked into Paradise Lost, so did Rock Hard. He arrived in a flamboyant pink-colored Cadillac, borrowed from a Florida relative who sold cosmetics, and was escorted into the resort with an entourage of four very beefy and muscular-looking security guards. Each of his

"Rock Hard Crew" wore matching pink t-shirts with Rock's face on it, and the words, "He's so Hard." Rock himself was dressed in a pink suit coat, unbuttoned pink shirt and matching pink shorts—that is, tight pink short-shorts. Because Rock was only five foot, three inches tall, he wore specially made, pink, high-top platform sneakers with an imprinted picture of himself on each one. Cradled under his right arm, he carried with him his pride and joy possession, "Stiffy," his dyed-pink poodle, who actually was a bitch, in heat, that is.

Rock was given royalty treatment during his check-in as he was one of the main porn stars attending the convention. He was as big a star as Johnny Rains was, not that Rock or many people knew yet that Johnny was no longer attending the convention because he was dead, and that his death was still being covered up. But Rock attracted a whole different and adoring fanbase in an ever-changing porn industry.

What first started out in the 1930s as silent, black-and-white, "underground" pornographic films of a man and woman doing "it," the entire movie "sex" scene quickly grew with different matches, or pairings, of different people: Two girls. Two girls and a guy. Two guys and a girl. Two guys and two girls. Any possible pairing of guys and girls and any other number of multiple participants. All sizes and all shapes. No names, just faces, even though some guys wore black Zorro-type eye masks to hide their identity from their family or friends or married significant others. The basic rule was that everyone was butt naked. However, some porn guys still wore their socks while being filmed having sex—must have had cold feet. Big name movie stars like Marilyn Monroe were even rumored to have jumpstarted their careers doing porn. And many did.

With the American public able to buy 8mm home movie projectors in the '50s and '60s, movie film loops of all of these combinations of participants going at it was big. Sold either through the mail or under the counter, movie or magazine porn was looked upon as "evil sex" by religious groups and righteous politicians, who actually practiced all this "evil" behind their own closed bedroom doors or secret hotel rendezvous. There were even some "forbidden" film loops, as they were called, of women with pets, usually a dog or a donkey. Just another way to attract the curious watcher, have a job, and to make a buck.

The '70s saw the advent of name porn actors and actresses. The most popular was Linda Lovelace, for her "special talent" in her role in the movie *Deep Throat,* and John Holmes for his big "part" (he also had a footlong penis) in the movie *The Devil in Miss Jones*. He actually played a horny naked devil, not that it mattered.

Porn exploded when prerecorded home video machines and video tapes hit the market in the '80s. X-rated movie theaters closed with their sticky and soiled seats, and more porn video tapes were sold than popular children's and family movies. Of course, the religious groups still protested, as did the politicians. But it was mostly "blah-blah-blah" to promote an agenda or create a name recognition. Sadly, many of these same people eventually got arrested for some naughty and nasty personal "sexcapades" of their own.

Porn really "exploded" in sales and became a worldwide epidemic with home-owned computers and the internet. Just one click of the finger and it was free in anyone's house, or for immediate purchase by the discerning collector.

As a result of all of this, sex became more open to the public. Naturist or nudist resorts grew worldwide as people sunned during the day and had fun during the night. Swingers and Swinger Clubs became *en vogue*. Boyfriends, girlfriends, people of all ages and all shapes and sizes, all colors and all nationalities used their digital cameras and phones to post images of themselves doing just about everything with everyone in every imaginable and unimaginable position. Sodom and Gomorrah? The end of civilization as we once knew it? The beginning of the end? Or, just the dawn of a new lifestyle without conventional morals, or any whatsoever? Whatever it was, it was, and still is today, at the "full bare-ass" Paradise Lost Resort Nude-a-Rama Convention, with everyone and anyone who wanted to participate. From plain folk who liked "the sun," to strange folk who liked "the fun." From husbands and wives looking for something different, to politicians and celebrities who already were doing the different. Sprinkle in the gawking fans, the wannabe future porn stars and the current ones. They were all there. Even a porn "Queen" with a big dick, two dicks in disguise hunting a Killer, and a Killer who liked to suck someone's blood. This was certainly the place to be, and for some, for sure, certainly the place to die.

When Rock Hard entered his celebrity suite, he didn't have the same amenities waiting for him as Parker and McKenna did. No, Rock was a "special" guest, and so he had something extra special that the management had pre-arranged just for him. In place of the typical guest "fruit basket," there on the heart-shaped bed sat an older man wearing a complete boy scout uniform, holding a long-stemmed, red rose.

"My, my, my. I do love a 'man' in a boy's uniform." Rock licked his lips and smiled happily for this pleasant surprise.

Rock's bodyguards closed the room door behind them, leaving Rock alone, while still holding his Stiffy.

The man on the bed was older than Rock—old enough to be his father. His beige uniform had the typical boy scout merit badges and patches sewn on the short-sleeved shirt with pocket flaps. He wore tight olive-green scout shorts with the official belt and brass buckle, a Boy Scouts of America logo embroidered on knee-high socks, and a matching scout cap. He even wore the gold-and-green scout neckerchief, which, from a fashion standpoint, made the whole ensemble come together.

Placing his precious pink poodle gently on the floor beside him, Rock tapped his sneaker heels together, straightened his slightly paunchy body, and saluted military style in a serious, yet comical, gesture.

"Movie Star Rock Hard reporting for duty."

Forming a pretend trumpet with his two hands, Rock started to make strange spitting musical sounds as if performing in a military band. Pumping his fingers on imaginary trumpet valves and pushing an imaginary slide in and out, Rock marched in an exaggerated swishing manner as he paraded around the suite, and finally over to the where the man sat quietly and patiently on the queen-sized bed. He stopped, and saluted again, and slowly licked his lips in greater anticipation.

"I just love a parade. They are so much fun and exciting!" Rock exclaimed out loud while somewhat out of breath from his parade prancing, and while clapping his hands together happily.

Without hesitation, Rock immediately, and quietly, knelt in front of the waiting man-scout, knowing exactly what his "scouting" assignment was. Rubbing his hands up and down on the man's bare knees, Rock felt a secret pleasure noticing as how the man was nicely built with freshly shaved legs.

As Rock started to undo the zipper on scout's shorts, he looked directly into the man's eyes and whispered, "I do hope to get a merit badge for what I plan to do to you."

The man-scout smiled and took his cap off, placing it on Rock's head.

As if bobbing for apples in a water bucket, Rock Hard moved his head up and down while humming a military tune. He was eagerly on his way to earning a special one-of-a-kind "pleasuring" badge, which he most certainly deserved for performing his patriotic pornographic duty.

From above, and unseen to the participants below, a hidden video camera in the overhead mirror had been activated the whole time, and secretly recorded the two men.

CHAPTER 14

Everyone was naked.

From where Jamie stood next to the bright aqua-colored pool of the Paradise Lost Resort, a hundred-plus people were sunning, splashing, or surveying each other, all in the nude. Everywhere she looked—boobs, buns, boobs, buns, boobs, buns, and more. And here she was, a part of it, showing her boobs, buns, and more, and so was her pretend boyfriend Jim Stanton, aka Jim McKenna, who was definitely showing more. She squeezed his hand in both anticipation and trepidation. The two undercover cops were definitely "uncovered" for the whole resort to see.

A tall, busty, attractive blonde wearing only high heels passed closely by, giving them a very enticing smile. McKenna awkwardly smiled back.

"Actually, I think she smiled at you," he said softly to Jamie. And he was probably right.

This place wasn't just for getting a tan. It was for meeting a man or a woman, and not for just talking about the weather.

A soft mid-afternoon Florida breeze touched both their naked bodies. It actually felt good. Jamie's long hair blew softly across her face. They looked at each other and laughed.

"Well, I always wanted a better tan," Jamie said candidly, while punctuating their laughter with a smile.

The sound of the nearby splashing two-story waterfall in the main pool of the Paradise Lost Resort blended with the piped-in music. The main resort pool was very large, and heart shaped. It was mostly for walking around waist deep and conversing with other guests. In the center was the circular giant waterfall shaped into a man-made working replica of a tropical volcano. Once an hour it blew artificial smoke high into the air, mixed with different-sized bubbles to the "oohs" and "aahs" of the mostly inebriated, naked watchers.

A built-in pool bar was adjacent to the waterfall. It had several heart-shaped bar stools in the water that one could easily swim up to, or just wade to. It was already filled with a dozen or so happy and laughing patrons, mostly in their early 30s. From Jamie's first investigative analysis of the entire pool area, there was a mixture of ages here, ranging from twenty-something to fifty-something. There were no kids, no families. Obviously, this was not the resort for them. And just about everyone here looked attractive naked. Obviously, this was the resort for them.

McKenna did a quick look to the pool and then back to Jamie.

"Why don't I wander over to the pool bar and get us something to drink while you find some pool chairs so we can sit and blend in, and talk with some guests?"

"Are you sure you're just not going after that smiling blonde?" she casually teased him.

"If I were, it would be to get a name and number for you," Jim chided her.

Jamie blushed, shook her head lightly, and walked towards some open chairs alongside the huge pool.

All the chairs were the same—full-length wooden lounge chairs, which could be adjusted to sit upright or flattened to lie down on. Rows and rows of them, either already filled with people, or a few empty chairs scattered here and there.

Jamie saw two together in between a young-looking couple holding hands, and a middle-aged woman reading a Danielle Steel romance novel.

"These two taken?"

"Hopefully, by you?" The man tipped his sunglasses upwards to get a better look at her.

Jamie half smiled politely. "Thanks. Guests or members?"

"Both. We're here for the convention. I'm a member. This is my girlfriend, Tina. Her first time."

"Yeah, mine too. I'm Jamie. So, what do you think of the place, Tina?"

She sat up in her lounge chair and casually wrapped her arms around her knees. She was probably mid- to late-20s, with short auburn hair, and small, but nice-looking, perky breasts.

"Absolutely nothing like it. We've been to a few nude beaches near Miami, but there are always a lot of creeps who just go to stare. Not here. This place has class."

"And hot-looking women like you," her boyfriend said, continuing to size up Jamie, which made her slightly uncomfortable, never having sat with a strange, naked man before.

"And hunky-looking guys like him," Tina added, as she watched a man walking towards them.

Jim approached with two tropical drinks in plastic-stemmed glasses.

"Yeah, he's a hunk, alright; he's my boyfriend, Jim."

Jamie reached for the drink he extended to her, and then nodded for him to join the conversation.

"Jim, this is..."

"Tina." She held out her hand to touch his.

"Jeff." Her boyfriend just waved his one hand in a hello gesture and put his sunglasses back down over his eyes.

"Where you from?" Tina asked, while taking her arms off her legs and sitting back casually on the edge of the lounge chair, revealing her body to Jim.

"Up north. New York State. We're here on vacation, first stop for some tanning in the sun to make our New York friends jealous when we go back next week. We're also here for a few days to check out the convention," Jim said matter of factly, having their background story well-rehearsed for conversations just like this.

"Then off to Disney. I always wanted to meet Mickey and Minnie," Jamie added.

Tina laughed. "Yeah, Disney's cool, but it would be more fun, though, if they were naked. We really enjoy being nude. We're excited about the convention. Lots of fun people to get to know. There's a bunch of planned sex seminars. We're soft swingers; we pretty much like to watch. How about you guys?"

"Well, mostly for the sun and..." Jim started to answer.

"...the convention. We're 'newbies.' We also like to watch," Jamie quickly jumped in.

"You're at the right place. There's a lot to watch here, and after the dances at night there's a lot to take part in if you want to," Jeff spoke up while laying back on the lounge chair and placing each leg on either side purposely exposing himself to Jamie.

She avoided his pose and looked back at Tina.

"Sounds interesting. How does it happen?"

"Each night there's a dance. It gets touchy-feely on the dance floor, and then it leads to mostly private parties, by invitation. There's also some outdoor stuff that goes on by the four, giant conversation jacuzzis on the other side of the pool. Good place to watch or join in casually. There's also a porn awards presentation and a gala nude masquerade party tomorrow night," Tina replied, apparently knowing a bit more than a first-timer would know.

It was Jim's turn to add to the conversation.

"Hmm. Quite a place. We heard all about this convention on the internet and were excited to come here. But I guess it's not all fun and games. Did you hear about the murder last night?"

"Yeah, kinda sketchy, although they're saying it was an accident. Heard a few rumors. Some guy died after midnight. Don't know much; no one seems to know much, or really cares, not in a place like this," Jeff answered while he started to casually scratch his leg close to where it met his waist, obviously trying to get Jamie's attention again.

"Apparently, it happened in this pool. Kind of weird, sitting here next to where a person drowned. Probably had too much to drink." Jamie again looked away and back to Tina.

"Had his blood drained out of him." Jim emphasized that point, looking for a reaction. Maybe they knew something; maybe a lot of people knew something. It was his and Jamie's job to find out that "something."

"What! No shit. You're kidding?" Tina exclaimed.

"Yeah, one of the porn stars. Not sure which one." Jamie tried to bait Tina to see if she knew more than she was willing to let on.

"Hope it wasn't Rock Hard; he's my favorite," Tina responded as if she honestly didn't know anything.

"Rock Hard. Ha. Quite an interesting name," Jim chuckled, hiding the truth that he really knew who was killed, while admitting out loud that this mentioned name was quite amusing for a porn star.

"And quite an interesting guy, if you want to call him that. He's queerer than a three-dollar bill, but 'hung' like a horse," Jeff stated more or less, as not really being a fan of this "Rock Hard" porn guy.

"So, who was it?" Tina asked, seriously interested.

"Some other porn guy named Rains," Jim continued like he didn't know much about him, although he did from the quick internet check on him before they arrived here.

"Johnny Rains! Wow. We saw him at the autograph session last night. He had just arrived and seemed to always have a drink in his hand. Quite a 'ladies' guy. I liked him a lot. How did you find this out?" Tina continued, unknowingly revealing herself as a closet porn-movie fan.

"Overheard people talking at the bar. There was another body discovered later," Jim continued.

"What? Really, no shit?" Tina was sincerely shocked.

"Nah, no shit; just a body." Jamie made a joke of the situation.

They all laughed.

Jim and Jamie looked at each other, both realizing that they were obviously wasting their investigative time with these two.

Jeff glanced at the watch he was wearing. Clothes weren't permitted, but watches were.

"Tina and I are getting a planned couple massage at 4 at the resort spa, but we'll be at the resort club tonight. Maybe have a drink there?"

"Sure. We'll be there," Jim nodded.

"Starts at 9. And save a dance for me." Tina gave Jim a sexy look as she opened her legs very wide while getting off her lounge chair.

"Oh, I'm sure he will. Jim really likes to dance. Especially the Twist," Jamie responded cutely to make light of what Tina just did was okay with her.

"Oh, and I like a good 'twist' now and then, if you know what I mean. Put me on your dance card." Tina rolled her bare shoulders directly at Jim, adding another little flirtatious punctuation to her goodbye, and apparently indicating that she was more than just someone who liked to watch.

"Sure. See you later." Jim smiled politely, although holding back how he really felt about the situation Jamie had just put him in.

As they left, a nearby pool guy came and picked up their towels from the empty chairs and replaced them with fresh ones. As quickly as he appeared, he quickly left.

"Hey, why did you say that about me dancing?" Jim questioned her comment in a joking manner.

"With those abs you got, Mister, and the way she stared at you, it was obvious you looked like someone who likes to do the 'Twist,' or whatever it's called here!"

McKenna shook his head. He was beginning to appreciate her sense of humor. It would definitely make this strange working arrangement better if they actually became more comfortable together in the surroundings. She certainly was trying, and he knew it had to be challenging for her to be here as they were without a stitch of clothes, as it was for him too.

"Okay. I'll remember that," McKenna smugly replied while giving a little twist of his hips.

Jamie liked his attitude, his voice, and how he spoke to her. She liked talking to him, she liked looking at him, and she liked the way he looked at her, too. They came here as working partners and she felt as if they were now on a fast track to becoming friends, or maybe more.

"Let's take a stroll over to the boutique shop where they found the second body. Watch for security cameras, too. I saw one near the phony volcano in the pool, it was hidden above the bar near a palm tree. But if they have cameras placed throughout, maybe they have images of the killer. Not sure how much sound they can pick up, so we should be careful of what we say."

"And what we do," Jamie added as they stood up and reached for his hand. It was time to play "couples" again. And it was starting to feel real for her, as she enjoyed the touch of his warm hand in hers.

"And say, Mister, that drink you brought me? I didn't taste any alcohol. What was it?"

"Well, I thought we should stay clear headed, being in the sun. You know alcohol hits you quicker in the sun. So, I ordered you a special drink."

"Aha. I bet you got me a kid's drink. It was non-alcoholic; it tasted like plain ginger ale—a Shirley Temple?" she looked at him directly as if interrogating him.

"You know, if I didn't know better, I'd think you were a detective. Actually, it was called a 'Naked' Shirley Temple!"

Jamie really laughed at that, and so did McKenna.

As they walked away from the pool holding hands, they smiled to some close-by lounging guests who looked at them. The sun and warm breeze on her naked body made her feel relaxed, especially after the good laugh they just shared. This moment, this place, this man holding her hand, was something she hadn't experienced in a long time with her high-pressure police job, and the quiet, after-work home life to which she was accustomed. As a detective, Jamie wasn't quite sure if naked people were friendlier and more relaxed because they didn't need clothes to create an "identity," or if they were interested in something more, whether appreciating and showing off their bodies, or wanting to meet and see someone for who they really were. She thought about what a different world they were now in, and a part of—a world hidden from the outside reality of routine jobs and routine lives. This was certainly not a routine place. This was a place that she had never known about, or even thought about. But it was becoming a place that she began to feel more interested in, more comfortable in, and more like the attractive woman she really was. She smiled to herself.

For Jamie Parker, Paradise Lost might just actually be her "Paradise Found."

As they walked way, not looking like a "pretend" couple, but like a real couple, neither knew a mysterious set of eyes had been watching them the whole time and now continued to follow them.

For Jamie Parker, "Paradise Found" was soon to become Paradise "Hell."

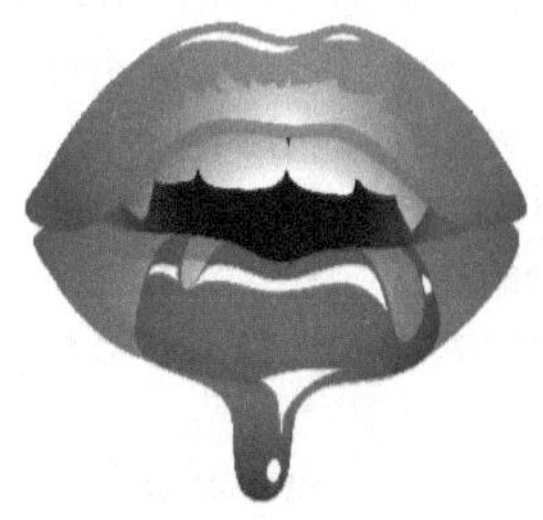

CHAPTER 15

They all hung upside down, tied at their ankles, with their outstretched arms mere inches away from the smooth tile floor below. There were five of them. They were all swaying slightly like slabs of meat hanging in a warehouse. They were alone. They were naked. They were almost dead. Whatever life was still left in them, if they could scream, they would have. But they were too weak to even whisper. And if they could be heard, they would be begging for death. Any thoughts of mercy were long gone.

Three were men, two were women. All shapely, all attractive. Whatever their ages were, it didn't really matter anymore. How long they had hung upside down, they didn't know, nor did that matter to them, as time no longer existed in their state. But, if they were still able to consciously form thoughts, they knew their lives would soon end.

Each had a shiny silver IV needle inserted into their right hanging arm, attached to long, transparent, vinyl tubing. Dark red blood was draining from their bodies into large, ancient-looking silver containers placed next to each one of them on the floor. An emblem of an upside-down crucifix was affixed to each container in a matching blood-red color. The entire room was very sterile looking. With plain white walls on all four sides, it could easily pass for an operating room in a hospital. Maybe it was. Large circular fluorescent lights were tucked neatly into the white ceiling panels above. Across the ceiling, parallel to the floor, was an iron beam with a series of moveable, mechanical pulleys, each with thick, attached ropes that held the five hanging victims.

Two men in white surgical gowns entered from a metal door, which opened to the far left of the room. The taller of the two was in his late 60s, with a full head of silver hair, and a single name, Morbius. He had a look of authority about him. Walking with the aid of a cane, he favored a slight limp, which seemed to make one foot drag with each step. The other man, Doctor Steffens, was in his 40s, a renown blood specialist who was the world's leading expert in modified DNA genetic blood transfusions. Although younger, he looked older, as he was prematurely balding and looked extremely stressed. He was of medium height, wore large black-rimmed glasses, and carried a clipboard with medical notes in one hand. His other hand was making punctuated gestures, as he appeared very concerned while talking quite rapidly.

"The latest analysis of the donor blood types indicates a full set of all thirty substances on the surface of their red blood cells, but the retransfusional protocol continues to fail. We've used combinations of all their blood and still no indication of any change. Her ingestion of new blood, combined with her aging tissue, has no compatibility with any of the blood types we already tried, and each new transfusion potentially opens the possibility of greater risk. We still need to find the source of the origin. It holds the secret to our living…"

"Or, not living," the older man interrupted, paused, then continued.

"The paradox is that she can't die like you, Steffens. Her suffering grows worse each day, each hour, each minute. As does mine. Her desires and needs are becoming more insatiable. Alexandria's stabilization is becoming less controlled. But tonight, now that they've arrived, there are plans in place for them."

"She's the one, isn't she?"

Morbius gave him a very wide and very wicked smile. And in that smile, many sharp and different-sized teeth were revealed. Some perfect, some rotted. Without any direct reply to the question asked, the disturbing smile slowly went away, and he changed his attention and looked at his watch.

"Time will tell; it always does. And soon, finally...we will know."

Steffens nodded his head in silent agreement.

Morbius walked around the closest hanging body, almost like they weren't even there to him. He continued, "But until then, I want you to further explore their ABO blood group system and analyze the options of the A and B antigens. Use the new diagnostic procedure we discussed on their sexual organ tissues. That might also hold a clue."

"Should I wait till they're dead?"

The older man looked at each one of them for a brief moment. Not with a look of compassion, or even a trace of feeling. But rather a look of unconcern.

"No, why wait? Death becomes them now. They'll probably embrace the suffering."

Morbius stood next to one of the hanging victims and without care, or caution, pulled the inserted transfusion needle and attached hose away from their arm. Having most of their blood already removed, only a few red drops flowed from the needle mark left in the arm. He took his index finger and touched the small flow of lingering blood, bringing it to his mouth where he licked it slowly, savoring it. Without any regard for his reaction, he suddenly spit it out onto the hanging naked body, and, without a word, turned and left. The sound of his cane on the floor echoed in the otherwise silent room.

Steffens remained, looking at the five hanging bodies. Studying them, to make his choice.

Nearby was a small metal, medical table on wheels with an array of surgical instruments and a large glass bowl. His fingers touched each tool, one by one, and stopped on one in particular. It was a small battery-operated hand drill, with a circular spinning saw blade at its tip. Before picking it up, he put on the pair of latex surgical gloves next to the tools. He snapped the gloves snuggly at the wrist, making the only recent sound in the room. Turning the drill on, he stared at its spinning motion, both fascinated by it and somewhat lost in thought about how to proceed. The drill made a humming, almost hypnotizing sound. He knew what he had to do, and he did. He casually reached over and grabbed one leg of the man who had the needle removed. Temporarily, while holding the bare leg to steady himself and the hanging body, he brought the whirring saw blade towards the intended surgical area. With latex gloves protecting his hands, he grabbed the man's body part with his fingers and stretched it by its tip, as far as it would go. The sharp rotating saw blade slowly made a clean and total cut into the human flesh.

There was no scream from the upside-down patient, only a slight movement of his hanging body trembling with a shocked spasm, reacting to the brutal surgery which had been done without any anesthesia. It had to have been painful. It had to have been horrific. Actually, it was both. But it happened, and then it was over. And the naked man was now hanging dead.

The smell of fresh burning flesh remained in the air as he turned off the surgical device.

A bloodied, sawed-off penis with exposed tissues was tossed into the open glass bowl on the table.

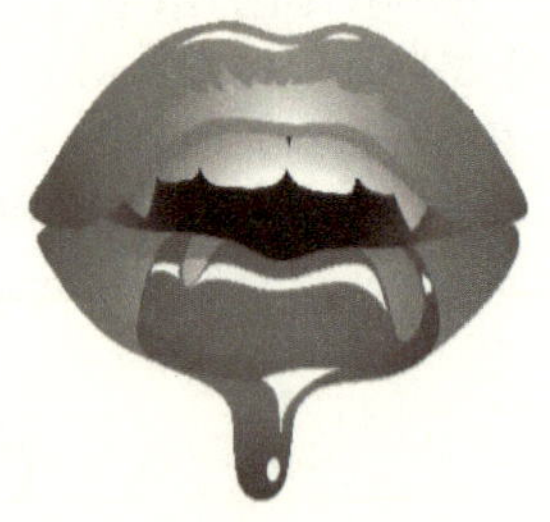

CHAPTER 16

"*Well, if everyone else is looking, I guess I'm going to, too,*" Jamie thought to herself while fighting the internal temptation. It had been difficult to keep her eyes above waist level for so long, ever since they arrived here, but she couldn't hide the temptation anymore. Even McKenna had looked more than once, and it wasn't in the same way he would look if he were a cop doing an investigation, which, of course, he was. And it wasn't just a "peek-a-boo" look. So, if he could, she would, and she did. And she was shocked to see big ones, little ones, and some in-between-size ones also. And, of course, they all came in different colors. That was expected. But so many of them? She shook her head in disbelief with a bit of amazement mixed in. "Toe rings." Just about everyone here was wearing toe rings. Not just the women, but a lot of the men, too.

McKenna saw her looking and laughed.

"You know, you should have some of those to make your wardrobe complete," he commented to her.

She looked back at him somewhat amused.

"What wardrobe? I'm naked!"

"Isn't there the expression, 'Toe rings are a girl's best friend'?"

"Actually, the word is 'Diamonds,' and if you haven't noticed, I'm a woman; not a girl!"

"Oh, I've noticed. And quite an attractive woman, too," he replied warmly, maybe in a bit of playful and kidding tone, as young couples do, but certainly with a look of truth.

This made her blush, with a smile mixed in.

"Why, Jim, I think I'm going to have to buy 'you' a special toe ring for saying something so nice," Jamie replied smugly. "So, let's check out that boutique, probably lots of rings and 'things' to look at."

Whether they were playing along for the security cameras to see, or whether it was what they really meant, only they knew. And they did, as Jamie moved closer to him by moving her hand from his hand and holding onto his arm. And he did, as he moved closer to her, as their naked bodies brushed against each other for the first time. But, not the last time.

Everything appeared normal at the resort boutique. The shop was open, modest sized, with several guests casually looking at sexy lingerie, an assortment of adult toys, and, of course, toe rings. There was no sign of anything strange having happened there earlier that day, like a naked man propped up in the window, advertising death. It appeared as if everything here was business as usual. But appearances can be deceiving, especially when the clothes come off. It was all a cover-up. And it was time to find out more.

An attractive twenty-something-year-old female clerk approached them. She was only wearing a thin gold waist chain, two nipple rings, and lots of toe rings. Perfect body, perfect smile, perfect place to "show off" the merchandise.

"Can I help you?"

McKenna smiled back politely and took the lead part in their pre-planned charade.

"Actually, my girlfriend saw a piece of clothing on the middle mannequin in the window last night. But it appears to have been removed." Laughing at his unintended pun with his choice of words, "I mean taken off." He chuckled at his words again.

She didn't get it.

"Let me look. Hmm. You're right. That lingerie in the window display must have been just put there. Let me ask the store manager. I'm new here. It wasn't there yesterday."

"Of course not," McKenna thought to himself. *"When they took the dead body off the attached display wires and mannequin, they must have removed the outfit behind it, as it may have contained evidence related to the murder."*

While the young clerk talked to her manager, Jamie quickly looked inside the open window display. *"No sign of blood, or any apparent clues."* She knew that her quick, visual examination was just that. But everything appeared freshly clean, too clean. Dust on the window ledge, but none on the immediate display floor, and the window looked like it had fresh streaks from a recent washing. Whatever clues there may have been, they were well scrubbed away.

"I'm sorry, but the manager says that the item was sold earlier today. Perhaps you may want to see something similar?"

Jamie's turn to play the rehearsed part.

"I heard someone say that a dead body was found in the store window this morning. Is that true?"

"Jeez, I haven't heard that. A dead body!" The clerk was definitely shocked. Apparently, she knew nothing about this.

Some other nearby guests overheard the comment and turned their attention towards them.

The store manager approached. She was in her 50s, but in excellent shape, with a definite boob job.

"I can assure you there was no body in the window. A mannequin did fall during the shop's closed hours. That's what people saw. I straightened it up myself this morning when I arrived." Her demeanor was polite and professional, and she wanted to immediately change the story. Obviously, she was a good liar and also well-rehearsed.

"Someone also said they found a body in the pool," Jamie continued.

"Again, I can assure you that was a rumor. A lot of guests who may have had a bit too much to drink or partied too hard are sometimes seen floating in the pool," the manager replied casually as if she was revealing a somewhat typical fact of life here.

"Face down?" Jamie questioned a bit sarcastically.

"All a rumor. Just a rumor. This resort has never had any such thing happen here unless, again, someone accidentally fell in the pool. On behalf of your, and all our guests' enjoyment while here, we would appreciate you pay no attention to silly rumors. Please enjoy your stay here with some fun in the sun." She gave them a very obvious and very fake smile, then continued, "Perhaps I can interest you in today's special, toe rings?"

McKenna and Jamie looked at each other.

"No thanks. My boyfriend has fat, stubby-looking toes." Jamie gave a very obvious and very fake smile back to her, and grabbed McKenna's arm again, giving it a slight squeeze, which was a planned and agreed exit cue.

And they left.

They both knew. There was nothing else to get from the manager. Whatever happened here was definitely being covered up. For sure, not to scare the guests, but also for another reason, yet to be determined. It was a clue to what was becoming an interesting puzzle.

"And by the way, I do not have fat..."

"And you wouldn't look good in those silly rings either," Jamie interrupted, and grabbed his hand again as they both shared a laugh and walked towards the resort lobby.

"So, the plan is to go to the Meet and Greet and try to find someone to share some insight on how that Johnny character ended up in the pool, who he left the dance with, and how the dead guy in the boutique window ties in."

McKenna nodded in agreement. He then added to what she laid out.

"If Winston, one of the owners I met this morning, is there, you might want to work into a conversation with him. See if you can get anything from him. From the way he acted this morning, there is something more going on that he knows about. He just didn't want the cops to know. I don't think he'd recognize me with my new hair color and new outfit—butt naked, but I don't want to take a chance."

"Agreed. Just point him out to me. The event should be taking place shortly in the main lobby. There'll be some food and drinks, and more Shirley Temples, I presume, but before I go, I need to stop back at our room to freshen up."

McKenna nodded again. He knew she probably needed a few moments to herself, after all, she probably felt like Alice in Wonderland as much as he felt like Christopher Columbus in uncharted territory.

"Sure. But, please don't take too much time deciding what to wear tonight," he chuckled wryly.

She just turned her eyes upwards and shook her head cutely in reply.

He continued, back in a serious voice, "So, I'll meet you in the lobby in about a half an hour. In the meantime, I'll do some walking around, checking out the resort."

Jamie was quick to take a turn and chide him as to what she pretended he was really going to do.

"Check out the resort. Right. You're probably going looking for that woman who gave you the once-over at the pool."

"Oh, the one in the pink shorts with the light blue top and the yellow ribbon in her hair?"

"Yeah, that's her, minus all the clothes."

"And minus the ribbon. Don't forget the ribbon," he kidded her back.

"Touché," she punctuated his remark.

They both smiled at the playfulness of the moment.

McKenna continued, "Hmm. Well, maybe you should be aware of the two guys who checked you out when we walked to the boutique. They seemed pretty 'interested' in you by the way they stared."

Jamie cocked her head slightly and raised an eyebrow before replying. "Nice try, Sherlock. They were gay and making eyes at you. Remember, I'm the detective, and you're just the big, tough cop who's gonna catch the bad guy when I figure it out."

"Hopefully, it will be soon, so I can get my clothes back on," McKenna concluded.

"Really? So, you can get your clothes back on?" Jamie replied with a serious, and maybe somewhat disappointed tone in her question.

"Well, I meant 'soon' as in catching the Killer, but as for the clothes..."

He paused, and without hesitation surprised her by leaning in and kissing her softly on her cheek.

"...well..., the sun feels kinda nice." He brought his head back and finished his sentence softly with a sincere smile.

His eyes met hers for a brief, but seemingly long moment, as he stood close to her, and reached out and touched her hair, moving it away from where the sudden wind had blown it gently across her face. It was apparent that he may have wanted to say more. But instead, he said it with another smile.

"See you at the lobby."

He turned and left her standing, thinking about what just happened.

"Was that a real sign of affection? Did he kiss me because of how he felt about me? Or was that part of the act we're playing in, in case we're being watched?" Her analytical detective mind raced with an assortment of "what ifs." Jamie slowly touched her cheek where his lips had just been. She suddenly felt warm all over. She thought about his words, "The sun feels kinda nice," and it did, right now, right then, on her naked body as she looked at his, as he walked away. Yes, the sun did feel kinda nice, real nice. So did his kiss.

CHAPTER 17

Three black limos drove up to the front lobby entrance of Paradise Lost Resort. Winston and two security men were waiting outside in the warm Florida air. They stood, fully dressed, in front of a just-placed, roped-off barricade for this anticipated arrival. A two-deep crowd of scantily clad to fully clad spectators, with a few naked people mixed in, stood behind the ropes patiently waiting. The resort valet opened the side door of the first limo facing the entrance, and two platinum blonde female porn stars in sunglasses stepped out, showing long, bare legs first. Wearing identically matching, sparkly, gold-sequined "miniest" of miniskirts, with the tightest of tight-fitting tiny tops covering busts the size of overripe cantaloupes, and the highest of high 7-inch stilettos, they stood and posed to the "oohs" and "aahs" of the gawking onlookers.

They were the Barbee Doll twins, Bar and Bee, superstars of erotica fame. They smiled, puckered their lips, and gave naughty winks with their beautiful, matching blue eyes, while waving their open hands like the Queen of England, back and forth and in synched rhythm. After being photographed and ogled by the waiting fans, they each stepped to one side of the next limo, which pulled up as theirs pulled away. Blowing kisses to the crowd, the twin beauties stepped simultaneously backwards, and stood next to the vehicle's opening doors, as if having been rehearsed for a scene in one of their X-rated movies. This time, in place of long curvaceous legs, out came two short, stubby, bare black legs, followed by a pink-pantied and topless, four-foot-seven-inch female "little person," Bridgett the Midget. She swayed back and forth with a "look-at-me attitude" while her hands pumped high above and she danced to her own music in her head. She suddenly stopped and slowly pointed her small fingers at two large, flashing pink, lit pasties covering her nipples. The crowd went wild with applause as she pulled off her pasties and tossed them high into the air for the waiting and waving outstretched hands. Another burst of "oohs" and "aahs" was followed with the squeaky voice of an older gay man yelling, "Bridgett, I love you!"

But the show wasn't quite over. Following behind was her Native American lesbian lover, Little Beaver, a little person in a brown thong and fringed top, wearing an Indian headdress, while brandishing a small cupid-like plastic archery bow with rubber-tipped arrows. She took aim and shot directly at Bridgett's nearly bare ass, which just happened to be bent over facing her at this moment and wiggling back and forth. The rubber suction tip stuck to her butt and Little Beaver let out a loud "sort-of" Indian "war whoop," while doing a little dance. That brought a roar of approval from the onlookers.

As the final of the three limos pulled up to the resort entrance, the two little ladies stepped aside and joined the two towering other ladies waiting for the "main star" of this anticipated arrival. An ornate, handcrafted man's leather cowboy boot, studded in glistening diamonds, touched the pavement first.

Slowly, purposely, and theatrically from the limo came Hollywood's legendary leading male porn performer, and now richer than rich, porno world's "numero-uno" producer and organizer of this convention, the legendary Jack Hammer. At six-foot-two, athletically proportioned, and poured into a black, tailor-made, tight-fitting leather suit, minus a shirt, and with shoulder-length black hair, he was the most handsome and alluring male in the entire porn industry. Jack smiled, opened his two hands and threw into the air an assortment of colored condoms, all wrapped with a glow-in-the-dark image of his smiling face. Yells and whistles accompanied him and the four odd-sized female entourage, as Winston and his bodyguards led them through the adoring crowd and towards the main lobby.

Walking past one of the two giant outdoor birdcages, a perched parrot flapped his wings and squawked out loud, "It's Hammer Time." The parrot started to dance.

Jack stopped and smiled at the caged parrot, appreciating what it just said, and was now doing. Flashing that "sullen" movie star look, that was definitely his and his alone, Jack posed next to the birdcage for a candid photo for an excited naked female fan. The bird responded by bobbing its head up and down and pooping.

"Send the bird an extra bag of seed and put it on my account," Hammer mentioned to Winston as they entered the lobby.

Without expression to the odd request, Winston nodded and then turned and rolled his eyes.

As they walked into the huge lobby entrance, Jack leaned close to him and whispered a few words for his ears only.

"We need to talk," Hammer spoke sternly.

Again, Winston nodded, and added something quietly and privately back to him, making certain no one could hear his response, or whatever conversation was to follow, while turning and leading them through the main lobby and past the resort's check-in area.

"All of the ladies' accommodations are ready," Winston spoke out loud as they walked, returning to the moment at hand.

Reaching the main hallway leading to the various resort rooms, Winston turned from the four women and beckoned to one of the naked bellmen with a professional and fake smile, "Suites 201 and 202."

Each of the towering Barbee twins leaned forward in sync and gave Jack a kiss on his cheeks at the same time. The midgets, being midgets, just blew kisses upwards.

Winston turned back to Jack and, with a troubled look, he spoke softly as the ladies were escorted away. "If you follow me, I'll show you what we know."

Hammer showed no real expression of response, except for the few fake smiles he continued to do for nearby remaining people still trying to get a peek at him and his entourage.

"There's more than two?" he asked solemnly, while looking directly at Winston with a gaze intended only for him to see. A look that that indicated a foreboding event to follow. And it would be not only foreboding, but frightening and horrific.

Together they walked to a private hallway behind the front reception desk, which led to a closed door at its end. Winston knocked twice on the unmarked door, waited a moment, unlocked it with a key, and let Hammer in first. Looking behind him to make sure they were alone, he entered, and closed the door behind him.

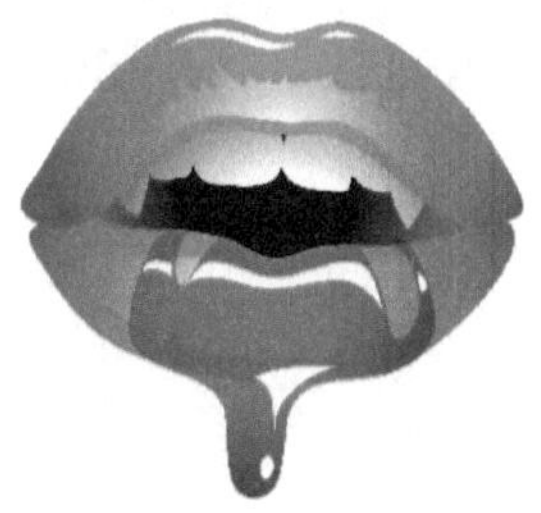

CHAPTER 18

As McKenna strolled around the large pool area feeling the warm summer breeze on his bare body, he sensed that he was being watched. His intuitive personal "cop" radar kicked in. He felt it before in other police situations and he was always right. And he was right now, too. He stopped close to the edge of the main pool and looked into the water reflection. His image moved slightly from some nearby movement in the water. Two naked women were walking through the shallow end, enjoying the sun. They also seemed to be enjoying him as they gave him more than a once-over. They smiled; he smiled back. But he knew that they weren't the only ones who were watching him. And he was right, there was someone else. He also felt that he was being followed. And he was right again. A middle-aged man walked next to him and, without looking at him but staring at his image in the pool, started a conversation.

"A beautiful day, don't you think?"

McKenna glanced back at him. He was about the same height, a few years older, slender, not really athletic or muscular by any means, just a normal-looking guy. Almost normal. But something caught his attention. McKenna noticed an unusual tattoo on the man's shoulder that was closest to him. It appeared to be a circle with an upside-down religious cross in it. It was etched in black and red and there was almost an eerie glow from it. Not that it was a freshly made, wet-looking tattoo, but there appeared to be an eerie emanation, almost as if the cross wasn't just an image, but was tangible and actually inserted in his skin.

"Yeah," McKenna nonchalantly replied, "it's a beautiful day."

And then he saw it. There, on this stranger's neck, between the jaw and the shoulder were two small puncture marks. Two very small holes, bigger than pin pricks, but small enough to be missed at first, unless one had a trained eye to see such things. McKenna did, being "the consummate cop" he was. And as he looked at these two small holes, it became more apparent to him that they looked like bite marks.

The stranger casually put his hand directly onto his neck as if slightly rubbing, while hiding the spot McKenna looked at. He paused, turned to McKenna, and put his hand back down.

"There are lots of interesting people here to look at. Some more interesting than others. I'd be careful not to look too much. You never know quite what you might 'actually see.' You might get hurt; eye strain can be painful. Naked people, especially naked women, can be quite alluring."

And with those words, he abruptly turned and walked away.

"Hurt? Might see? Be careful?" Were these choices of words meant especially for him? Did someone recognize him? Was someone watching him? *"Who was that guy? And the bite marks?"*

McKenna quickly turned to follow him, and almost immediately collided into the body of a beautiful, young naked woman carrying a tray full of drinks. She was no more than twenty and was obviously a resort-employed pool girl who got drinks for the lazy sunning patrons.

Surprisingly, none of the drinks spilled or fell from the tray that she carried in one hand. Her other hand was on his chest, as she tried to block a collision. She let it remain there a moment, then smiled at him, pleasantly unconcerned, and maybe something more.

"Can I get you a drink?"

"Great line," he thought to himself. Never had a naked woman, and a pretty one at that, ask him if he wanted a drink after almost bumping into each other, nude. They usually had other intentions.

"Ah, no thanks. Not now."

He smiled back, and then buried his thoughts on her as he resumed his police role and continued in pursuit after the stranger. But he was gone. He had disappeared into a crowd of people who were coming from an outdoor yoga class McKenna had passed a while back. McKenna stood looking in all directions, but also didn't want it to seem too obvious to anyone who may be watching him. The stranger was gone and that was all there was to it. McKenna turned away to go back to where he stood by the pool and almost turned again into the same resort pool girl. She had completed her drink delivery and was on her way back to the bar to pick up more.

"Whoa!" he exclaimed, as they almost collided again.

She smiled and quickly walked around him hurrying off to the nearby outside cabana bar. Her high heels left a trail of clicking sounds on the stone sidewalk as she moved away. He looked at her tight backside, her nice suntanned shape, and the long smooth-looking legs that led his eyes up and back down. He slowly shook his head and almost laughed.

"Way too young, besides..."

She suddenly turned back to look at him almost as if she knew he'd be looking. She smiled even more and turned back away.

This time he laughed.

"Excuse me. Do you know the time?" a female voice from behind caught his attention and quickly returned him to the "here and now."

McKenna turned to answer the question and was immediately taken aback. Two naked 30-something, well-tanned, and very attractive women stood before him, holding tennis rackets and one tossing a tennis ball in the air in a teasing manner. With the late afternoon sun behind them, they were surrounded in a bright, almost angelic, yellowish glow. If this were heaven, every man's fantasy would have come true. The one who spoke was tall with shoulder-length, curly blonde hair, very large breasts, and an impressive athletic figure. She had a bit of a French accent. The other woman was equally tall and equally blessed with a similar figure, with long brown hair that almost reached her waist and draped her body, eyes that were very alluring, and an interesting smile that included licking her bottom lip back and forth as she gave him the once-over, more than once, and "more than over."

Telling time was easy for McKenna, as the only item he wore was a watch on his left wrist.

"Four-fifteen," he replied with a nice, warm smile.

"Oh, great! We have time for a few more games before the cocktail party," she genuinely smiled back, replying both to him and the other woman.

And as if on cue, the brown-haired woman stepped closer to her friend and put her arm around her naked waist.

"Tennis is our favorite outdoor sport. We like to play a lot of games. Maybe you would like to join us in a threesome?"

McKenna's mind raced in both policeman's logic, analyzing innuendo-type word association, and ending on a naked man's wishful thinking. He struggled to find the right and polite answer, but he did.

"A threesome! Well, I appreciate the offer, but I haven't played tennis in a long time. I might be a bit rusty."

"Oh, that's okay. We would be very easy on you and we could even take turns helping you get rid of the 'rust,'" she coyly responded in a teasing tone.

The two women looked at each other with a devilish smile. Obviously, their choice of words was more than just talking or thinking about the game of tennis. It was very apparent that they both seemed to have more in mind than playing a tennis game with him.

McKenna kept his thoughts in check and knew he was here on assignment first and foremost and had to get back on track by checking out the grounds and people. He quickly answered back with a question of his own.

"You have a French accent. Are you here on vacation?"

"Yes. We're sisters. I am Eva," said the brown-haired woman, "and this is Bretta. We came here for the convention. We love the sun and we love to have fun in the sun. Nudism is very popular in France. And this place is so beautiful. It's our first time here. And today's sun is so warm and invigorating. Don't you feel good being nude?"

The surrounding view of the pool and the two women before him was quite breathtaking.

"Never felt better in my life," he replied sincerely.

"Then come play with us. You can feel even better," Eva responded softly as she stepped closer to him and reached out and touched his chest. She gently moved her one finger slowly down the middle of it, very slowly, and finally stopping above his waist, where she circled the finger playfully before removing it. Her eyes never left his.

McKenna took a deep breath and let it out with a slight chuckle to himself.

"You know, I just realized my wife is waiting for me back in the room. So, I'm sorry, but I may have to take a raincheck on the invitation." He nodded in a way of saying yes but no.

"Raincheck?" Bretta asked.

"That's an American expression; it means another time." McKenna kept his eyes to her eyes. *"Above the neckline, Mister,"* he thought to himself, fighting any temptation that tried to cross his mind.

"Oh. Well, maybe you can bring your wife with you in that 'other time,' especially if she likes to play games, too." Eva winked at him.

"I'll certainly keep that in mind," McKenna playfully responded with a wink of his own.

And with the only French words he knew, *"Au revoir,"* he smiled, ended the conversation, and turned and walked back towards the main building.

As he walked away, he was tempted to look back, like the barmaid had done to him. However, he already knew that they were looking at him and, most likely, at his tight, athletic ass. He also knew that they were more interested in him than playing a game of tennis. After all, cops are supposed to know these things.

Before returning to his room to freshen up, McKenna stopped for a moment at the edge of the main pool looking back at the incredible "paradise-like" surroundings—the sound of the splashing waterfall, mingled with the happy voices of naked guests strolling waist deep in the water or sitting at the in-pool bar. Some upbeat, but relaxing tropical music was piped in and around the area on hidden speakers.

No wonder this place had a name like it did. Paradise Lost. This place was incredible and beyond his wildest imagination. Having played sports and taken care of his body certainly paid off in a place like this. It worked both ways. This was like an adult "candy store," and there was plenty of eye candy to look at, and certainly a lot of potential candy to taste. Definitely, a lot of candy. For him, as a man, and probably for a lot of women who were here either for fun in the sun or just plain "fun," it worked both ways.

And then he thought of Jamie.

"Jamie," he nodded slowly to himself. *"I hardly know her, and yet..."*

McKenna thought of their situation, here together, tracking and finding a killer.

This morning, when he showered and prepared for the workday ahead in his mind, he never in a million years would have imagined being totally nude on an assignment in a nudist resort with attractive, naked women all over the place and a naked woman by his side. And a beautiful one, too. He shook his head slowly, back and forth, thinking of all this as he felt the warm afternoon sun touch his skin. Actually, it felt good to be without clothes. He had never told anyone, especially Jamie, that there was another time without clothes besides the childhood experience that he shared with her earlier. He recalled the one time in his high school years when he and a group of his classmates wandered away from a school-organized picnic and went to a nearby pond where many of them enjoyed their first taste of "skinny dipping." At first, he remembered how everybody was shy and reserved, daring each other to take off their clothes. And slowly everyone did. Some held their hands in front of their private parts before getting into the water, while others, especially some of the girls, just took it all off like it belonged off. And after a few moments without clothes, it was "fun in the sun" for all of them, just like little kids doing something they didn't want their parents or anyone to know but themselves. They laughed, they splashed, they swam. Totally nude. It was their "agreed-to-keep" secret. It wasn't sexual; it was just fun. And, even though that was a long time ago, he had to admit to himself that he enjoyed the freedom of being without a uniform, without any clothing, just being himself, a feeling that sometimes got lost and buried in the outside world he lived in, but not today. Maybe that one secret moment in time helped prepare him for this day. Certainly, he was a little shy at first being naked in front of Jamie, as he hardly knew her, or knew anything about her. But when they stood in front of each other for the first time without clothing, it seemed so natural. And now, here, at this moment, as he reflected on that memory long ago, it seemed even more natural. It truly was a paradise of sorts.

The only thing he really missed was his revolver. Several times today he reached towards where his gun normally sat in its waist holster. It was just a matter of routine to check for it, having done it so many times and, with instinct of a cop, to make sure it was there and ready for him. And now he felt naked without it. He laughed to himself. *"Naked' without my gun; how funny is that? I am naked!"*

Here he was, without his weapon, with only his training and skills to use in any dangerous situation that might arise. He was quite confident in his police skills, having been at the top of his class in boxing and running at the police academy he attended. He was also a star college athlete, the team quarterback at Florida State. At that time, he was so well conditioned and adept with his football skills that a potential NFL career was on his horizon, as his team kept winning and winning, with him leading them to a bowl conference game. And then the unexpected happened. A blindside hit by a 300-pound tackler, who had a chip on his shoulder and who actually fell on him and broke both his own shoulder and McKenna's in an unforgettable goal line, game-winning touchdown. Surgery repaired his shoulder, but it was so badly damaged, the team's doctors and his coach told him that another hit like that would leave him a cripple. So, the college major in criminal law paid off as he graduated with honors and was immediately accepted into the State Law Enforcement Academy. Strength training and a winning resolve to overcome the adversity of his shoulder injury allowed him to beat the odds the doctors gave him, and he healed himself to some form of normal. But his football days were over. He did miss the game, but to rehabilitate his shoulder, he did learn to play a mean game of tennis. But not naked tennis.

As he stood in the moment of what he had just experienced, the only danger he thought about seemed to come from the sexually hungry-looking women he had just met and a few others who certainly gave him "more" than a glance. They certainly fit the definition of "swingers," not that he was that familiar with the whole swinging scene, but he had read about it and knew a little bit about this place and the lifestyle convention he was now in the middle of.

And then his thoughts returned to Jamie.

He recalled how her hand had touched his, and how it felt. It actually felt nice. It had been a long time since he felt the touch of another woman. Not that he couldn't have, for he knew that he was thought of as a handsome man, and a lot of his fellow officers always wanted to fix him up with a sister or a friend. He always said no. He just put his focus on himself as a cop and his career. It was apparent to everyone who met him that he was a dedicated cop. Some said he was "married to his work." And, in retrospect, as he looked back at his life in law enforcement, he was. There was a time when he shared part of his life with a woman; but after four years of playing house, living together, and planning on staying together, she ended the relationship with an ultimatum. She didn't want the man she loved to die in some "heroic-cop vs. bad-guy scenario," so she gave him a choice: to be with her and find a new career, or be without her and stay in law enforcement. And he chose. It wasn't easy; it was actually very emotionally painful, and the pain still lingered. He always felt that they were close to getting married and he even told her how much he wanted to share his life with her and start a family, together, forever. Romantic words, spoken, shared, but now forgotten. She stuck to her words; he stayed in his career. That was three years ago. And in those three years since, no woman ever caught his attention, nor did he want one to, not even the day he first met Jamie when she was introduced to him. Nor today, the day they got this unusual and unbelievable undercover assignment to play a romantic couple while totally "uncovered." Totally naked. Not naked, as if in a brief romantic fling as most sexually active and interested people find themselves naked, but naked in a working situation, where all that mattered was that they had an assignment to find a killer.

Water splashed on his nude body, suddenly and accidentally, from a young couple nearby, embracing and falling together in a moment of playful fun into the pool close to where he stood. They didn't care. Neither did he. He smiled to himself as he wiped some of the water off with his bare hand. His "bare" hand. And here he was, bare all over—bare naked.

"This is turning into one interesting assignment," he said almost loud enough to actually be heard as spoken words. When this assignment was done, he knew no one would ever believe him, even if he had enough courage to tell anyone about it. He couldn't even believe it himself. But he knew from the moment he took his clothes off today, and she took her clothes off, that this was going to be something different, for sure. Something that, as a police officer, he had no grasp on, nor any idea where it would lead. Besides finding a killer, maybe it would become something more, something special, something they were meant to share together. Maybe be together. Yes, he acknowledged to himself, it was turning into a very interesting assignment. Maybe something long overdue, like finding a reawakening in his lost love life. And maybe hers, too.

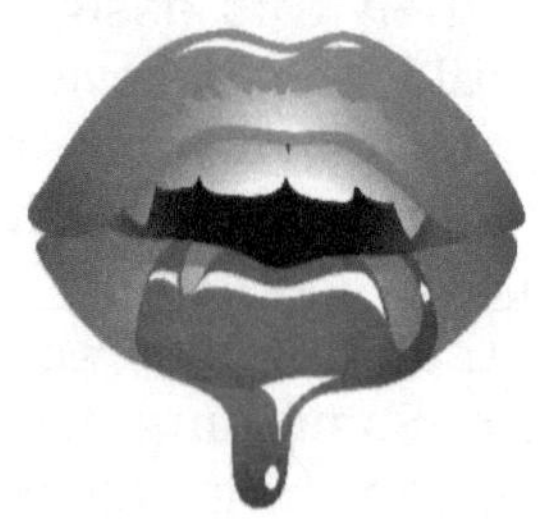

CHAPTER 19

The warm water sprayed across her perfectly shaped breasts and flowed gently down and across her naked body. It was as if a thousand fingers were caressing her. It felt good, real good. Eyes closed, head slowly turning back and forth, Jamie savored the moment, lost in all thoughts, just feeling the comfort of a long, long, hot shower. How long she had been in it didn't matter. How long had McKenna been in her thoughts really mattered. A police detective she was; but she wanted to be a woman again. It had been so long, too long, since she had thoughts like this. Thoughts of being touched, being held, being kissed. Thoughts that made her heart beat a few times faster. Thoughts that reminded her of a long, hidden passion that still existed somewhere beneath her professional daily demeanor. Being "a woman." Being loved again. Being in love again. Being with someone again. Someone. McKenna? James McKenna. Someone who had suddenly been thrust into her life and who had suddenly, unexpectedly, awakened something within her. Was it just his attractive, naked, athletic-looking body that turned her desirous thoughts back on, or was it the gentleness in his voice, the charm in his look, or the feeling that came from his eyes as he looked at her, and she looked at him.

"Awkward, Jamie. Get control," she mused to herself. This whole nude thing was like being a kid in Disneyland, except, instead of characters in costumes, all the characters here were naked. *"Naked. And I'm enjoying it! I'm not even this naked in front of Bentley,"* she laughed out loud to herself. Laughed, and shook her head, to let the water splash the tiled shower walls. Laughed to relax her mind and to relax her body. Laughed to enjoy the moment, for there was never a moment like this before and, in the back of her mind, she couldn't even fathom another moment like this in the future—finding a killer in a nudist resort while discovering sexual feelings again with a naked cop. *"Now that's one heck of an assignment. And I'm being paid by taxpayer dollars to do this job."* She rolled her eyes thinking about this and laughed again. *"Okay, girl, time for the shower to end, and time to get your wandering mind back to work."*

Standing before a full-length mirror in the bathroom, she toweled herself off. A few water drops remained, glistening on her slightly tanned skin in the overhead light, maybe purposely missed, or maybe left so she could look at them in the mirror, while she looked at herself. She turned slowly to the right and then to the left. She admired her figure. Her skin was toned, her breasts were firm, and her ass didn't jiggle. It just had a nice curvy shape. She was glad she took care of herself. Yes, she had looked at some, or maybe a lot of the naked and beautiful women here, and she knew they looked back at her. She held her own when it came to "having" a nice, attractive shape, although she wouldn't admit it to herself nor did she flaunt it, but her inner confidence told her so, and so did the image in the mirror.

"Not bad for a naked cop. No, not bad at all, and thank God for my morning runs and a touch or two of good genetics." She smiled at herself in the mirror, and her reflection smiled back.

The door to the hotel room opened, and McKenna called out so as not to scare her or surprise her. Or maybe, just to be polite. Jamie still had some figuring out to do with him, and being a pretty darn good detective, so she was told, and so she told herself, she knew she'd figure him out, if not more.

"Jamie, I'm back."

She wrapped the wet towel around herself, not exactly knowing why she did this, other than that's the basic daily routine she did when she showered. Opening the bathroom door slightly, she peeked out.

"I'll be out in a minute. And," with a pause in her voice, "do your eyes hurt?"

"What a silly thing to say!" she questioned herself. Was there a bit of jealousy in her question? Was she imagining that he was busy enjoying all the naked ladies instead of looking for clues?

"Sorry, I meant..." she quickly continued, only to be interrupted by his friendly response.

"Actually, my eyes do hurt. We need to get some better sunglasses if we spend a lot of time walking around the grounds."

She smiled, half believing him.

"I'll be out in a minute."

"Great! I want to shower before we go to the Meet and Greet activity. I won't take long. Don't have to decide what to wear," McKenna teased.

She looked at him as he stood in the shadows and light from the patio door. *"God, he is handsome."* Her brain raced in overdrive. She slightly bit her lip and quickly replied, so he wouldn't pick up on her "once-over."

"Yeah, it won't take me long either. I actually have nothing to wear."

They both shared a laugh, and she returned to the bathroom. But without saying it, or giving it away, he had felt her "once-over." He had felt it before from other women earlier today, several times, but this time, he enjoyed it.

When it was McKenna's turn to shower, he left the bathroom door partially open. Jamie, first as a detective, noticed this. Secondly, as a woman, it made her think. Did he do this on purpose? Did he want me to peek? *"Ha!"* she caught herself with a short laugh. Peek? What else was left to see? Except she wanted to see more, and she did.

As the hot water and steam swirled around him, and with his back to her, she watched his hands lather his muscular and toned frame. Whether it was the heat from the shower, or the heat from the warm afternoon breeze emanating from the open patio door, she felt hot all over. Real hot. And without thinking or stopping herself, her two hands slowly moved in two different directions, timed as if they knew what to do and where to go without any further instructions. Her left hand lightly caressed her right breast, moving slowly across her taut skin and circling her partially aroused nipple. Her right hand reached below her waist and brushed lightly across her womanhood. It felt good, too good. And he looked good, too good. The sensual moment was so unexpected, so exciting, she never wanted it to stop or let it end. He turned in the shower with water pouring across his face and muscular chest. Through the glass shower door, she could see him fully naked, facing her. The water that splashed off his incredible-looking body seemed to be dancing in the air in all directions. It seemed to cover him and uncover him simultaneously, while purposely teasing her womanly senses. Her eyes followed his body, beginning at the top, and moving towards and stopping at his...

His eyes opened, and she backed away from his sight. Had he seen her? Did she want him to see her? Did he know she was watching? Did he want her to watch?

Her hands stopped where they were, and with what they were doing, and she returned both to rest on the front of her hips. She took a deep breath. A long deep breath. *"Cold water would be good right now—real good,"* she thought to herself. *"Lots of cold water."*

She heard the shower end and she moved away from the bathroom door and back towards the open patio door. She didn't know what to do. She didn't know what to say. She didn't know, and yet, she did. He had aroused her, and she knew she could and would arouse him. *"Later,"* she thought to herself. *"Get control, Jamie. Later."* And she felt that "later" would come sooner than expected. And she couldn't wait.

Outside the patio door, and just past the adjacent flower gardens, the sounds of people having fun in the giant outdoor swimming pool, mixed with soft, tropical music, brought her mindset back to where it needed to be. Not that she wanted it to, but she knew she needed it to. The "moment" would be tucked in her memory and the next moment of "later" would have to wait. She reminded herself that she had a job to do, and he had a job to do. That's what brought them here. They had a job to do together. Together. That single, simple, and yet complex word, made her smile.

Little did she know that while she had watched him, and maybe while he had watched her, someone else was watching them.

A mysterious figure stood outside, unseen, in the not so far away, and stared at their open patio door.

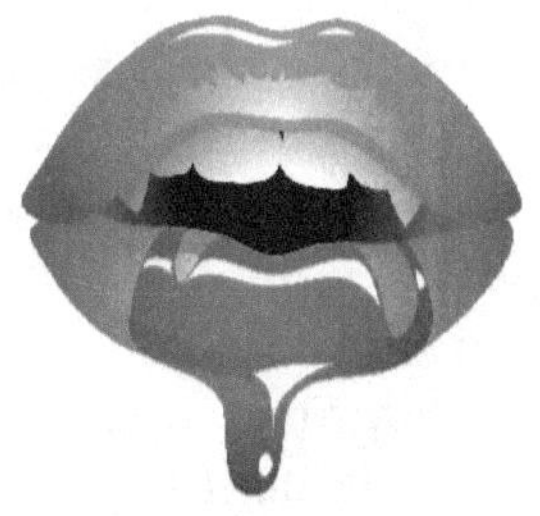

CHAPTER 20

"*How do I meet and greet a naked person? Do I just shake a bare hand at arm's length, or do I lean close and hug a nude body? And what if 'something' gets in the way? After all, we all have different-sized anatomical parts, and sometimes those parts do get in the way, whether they're male or female. And in this resort world of completely naked people, parts aren't just parts. Some parts are much more,*" Jamie thought to herself as she and McKenna entered the resort ballroom holding hands while playing the part of a couple, while possibly, or actually, becoming a couple. Here they were, at the "The Paradise Lost Nude-a-Rama Meet-and-Greet Evening Program," the official beginning to the resort-sponsored convention. Tonight, every resort guest was welcome to free food, free drinks, free looks and see, and maybe even a free "feel" fest of fun, wrapped around vendors promoting and selling their latest sexual paraphernalia, along with porn stars talking about their latest movies and projects. They were all here, in one large ballroom, about two-hundred-plus assorted people of assorted sizes—big, small, tall, short, big-busted, small-busted, some longer than the others and maybe others measured somewhere in between, and, amongst them, possibly the mysterious "Killer."

"We'll stay together to see if we can pick up anything from anyone who might have heard something or knows anything about the two murders," McKenna said to Jamie in a low voice as he leaned close to her ear.

She nodded slightly and squeezed his hand tightly, not out of fear, but out of security. Even though she was beginning to get accustomed to seeing people without clothes and had already seen a lot of them throughout the pool area, she had not experienced, or imagined, this many at once, all in one place, all together, bare naked.

"Different, huh?" McKenna quipped while keeping his eyes forward surveying the crowd.

"Yeah, quite different. I guess the 'key' is to keep the chin up," Jamie added.

McKenna chuckled, "Just be careful not to bump into anyone. You don't want to leave a bruise, or get one in return." McKenna slightly nodded to his left as a semi-aroused man in his early thirties pointed his way past them.

Jamie glanced at his appendage, then looked away. "Oh, dear God," she said, rolling her eyes.

"Like you said, my dear, keep your chin up," McKenna added, almost with a laugh.

She shook her head slightly in amazement of everything she was experiencing. And it certainly was an experience.

"Okay..." she started to ask, then paused with a hesitation of should she, or shouldn't she. But she did. "I have a question."

"Hmm." He knew what was coming, so he played along. "A detective's question?"

"Well, let's just say it is."

"Okay, let's just say it is," he replied with a sense of humor in his voice.

"With all the beautiful women here, everywhere you look, how do you...?" She quickly changed her words. "I mean...how does a guy keep it from...?"

"It from?" McKenna repeated coyly.

"Changing directions?"

There was a brief pause between them as Jamie waited for an answer, an explanation or...

"Oh, as in which way is North and which way is South?" McKenna asked her, using the euphemisms for up and down, as if this was relevant in giving her an answer.

"Yeah, directions. Exactly." Jamie nodded and looked at him to see how he would answer this, or maybe find a way to not answer this.

"I guess it depends what you're looking at."

"Or thinking about?" she asked, wanting more of an answer, especially since she was stark naked in front of him, as she was most of the day, holding his hand, and their bodies lightly touching. How did he not have a reaction? How did he stop his libido-driven thoughts?

"I'm thinking about the case we have to solve," he replied quite casually, as if that was all he had to do.

She cocked her head, not fully satisfied with the answer.

"And sometimes sports," McKenna finished and smiled at her.

"And right now..." he said, as his eyes looked directly into hers, "...the Super Bowl."

Jamie sighed, then broke into a short laugh. For a tough guy, he actually had a sense of humor. And, he probably could show "directions" when and if he wanted to.

She squeezed his hand again, this time in a more, gentle way.

The ballroom was quite large and opulent, just like the rest of the resort. No money was spared in creating a "Sodom and Gomorrah" look. Two-story-high floor-to-ceiling windows faced the outer pool. From outside, the remaining moments of twilight were blending with a series of colored mini-spotlights, illuminating the never-ending surrounding grounds and the always-flowing, man-made pool waterfall in a breathtaking glow. An adjacent ballroom wall was equally stunning, filled with the most amazing, colorful, and most expensive, original, giant-sized paintings and photos of erotic art. Another wall had billowing and swirling golden silk tapestries hanging from the ceiling, each as a backdrop to several pearly white, Romanesque, life-sized marble statues of naked men and women. Every angle of the room was striking and worthy of more than just a quick look or limited attention. With naked people eating, drinking, laughing, playfully kissing, and touching, this "Meet and Greet" was really "Sodom and Gomorrah."

The entrance to the room was equally breathtaking with two fifteen-foot-high, gold-leaf, stained-glass doors opened halfway, each with one of the Barbee Doll girls smiling and kissing everyone on their cheek as they entered. The face cheek.

In the center of the ballroom, eight-feet high above the floor on a rotating dais, was a giant white grand piano. A naked pianist was seated on a white bench, filling the room with classical and soothing piano music. Giant ice sculptures of flamingoes, swans, and naked men and women surrounded the rotating dais. Although the room was warm enough to be comfortable without clothes, the ice statues each had a special refrigerated cooling system installed underneath to keep them from melting.

As Jamie and McKenna made their way into the room, they maneuvered politely and carefully through a clustered crowd of totally nude resort guests and invited porn stars.

Jamie and McKenna had heard about the special autograph session in the lobby for early arrivals the night before they arrived. Tonight was the actual start of the convention, as they learned from the literature left in each hotel room.

"Might as well get us a drink and some food," McKenna said to Jamie and she nodded a response.

"Well, not too much food. Don't want my tummy to show," Jamie casually replied while rubbing her bare midriff with one hand.

McKenna looked at her, then her tummy, then back to her, and smiled.

"Chin up, Mister," she stated, half playfully, half seriously. She didn't want him to see anything that might make a change in his "direction."

"Of course, darling," he replied, this time with a squeeze of her hand.

"Drink?" A tall, attractive, mid-20s, naked bargirl with a tray full of assorted drinks stood before them. She looked at McKenna and most definitely didn't keep her "chin up."

"Sure. What do you have?"

"Well, depends on what you want?" The naked bargirl replied more than friendly.

"Chardonnay," Jamie interrupted sternly, not exactly pleased at how this 20-something nudie was eyeing McKenna.

"Wine for me, too," McKenna added, keeping his chin up, while catching the tone in Jamie's voice.

The girl extended the tray with two wine glasses now pointed towards them.

"My name's Aleena. Just ask for me if you want anything special."

"To drink?" Jamie asked with a look of irritation.

She looked at Jamie and coyly smiled.

"That can be arranged, too, of course, and, the offer is for you, also." Her eyes gave Jamie the more-than-once-over with a naughty smile mixed between.

A passing naked couple interrupted the moment as they strolled up to the bargirl and reached for any type of drink they could grab. Apparently, they didn't care; just wanted to indulge on free drinks.

It was a good break for them to move away.

"A swinger?" Jamie looked at McKenna while raising one eyebrow in concern.

"Well, in a place like this, not sure. Could be just friendly."

"As a 'detective' talking to a cop, that was more than just friendly," Jamie smugly replied.

"As a 'cop' talking to a detective, I'm very content with what I have in my hand." He held up his glass to clink with hers, while he squeezed her other hand in his, matching his words, and maybe more.

"So, what do you think of the place? Quite a 'meet' market isn't it?" a man's voice interrupted them.

It was Jack Hammer, with the same confidence and cockiness as when he first arrived, except now he was naked. Naked, except for the many gold chains across his neck, and some hanging halfway down his chest. On his arm was a tall, black woman, with artificial breasts and long, black curly hair that draped her half-exposed bosoms.

"Quite a show, and the show hasn't even begun. Yet." Hammer took a sip from his wine glass and gave them both a sly smile. So did his friend attached to his arm. "I'm Jack Hammer, and this is Ebony. Maybe you've seen her work?"

"Loved her in *Ebony and Ivory,* her recent DVD. Quite a 'piece' of work." McKenna nodded to both with emphasis on certain spoken words.

Jamie turned to look at Jim, somewhat shocked at what he said.

"This is Jamie. I'm Jim. You're one of the main celebrities here tonight."

"Well, thank you for your kind words. I just think of myself as a just a regular guy with a few 'extra' trimmings." He moved his hand downwards as if to show off what he was talking about, and he certainly had "something" to show off.

"Jack Hammer, the Producer, Writer, and Actor. Well, yes, quite the 'package,' so we see," Jamie added and smiled directly at him.

It was McKenna's turn to look at her with a somewhat shocked, but mostly hidden look.

"Why, thank you, Jamie. They say all good things come in different-size packages," Hammer proudly added.

"Indeed, they do," Jamie replied, matter of factly, while keeping her eyes above his chin.

"So, are you pleased with the number of guests here for the convention?" McKenna quickly asked to change the course of conversation.

Hammer kept his eyes on Jamie as he replied to McKenna's question.

"Very pleased, especially with the beautiful guest I see in front of me." Hammer's words were more than just flirtatious.

Jamie politely smiled. In her mind, only one word registered, "Awkward."

A naked, burly, and bald security guard approached them and tapped Jack on the shoulder. The guard leaned close to him to say something only Jack could hear.

The sounds of the many guests, and the accompanying piano music, prevented both McKenna and Jamie from hearing anything that was being said.

Hammer nodded his head to the security man, who abruptly turned and left.

"I'm sorry. You'll have to excuse me. I have to speak to the event planner who is looking for me. I'll be making a welcoming speech later. In the meantime, do enjoy yourselves, and don't forget, tomorrow night's event is a masquerade-themed dance in the resort nightclub. He turned to look directly at Jamie while taking her free hand in his. "I hope you will save me a dance."

"I hope so, too." Jamie again smiled politely, continuing to play the "interested starstruck female" role, while leaving her hand in his for the moment, before finally letting it drop freely to her side.

Ivory smiled also, but not at her, but directly at McKenna.

As Jack began to turn away, McKenna blurted out, "Did you hear about the porn star found in the pool? You must have known him."

Hammer stopped abruptly, and slowly turned with a half-real and half-fake smile, while staring directly at McKenna.

"He accidentally fell in the pool and must have drowned. Had too much to drink. He was known to be a big drinker. It was a big problem with him; it even affected his on-camera performances. They weren't as 'big' as they used to be. Sad that he had an accident, but it shouldn't spoil our fun tonight, after all we're all here for fun, aren't we?"

Before he could turn again to leave, McKenna blurted out another comment, "We heard another body was found in the resort clothing shop, drained of all its blood."

There was an awkward pause as Hammer's half-fake smile became a full-fake smile. Was McKenna fishing for something, or did he feel that Hammer might know something, and his words or demeanor might indicate such? Or was this this just a game of cat and mouse between two naked, macho men who, from the looks they gave each other, weren't exactly wanting to be chummy friends?

"Just a rumor. I can assure you that it was a store mannequin someone placed in the window looking like that. Just a drunken prank. Lots of people drink and do funny things when they're in a place like this, and sometimes say regretful things, too," Hammer replied without hesitation, or much emotion, but with a definite emphasis on the word "regretful."

The smile slowly left his face, and he abruptly turned and left with Ivory still attached to his arm.

"Ahh, that was interesting," Jamie commented as she watched the two of them disappear into the adoring crowd that parted like the Red Sea before them.

"Yes, it was. Say, how did you know who he was?" McKenna asked quizzically.

"Display poster in the lobby. When I was on my way to our room earlier, I overheard some guests saying that he was here. He sure looked like he thought he was something special. Just putting two and two together. And how did you recognize her as in *Ebony and Ivory*?"

"Just a lucky guess. As a porn star with the name Ebony, I assumed there had to be an Ivory. One of the Beatles once sang a song 'Ebony and Ivory.' It just stuck out in my mind."

"Uh-huh," Jamie replied as if not believing a word he said.

"And what about Jack Hammer and the comment about his...?" McKenna quickly turned the conversation back to her.

"Package? Well, he certainly has a 'package of credentials'—producer, writer and actor. I'd call that quite a package. Wouldn't you agree?"

"Uh-huh," McKenna replied as if not believing, or maybe just barely believing that was what she really meant.

Another serving attendant came up to them. This time it was a young, handsome, naked male, mid-20s, carrying a tray of drinks. If he was a male model, he was definitely a "perfect ten." Perfect hair, perfect teeth, perfect physique, perfect...

"Drinks?" he asked with a look of perfect assurance in his eyes.

"No thanks. We'll get some food first," McKenna replied quickly, as he could see Jamie was at a loss of words staring at him.

McKenna took Jamie by her arm and escorted her away. As they walked toward the nearby food stations, she turned back one more time to look, and this time she didn't keep her chin up.

"My, my! From the fellow at the pool, to the fellow with the big package...of credentials, everyone wants to dance with you. Guess you'll have to create a dance card, and certainly save a space for my name on it," he teased her.

"Why, Jim, I didn't know cops liked to dance!" as she teased right back at him.

"Like you said earlier today, I like to twist." He looked at her defenselessly.

They both laughed.

Turning towards one of the nearby food stations, their nude bodies touched slightly together as they held hands walking through the crowded ballroom. Jamie's mind raced with so many thoughts. *"This place is like a shark frenzy—free food, free drinks, and possibly free sex. People filling plates, people downing one drink after another, people making innuendos, and some people staring at you as if they were trying to undress you, but we're all already undressed. This place is definitely something to see and be part of, a whole different lifestyle, something that words really can't describe, and here I am in the middle of it. And here I am becoming comfortable with it, and even beginning to like it. Who would have thought?"*

An unknown man's bare arm suddenly went around her waist, interrupting her thoughts and pulling her away from McKenna. A woman's bare arm went around McKenna's waist, as he turned to see what just happened.

"Hi, guys," a familiar man's voice greeted them and face smiled at them.

It was Tina and Jeff, the couple they met earlier at the pool.

"We've been looking all over for you. How do you like this? Isn't it crazy?" Jeff added.

McKenna was ready to pull Jamie back, maybe both as a cop protecting her, and maybe as a man who wanted her. He hesitated and decided to play along. After all, he thought to himself, *"She's a big girl and can fend for herself."* And she did, but not the way he expected.

She put her bare arm around Jeff, bringing their bodies closer together.

"So how was your massage?" Jamie asked him, as if pleased to see him.

"Let's just say a 'couple's' massage is a couple's massage." He smiled broadly, as if he were a "Cheshire cat" with a secret.

Tina just smiled in agreement and moved closer to Jim.

"So how was your afternoon? Find the killer yet?" Tina asked him.

Her out-of-the-blue comment made McKenna straighten up quickly. Did she know he was a cop here on assignment? Was their cover story blown? He was at a loss for immediate words.

"I mean, after what you said at the pool, I heard from another guest that there have been a few strange things going on here lately, and maybe you heard more," Tina continued, more matter of fact than a question.

"Actually, no." McKenna regained his composure and acted like her earlier comment was just what it was, a comment, nothing more. "But, what did you hear?"

"Something about a disappearance here two days ago, as the convention was being organized."

"Disappearance?" Jamie quickly asked, intrigued by a possible new development in this case.

"Yeah, some of the early guests—two couples from Atlanta—never made it back to their room that night," Tina continued.

"Was it reported to the local police?" McKenna questioned.

"Don't know. Although someone said there were cops here today nosing around," Jeff replied to McKenna's question.

McKenna said nothing to this, especially since he was one of the cops.

"Rumor is that the two couples heard about some free drugs at a private house party on the grounds, went to it, met some spooky-looking old guy, and they all headed off to a private bedroom, and neither couple has been seen since," Tina added.

"Maybe they're in another of the houses partying, or somewhere else in the resort?" McKenna tried to get more from her.

"Hmm, maybe, but it sounds odd." Tina shrugged her shoulders indicating that was all she knew.

"Like this place is normal?" Jamie looked at everyone with her response.

They all shared a laugh.

"Anyway, we're on our way now to a private party and we can invite friends. So, 'friends,' what do you think?" Jeff changed the subject back to the party.

"A private party, just like the one you mentioned?" Jamie asked, again, looking for something more. Her eyes went back and forth between Tina and Jeff.

"Yeah, like I just said, a lot of the homes built here on the grounds have some nightly private parties. They're a combination of those who like to watch, and those who like to be watched. The resort prefers that people keep it simple around the resort pool and jacuzzis, so just a little 'touchy, feely' fun is allowed, if you know what I mean. Even at the dance, touchy, feely is okay. Then people pair up and go off to their rooms or to a private party."

"Sounds interesting." McKenna glanced over to Jamie.

"Hell, yes. Tina here is quite interested in partying," Jeff blurted out like an excited young kid.

"It could be fun," Tina smiled casually.

"Yeah, it could." Jamie thought about it and nodded in agreement.

"Well, we've had a long afternoon, being our first time here, and we're going to get some of the food before it's all gone, mingle a bit with another drink, and then maybe..." McKenna paused, so as not to let them know their true intent, to look further into this new disappearance. "So, where is this party?"

"Finding the place is easy. Just follow the path behind the main pool and across the open-gated fencing to a row of houses. Fifth one on the left. Big red light over its address," Jeff replied.

"Which is?"

"Number 69. Pretty 'april-poe,' as they say in France," Jeff stated with a big, wide grin as if he were pleased with his show-off educated comment made in another language.

"Yeah, pretty *apropos,*" Jamie added with the correct pronunciation, and a smaller grin of her own. Obviously, Jeff wasn't the most educated person here, but as far as being here, education probably took second to endowment.

"Well, dinner first. Have to get some food to keep up the planned stamina. Maybe we'll catch you there later," McKenna concluded, making an excuse that was believable, yet really wasn't.

"Hey, and don't forget the dance, if not later tonight in the resort club, then definitely at the big masquerade party tomorrow," Jeff made sure to mention, as he directed his comment and accompanying stare right to Jamie.

"Don't worry. I'll be sure to put you on my dance card," Jamie replied politely.

"You're what?"

"Never mind," McKenna interrupted, to quickly change the subject.

"And I want to see Jim dance the Twist with me." Tina gave Jim a cute smile.

And then she leaned closer to him and shook a bit of herself. But having had her upper anatomy previously worked on, the original parts didn't move too much anymore, but they certainly kept a perfect shape.

"I also want to see how 'low' he can go," Tina added playfully, and partially licked her lower lip.

"So do I," Jeff quickly added, indicating he was more than just a voyeur, and maybe had an interest in more than just women.

He unexpectedly leaned forward and kissed Jamie on the face cheek, while squeezing her other lower cheek from behind.

Jamie tried not to appear shocked.

McKenna tried not to appear mad.

Tina reached over and kissed Jim on the lips briefly, then brought her mouth to his ear.

"I really do like to twist, but I much rather bump and grind."

Tina and Jeff both grabbed each other around their waists tightly, and with a wave of their open hands, turned and disappeared into the crowd.

"Definitely swingers," McKenna mused while nodding his head.

"He grabbed my ass!" Jamie exclaimed while shaking her head.

"Hmm. Do you expect me to arrest him? For grabbing your backside at a nudist and swinger resort party. What law would you say he broke?" McKenna asked as if one cop was talking to another.

"Well...what about trespassing?" she replied, maybe half seriously. Maybe.

McKenna rolled his eyes.

"I'll remember that," he added smugly.

"I hope you do," she replied with a hint of sarcasm, but also feeling naughty.

Then they both laughed at the whole situation and touched hands once again. McKenna took her hand in his.

"Let's get some food and then do some more snooping here. If need be, we can check out the party later. Interesting about the four missing people. I wonder if it has anything to do with the two murders?" Jamie asked as they walked together.

"You're the detective. Uncover the clues and I'll catch the killer."

They said no more, both knowing that, although this was certainly a surreal place with a unique mixture of adult fun and games, there was also a deepening mystery that needed to be solved before something else happened. And something would, soon, as an unseen person kept a close watch on them from afar. Far enough away from them, but close enough to give them both an uneasy feeling.

Jamie leaned closer to McKenna while keeping her voice low as not to be heard, "I can't help it, but I have a strange feeling we're being watched. I've had that feeling for some time."

They stopped and both looked around casually, not drawing any attention to what she just said, as if they were just interested in looking at all the goings on. Their hands remained tightly together, and Jamie even pointed towards one of the food stations as if that was where they should go next, while all the time scanning the guests. Looking for someone or something. McKenna had already shared his experience, talking with the mysterious stranger at the pool, with her. He had described him to her, and they both kept that in mind as they had walked through the ballroom to see if he was there.

"You know, in an investigative process, sometimes how a person dresses and how they act is a clue itself. This place here is proving to be a lot more complex. Everybody is dressed the same," Jamie spoke first as they continued walking.

"Birthday suits?"

"Exactly," Jamie replied, and they both shared a smile, even though they both knew it was a whole different lifestyle here, and that would make it a challenge to seek out clues. Although her comment had a sense of humor to it, it also had a sense of foreboding.

Not seeing anyone watching them directly, other than everyone looking at everyone indirectly, they approached a nearby food station. McKenna took two plates and handed her one.

Jamie suddenly felt "something" or someone bump into her. Startled, she turned and there was no one there. But there really was—just around the waistline.

"Excuse me, babe. Just looking for some pie," a raspy woman's voice came from below.

It was Bridgett the Midget, with an empty plate in one hand and a large black plastic vibrator in the other.

Jamie didn't want to appear too shocked, but this was the first time she had ever seen a naked little person.

"Where's the dessert station?" Bridgett looked over and up at McKenna.

McKenna, without pause, pointed towards the far wall by the window, obviously a bit too far and too high for Bridgett to see.

"It's over by the windows."

"Thanks, Sport. I just love eating dessert. Never can get too much pie. If you know what I mean." Bridgett winked.

And with that, she turned and disappeared into the surrounding crowd. Using her plate as a "prod" to let people know she was behind them and below them, and if they didn't see her immediately, they got a surprise jab of the vibrator to make them move.

"Oh, dear God! Now I've seen everything," Jamie said aloud, watching Bridgett "shock" a middle-aged couple in their protruding butts with her battery-driven device.

"Actually, I wouldn't be surprised if there's more to see."

And with that, Jamie took notice of his words, again trying to determine as a detective what he really meant, and as a woman if he meant what she heard him say.

"Let's get some air on the outside deck, and maybe get some of our 'normal' senses back. There's a whole lot of crazy going on here," Jamie said above the noisy crowd, while trying to avoid bumping into, or being bumped into, by the increasingly number of naked guests here.

With a plate full of finger foods in one hand, and a new glass of wine in the other, they worked their way to the large, open glass doors leading to the adjoining veranda. A long and beautifully constructed Romanesque marble railing wrapped along the full length of the area. Ornate tiki torches with soft blue-colored flames were placed equally throughout the winding exterior. At both ends of the veranda were a set of concrete steps which wound its way circularly down into the adjoining gardens and the nearby pool and jacuzzis. The rhythmic sound of the pool waterfall could be heard, but the pool itself was empty of people, as were the jacuzzis. Everyone was at the party.

The sun had just set and the remaining glow of ending daylight, mixed with the soft torch lights, created a relaxing, if not romantic atmosphere. Several other couples, and some groups of people stood throughout the veranda, eating, drinking, talking, kissing, or just "chilling" away from the large crowd in the ballroom.

Placing their plates on the wall ledge, McKenna turned and held his wine glass out to Jamie.

"I have a toast, and a confession to make."

Jamie took her glass away from her mouth and held it out touching his. Holding it there.

"Confession first. This morning, when the chief called us into his office and told us about this assignment, I was hesitant to work with you. I didn't even know you, other than from the few group meetings, and a few casual conversations we had in the office halls. Truth is, I've never had a female partner, and I've always been kind of a loner, especially in the past few years with some personal issues. And, of course, coming to this place, here, without...without our uniforms... has been more challenging than I can explain. But I want to tell you that the more we have been working together, the more I respect you as a partner, and you're making me feel more comfortable, if those are the right words. I know how to catch a killer while wearing clothes, but I can honestly say I've never caught one not wearing clothes. But I believe, with you, together, we will."

Jamie's eyes held on his, as his words drifted in her mind.

His eyes held onto hers. Her eyes shimmered enticingly at him. She was very beautiful, as the mixture of lighting draped her naked body. And he was a very handsome man.

"With you, together," she softly replied.

They touched glasses, slowly, meaningfully.

Their eyes held for a moment as they each sipped at their wine. It was the first time they really had a chance to look at each other like this. And they took the moment to make it last long, and to look deep. Deep enough to magically touch each other's heart, and make their hidden passion become more real. And, in that moment, he took a half step closer. As she did too. Their glasses slowly lowered as their eyes continued to express a secret feeling they both shared but had still not fully revealed. A feeling that maybe, just maybe...

A loud scream from the pool area suddenly broke their thoughts.

McKenna's body turned quickly toward the scream. There, by the edge of the pool, a woman was fighting off a tall man who held her by her arms. Without a word, McKenna put his wine glass on the ledge and ran towards the stairway. Jamie also put her glass down to follow him, when her arm was suddenly grabbed from behind.

It was Tina.

She had a look of complete confusion and utter distraught in her face.

Jamie tried to break free of her grip, but it was strong, way too strong.

"Jeff's disappeared." There was a tremor in her voice.

"What? I have to go. There's a..." Jamie quickly cut in while trying to break free of Tina's grasp on her.

"I think he's dead."

"What?" Jamie exclaimed, not at all having been prepared for what she just said.

Her eyes tried to follow McKenna, who by this time had gone down the steps, and was closing in on the man and woman struggling by the pool. Again, Jamie tried to break free.

"He's dead. I saw it. He's dead!" Tina screamed the words as tears swelled in her eyes.

By this time, a small crowd of on-lookers from the immediate area surrounded them, having been drawn by Tina's loud and out-of-control emotions. Jamie turned fully to Tina, and it was her turn to grab her, and shake her.

"What do you mean 'dead'?" Jamie shouted at her to bring Tina back to her senses.

"She bit him! She bit him!" Tina's eyes said it all, her words adding a certain feeling of horror to them.

And with those words, some of the nosey onlookers and nearby resort guests began to lose interest. After all, in a sex-charged place like this, and at a lifestyle convention that promoted swinging and other erotic situations, along with excessive drinking and drugs, "biting" was just part of the norm. But for Jamie, this was not the "norm" she was hearing; this was a clue she was looking for.

"Where did this happen? When? Quickly, take me there." Jamie's focus remained on Tina. Whatever McKenna was doing in the other situation, she knew he could handle himself.

In between the sobbing, Tina shook her head to clear her thoughts. Her senses were slowly returning to her.

"We were on our way to the party that we told you about when another couple approached us. They were friendly, real friendly, and the guy was real sexy, and I just started to kiss him, and when I opened my eyes to look over at Jeff with the other woman, I thought she was kissing his neck. He was moaning, but she was biting his neck. She bit into it, and she turned and looked directly at me, and blood dripped from her mouth. Lots of blood. She had fangs!"

"A vampire! My God, could the Killer we are looking for be a vampire?" Jamie's mind raced with both the words and images that Tina had described.

"There was blood all over him. It was pouring down his neck. He just stood there motionless. He was dead!"

Tina sank her face into Jamie's bosom and started to cry hysterically. Jamie held her tightly, rubbing her back to let her know that everything was okay, although by the description of what Tina saw, everything was far from okay. And then she thought about McKenna. From where she was standing with Tina, she couldn't see the pool or hear anything from it, especially with the few people who still stood blocking her view of the pool area. All she heard were just Tina's sobs, mixed with the continuing piano music and loud voices from inside the open ballroom doors. All she wanted to do right now was to get this situation under control and find McKenna. *"Where is he?"* she wondered with concern. *"He has to be okay, right? Or isn't he?"*

"Hey, you two having a little 'girl-girl' fun?" a man's voice suddenly called out from behind.

A voice Jamie recognized and, at first, thought it was the voice she wanted to hear. The voice of McKenna. But it wasn't. It was the voice of Jeff. A smiling Jeff, who looked anything but dead.

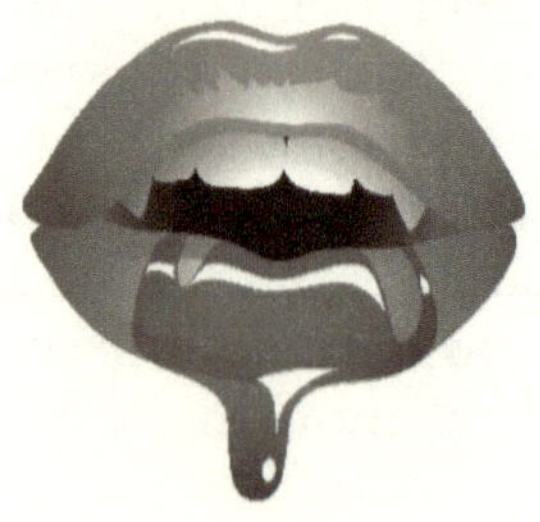

CHAPTER 21

As McKenna ran down the veranda concrete stairs towards the pool area where the woman and man were struggling, he realized what it really meant to be "fully" naked. Sure, several times throughout the day he "felt" naked, not having his gun on his side, which he had become so accustomed to as a cop, and yes, of course, he was "really" naked as he walked throughout the resort without clothes, but now he was "fully naked," as he had no shoes, and it hurt to run on the rough concrete stairs. And, he had a second problem. He was partially aroused. That, with no shoes and the rest of "everything" about having no clothes, now made his run and this moment somewhat awkward, if ever there was a word to describe a moment like this. He had let his "sports" defense down when he and Jamie came close to each other in that special moment a few minutes ago, and, as a result, he was now changing "directions." Not fully north, nor fully south, but somewhere in between, like on an applause meter. Really awkward. But being a cop 24x7, which had led to his previous relationship ending, so did this unusual moment come to an end, as "duty called" and his mind refocused on the immediate situation at the pool. And "things" slowly returned to normal. Sort of. It was still difficult for a guy, any guy, and especially him in this situation, to run naked and, of course, without shoes.

Screaming, the nude woman continued to struggle with her assailant as McKenna reached the pool area, which was otherwise unoccupied due to the party. From what he could see, she was probably late 20s, full figured, nicely tanned, with long brown hair. A pool towel was next to her on the ground. Apparently, she had gone for a late-night dip and hadn't come from the resort party. The man was tall, over six foot, but thin and remarkably white; not a trace of a suntan. Very unusual, for a place like this. It appeared as if he never went out in the sun. His long, jet black hair was slicked back into a pony tail, and his hands were wrapped tightly around her wrists as he was forcibly pulling her towards him. Maybe he was a drunk; maybe they were lovers in an argument. A cop like McKenna always thought about the "maybes." He was trained to evaluate the situation, and he also instinctively knew to do that. It was part of his personal makeup and part of being a well-trained cop. But in all the possible maybes, something was very different here and now, and something was definitely out of place. The man had clothes on, and the hands that held the struggling woman had long fingernails—very long and very sharp nails. As she struggled to break his hold, the fingernails cut into her, leaving a small stream of her blood flowing across her hands and onto the ground. But that was not all. He was growling. Not like a man, but like an animal.

"Let go of her!" McKenna ordered as he drew closer to their ongoing struggle.

And the strange man did, throwing the woman unexpectedly into the pool and turning quickly to face him. And in doing so, McKenna could see the assailant clearly for the first time in the evening shadows and surrounding pool lights. He had fangs.

McKenna quickly threw himself forward, knocking the stranger backwards a step or two as the man's long arms and hands reached out and grabbed McKenna by the neck. His forward-running motion and the slippery pool area surface made them both spin around and fall simultaneously into the water. Locked in battle, they sank beneath the pool's surface.

Although McKenna was in great physical shape and well adept at hand-to-hand combat, fighting beneath water was a new experience for him, especially with a much taller man. He couldn't use his fists to throw a punch, as the encompassing weight of the water prevented that. Nor could he use his feet to kick at his adversary. The water prevented that also. All he could do was wrestle with him underwater while holding his breath. And they did.

The spectrum of colored underwater pool lighting cast an odd and eerie glow on the fighting pair, as they thrashed back and forth in the water. Fortunately, the pool wasn't created for Olympic diving; it was a pleasure pool with different depths throughout, and they were only in neck-deep water. But it was still difficult to fight in.

The tall assailant was unexpectedly strong for a thin man, and his grip held McKenna down under the water, while his hands dug deep into McKenna's bare arms. So did his long fingernails. Traces of blood came from the open cuts as McKenna struggled to break free. But he couldn't. No matter how much he tried, he couldn't. But he had to. His life depended on it, and he finally did. Pushing a foot against the assailant's chest, he broke the man's grip and surfaced his face enough to fill his lungs with needed air. But not enough. The tall man surfaced also and grabbed McKenna tightly by the throat. And this time, the man's long, sharp fangs were closer to McKenna's vulnerable body—much closer. But this time, with both bodies thrashing somewhat above the water, McKenna was able to bring his hands out of the water, turn them sideways, and strike the stranger's ears. The force from the sudden blow stunned the attacker's equilibrium, resulting in the immediate release of his hands around McKenna's throat. And it worked, momentarily. The man's eyes opened wide in pain, momentarily. And then he attacked with more ferocity, coming straight forward in the water with his wide-open mouth and long fangs aimed directly at McKenna's neck. The fangs touched his skin, momentarily. McKenna's wet skin, and his ability to know how to twist and turn in combat, prevented the fangs from biting into his exposed throat as his assailant slipped and tumbled face-first past him, back into the water. Momentarily. And then he surfaced with a snarl, a menacing growl, and attacked McKenna again. His long arms and powerful hands grabbed onto McKenna's throat and forced him underwater again. This time, not momentarily. This time, for a longer period of time. McKenna was becoming exhausted and out of breath, and his ability to defend himself was lessening. Momentarily.

While held underwater, McKenna opened his eyes as wide as they could, looking for any way to escape from the deadly and seemingly unbreakable grip on his neck. The blurry image of the man he struggled with became clearer as McKenna regained his focus. The face of the man looked much older, much more wrinkled, much more evil than when he first saw it. This was not an ordinary man he struggled with. This was someone, or "something," very unordinary. And this was also no ordinary fight. This was an underwater fight to the death. And this man, this monster, this "whatever he was" was winning. And

McKenna, no matter how hard he fought back, no matter what he tried to break free, he was losing. But his inner strength wouldn't allow him to give up. It had never allowed him to give up. And he wouldn't now.

McKenna had one choice, and only one choice left, before the remaining air he held in his mouth was forced out.

Using all of his remaining strength, McKenna changed his fighting strategy. Instead of pushing away, trying to break free, this time he pushed himself into the grip of the man. It was a "martial arts" move he learned at the Academy, forcing his assailant's arms to bend sideways and inwards, and forcing him to release his hold. And he did.

McKenna's head surfaced. Air! Much needed air. Gasping aloud, he again filled his lungs. Momentarily.

The tall man's strong hands immediately grabbed the top of McKenna's wet head, forcing it straight down, back into, and beneath the swirling water. Forcing McKenna's whole body downward until he ended up on his knees at the bottom of the shallow water, submerged, struggling, fighting for his life, trying to break free again, trying to do anything and everything before...

A trail of air bubbles came to the water's surface as if in an endless parade. One after another, one after another. The struggle beneath the water appeared wavy and distorted from their movements. It was like a stretched Picasso-type painting, exaggerating the image, making it appear to be something other than what it was. Just blurs of flesh, and dark clothing mixed with some traces of blood. McKenna's blood. It looked unreal, but it was real, too real. The fight was becoming one-sided. A losing fight—for McKenna.

The air bubbles that surfaced came slower and slower, and finally stopped. There were no more.

The once distorted image in the pool's water came more into focus as the struggle finally ended. The tall man's clutched hands let go of McKenna's head, and McKenna's entire body slowly began to surface, face down, arms outstretched.

The mysterious assailant pulled himself out of the water and onto the surrounding pool area. Standing in his wet clothes, he appeared as if nothing had happened. He stood emotionless. He wasn't even breathing hard from the long fight. He turned his head looking for the woman who was thrown in the water earlier, but she was gone. Realizing she had escaped, he snarled his displeasure and abruptly left, darting between the lit areas and the shadowed areas, and disappearing into the surrounding darkness.

McKenna's body had come to the top of the water and floated calmly in the few remaining pool waves made from their struggle. Face down. Floating. Ever so lightly, ever so slightly. Ever so still.

Lifeless.

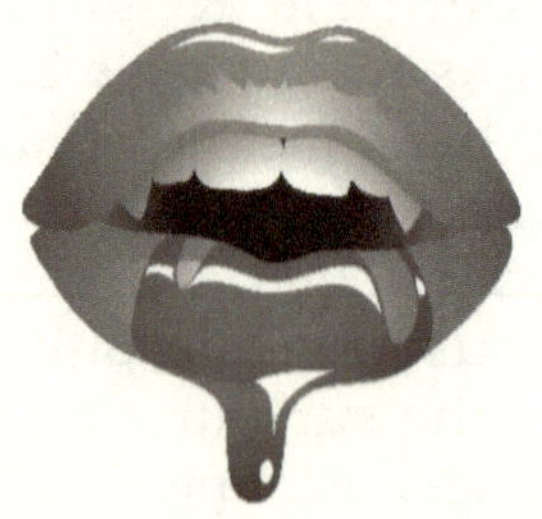

CHAPTER 22

"You're alive! Oh, my God, you're alive!" Tina exclaimed in a mixture of sudden shock and outright joy.

"Of course, I'm alive. What do you think? Do I look...dead?" Jeff smugly replied. "And why did you run away?"

"But I saw her bite you, bite you in the neck," Tina responded, somewhat confused.

"Oh, that was just an act," Jeff acknowledged like it was no big deal—an acknowledgement that almost felt rehearsed and not real.

"But I saw her teeth...her fangs!" Tina quickly added, while both questioning him and herself at the same time.

"That was just part of her costume for tomorrow night's masquerade party. She had fake plastic teeth. She's going to the party as a vampire."

"But the blood on her lips and your...?"

"There was no blood; you imagined that in the dim outdoor lighting. She had red lipstick on; it must have smeared from our kissing." Jeff's voice became stern, as if he was becoming annoyed and didn't want to answer more of her questions.

"She's not a vampire?" Tina continued.

"No, and there's no such things as vampires." This time his reply was filled with anger. It was a side of him that Tina was not that familiar with. It was almost if he were a different person from the fun-loving, laughing, flirtatious, and oversexed guy that she enjoyed being with. She looked away and down, hurt by the tone of his voice.

Jamie stepped closer and tried to look at his neck.

"Tina was really scared. Really worried," Jamie quickly interjected, deciding to defuse the situation before it escalated even more.

"So was I, when she ran away screaming," Jeff responded irritably. "She even scared our new friends just as we were having some fun. They got concerned with her actions and wandered off to the party."

He then turned away from Jamie and back to Tina.

"I came looking for you. Figured you'd be here. They still want to meet up later."

"But I'm sure I saw..."

"Nothing. Just your imagination." He punctuated his remark to her with an agitated look that was anything but friendly.

Jamie noticed two small red marks on the left side of his neck. Her detective senses aroused, she suspected that there was more to the story than what he was telling Tina.

"Looks like some type of mark on your neck." She looked directly at Jeff, trapping him in a lie.

He abruptly put his hand up to the area she was looking at and covered it with several fingers, almost pretending to wipe it away.

"I cut myself shaving. Bad blade. I was in a hurry." He looked at her tersely.

She took a step closer to get a better look and, as if to contradict him, commented, "Hmm, looks more like a..."

He turned to face Jamie, his eyes narrowing tightly and his demeanor becoming more disagreeable. His next words were anything but friendly as he raised his voice in response.

"I *said* I cut myself shaving!"

His eyes pierced into hers, giving Jamie an uneasy feeling. A very uneasy feeling.

Tina reacted to this also, taking a small step backward, not at all familiar with his cold and sharp tone of voice.

His eyes went back to Tina. It was apparent that he was not pleased with the direction of the conversation.

"We have to go. They'll be waiting for us." He looked directly at Tina as if issuing a command.

He turned his head sideways away from Jamie's immediate view of the marks on his neck.

"Okay, baby. Whatever you say," Tina agreed. It was apparent that she was shaken, but willing to do whatever he said. Quietly, she turned to her friend who had consoled her.

"Jamie, thanks for..."

Suddenly Jamie's thoughts returned to... *"McKenna! Where is he? Is he okay?"*

She glanced to the pool area where the confrontation had taken place a few minutes earlier. There was no one there. No woman, no man, no McKenna. Everything was quiet. Too quiet. The noisy guests who had been nearby when Tina ran up screaming had all dispersed. They lost their interest and either went back into the ballroom, finished their conversations, or left for some other activity, maybe a party, like Jeff had mentioned. It was now just the three of them. But where was McKenna? Something wasn't right. Her detective's intuition knew that, and so did her womanly instincts. Something was wrong. And she was right, as her eyes suddenly saw it. There, in the resort pool, floating in the water face down, was a body, a man's body.

"McKenna!" she exclaimed, quickly leaving Jeff and Tina and running toward the veranda stairs that led to the pool.

Jeff put his arm around Tina and held her close as they began to walk back towards the ballroom's open doors. Tina held onto him tightly, head buried in his shoulder and chest, lost in the relief that Jeff was okay, or so she thought. Jeff, paying no real attention to her, continued to watch Jamie run towards the pool, while his eyes narrowed even more and became two dark slits.

Jamie was running as fast as she could. And she could run fast. Her daily runs with her dog Bentley paid off as she made it to the edge of the pool in mere moments. And she didn't slow down or stop as she got closer. Without hesitation she dove directly into the water, quickly surfacing a few feet from the floating body. Her hands reached out, and underneath, quickly flipping the still body over. It was McKenna.

Her mind screamed with only one word.

"NO!"

That one word kept echoing over and over in her head as she held him in the water and pulled his body toward the pool's edge.

Using all her physical strength, and the fact that he was buoyant in the water, she easily reached the stairs in the shallow end of the pool. Even though his body had a muscular physique and weighed more than she expected, her inner emotional resolve, physical strength, and incredible willpower took control. Grabbing him under his shoulders, she pulled him up and out of the water onto the deck. Jamie laid him down on his back.

There was no movement. He lay still.

Not breathing, his body was becoming cold.

"NO!" she screamed again, this time loudly. Loud enough to wake the dead.

But still there was no movement.

Her heart beat faster—in overdrive. She knew what she had to do, and she did. She turned McKenna's head to the side to allow any water in his throat and mouth to drain. After repositioning his head again, she pinched and held his nose with one hand, while the other hand opened his mouth. She leaned directly forward, her lips surrounding his. Her breath becoming his, she forced her air into his mouth and down into his lungs. Changing position, she sat up and put both of her hands on his chest and pushed, once, twice, three times. And then she repeated the entire procedure again. Pinch nose, breathe air into his mouth, push on chest. Faster and faster. Nose. Mouth. Push. Everyone at the Academy had to know CPR. You never knew when it would be necessary. And it was necessary now, real necessary. She didn't want to lose him, especially since she had just found him. Found him to be a man she wanted to know more about, a man she wanted to be with, a man she was falling in love with. Nose, mouth, push on the chest. Again, and again. Her lips touched his. Again, and again. If this was their first kiss, she was determined—obsessed— to make sure it wouldn't be their last. Nose. Mouth. Push. Once, twice, three times, over and over, and over again and again. It didn't matter how long it would take. It didn't matter how tired she was becoming. All that mattered was McKenna. Nose, mouth, push. Again and again...until...

Exhausted, out of breath, arms feeling like jello, her mind and heart empty from all the physical and emotional efforts, she sat back on the cold concrete pool area. She sat back and stared at him. There would be no more "again and again." There would be no more "over and over." Jamie sat back holding his still body in her arms, tightly, next to her, and her eyes began to fill with tears, just a few tears, just a few. But she knew there would be a lot more. A lot more. Tears of realization. Realization that he was dead.

Dead.

And then she started to cry.

Suddenly, and unexpectedly, she was sprayed full in the face with a mouthful of water.

He was alive!

He coughed up more mouthfuls of water, some on her, some on himself. It really didn't matter as she sat him up, still holding him in her arms. All that mattered was that he was alive.

After getting the necessary oxygen into his lungs, his eyes slowly opened and looked directly into hers. As soon as he could, he spoke.

"Are you okay?" he asked as he continued to breathe heavily.

His first words weren't meant for himself but were meant for her. "Are you okay?" He was more concerned about her, and she understood the feeling in what he said, and how he said it. At this moment, this very moment, as she heard his words, and his eyes remained on hers, she had never, ever been more "okay." At this moment, all she knew, and all she cared about was that he was alive, and she was determined to never lose him again.

"Yes," she smiled softly. "I'm okay, now."

He was alive.

Whether it was from the warmth of her body while holding him, the so many, many breaths she gave him from her heart, or the intense need for him to never leave her, or maybe, just maybe, all of that and more. It didn't really matter. All that mattered was the moment.

And in that moment, her tears changed to laughter.

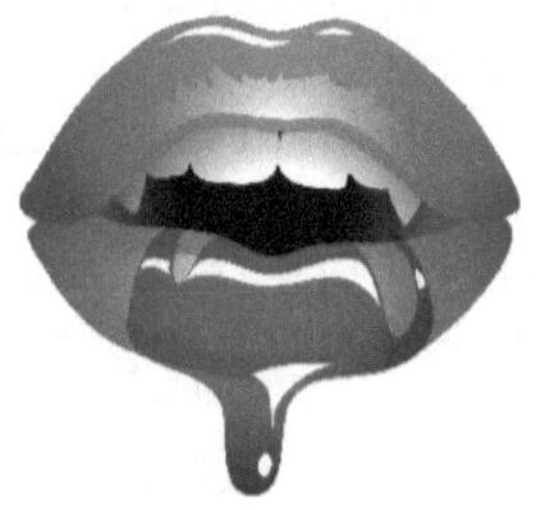

CHAPTER 23

"Well, other than the fact that they have the image of Popeye on them, it's the best I could find in my purse." Jamie surveyed all the colorful children's band-aids she had placed in different positions on his wounds. "Got them as a joke gift. Never knew when I would need them. Hmmm."

Returning to their resort bedroom, Jamie immediately attended to McKenna's cuts from the assailant's long fingernails. At the pool, she had picked up the towel that the attacked woman had left on the ground and used it as a compress to stop some of his bleeding until they returned to the room. The wounds weren't deep enough, or wide enough, to require stitching, and putting a lot of band-aids on him was the first logical solution. Unfortunately, if left on the way they were, they would certainly make him look a bit odd, if not conspicuous, especially without any clothing.

"Well, they don't exactly match the rest of your current outfit, so let's try Plan B," Jamie decided.

"Ouch." McKenna winced as Jamie quickly pulled off one of the many band-aids she had placed on

McKenna's bare shoulders, followed by removing five more.

A dab or two or her foundation makeup hid the cuts for the most part.

"Not bad," Jamie said out loud, while nodding to herself after her medical and cosmetic care.

"The makeup covers them up pretty well. But be careful of water. The makeup will come off if you go skinny dipping."

The reference to "skinny dipping" made him smile, as did she. Through most of the time she spent cleaning up his wounds and their walk back from the pool, he had been fairly quiet. He did tell her he had a lot to share with her but needed a few minutes to get his head and strength back together. The struggle in the water, and his coming back from Neptune's graveyard, had left McKenna exhausted. But he was feeling better with each passing moment.

"I can't believe he got away."

"I can't believe he almost drowned you," Jamie responded with a slight frown.

He let out a deep sigh.

"He was extremely strong. Actually, remarkably strong. And..."

McKenna hesitated, clearing his thoughts to make sure he had all of the "water out of his head" and was really prepared to say what he had to, and he did.

"He had fangs."

"What?" Jamie exclaimed.

"Fangs, like in long, sharp teeth," McKenna replied as a matter of fact, as if explaining the word to her.

"I know what fangs are. That's not *why* I was surprised, although I am by *what* you're telling me."

She cocked her head as if it was her turn to clear her thoughts and make sure she didn't have any "water on the brain" to cloud what she had to say.

"Jeff was attacked by a woman with fangs, too."

"What?" It was now McKenna's turn to show surprise.

Jamie repeated Tina's description of what she saw and then Jeff's arrival and his defense, and explained to McKenna why she didn't follow him immediately to the altercation at the pool.

McKenna sat in a somewhat stunned silence for a moment trying to piece it all together.

So did Jamie. After all, she was the detective, and she usually had a way of figuring out how to add up the facts.

"A vampire?" McKenna mused.

"Or vampires!" Jamie corrected his thinking. "You were fighting a man with fangs. Jeff was kissed by a woman with fangs."

"The marks on the earlier victim's necks..." he thought out loud.

"Which could have been made by fangs," Jamie replied.

"Or maybe just long teeth." McKenna couldn't admit, and wouldn't admit, that vampires existed. He was familiar with chasing and catching killers. Big ones, small ones, tall ones, short ones. Killers. All sizes and all shapes. But vampires?

He stood up and looked at Jamie, not believing what he was going to say.

"Dracula?"

He paused. She paused. They both paused, thinking about what he just said.

"Or, maybe Mr. and Mrs. Dracula," Jamie added, punctuating the possible answer, as if they really could exist.

Neither knew how to react at this comment, nor what to make of this. All they knew, as a seasoned cop and a well-respected detective, was that, right now, two plus two didn't quite equal four. This was something outside the norm, something that was quite unnatural, to say the least.

"How can this be possible?" McKenna asked both himself and Jamie.

Jamie frowned a bit, trying to think about the right answer to give, but couldn't. Her trained investigative mind kept reviewing the recent occurrences and possible clues. Vampires. Really?

While she was lost in thought, McKenna studied her face. Yes, he had looked at her many times throughout the day and, yes, he had fought hard with his own male libido to keep his "chin up," and he did most of the time. But right now, in the subdued room lighting with her so close to him treating his wounds, all that was changing. As he thought about his "confession" to her on the ballroom veranda and how she saved him from the pool, he was coming to a profound realization—a realization which was becoming more apparent each time he looked at her. He was looking at her as a woman. He found himself very attracted to her, perhaps a lot more than he could put in words. And whether this was the appropriate moment to say it or not, he did.

"You know, you're very beautiful when you're doing your detective thing," he said softly.

Jamie came out of her analytical thoughts and looked back at him. *Very beautiful...detective thing.* She tried to process the meaning behind his words. Not knowing the exact "right answer" to give him, she responded, "And you're very handsome with...your wounds."

The smiles they gave each other were more than just smiles. They were visible "feelings." Special feelings that had been surfacing between them, here and there, throughout the day, which they now were showing and sharing together. Although they were both professionals in their jobs, they were both somewhat shy in their emotions. But after a day of being naked together, their initial shyness finally disappeared and their emotions finally surfaced.

And then their eyes met. They met for a long, long moment.

"Thank you for rescuing me at the pool." His words meant more than what he spoke.

"Thank you for letting me rescue you." Her words spoke more than what she meant.

Their closeness became even closer, and in their silence, his hand gently reached out and lightly touched her face. Her hand also reached out and lightly touched his chest. He stepped closer, and so did she. There was no more distance, or space, between them. Their naked bodies were fully touching each other for the first time...locked together. His hand slowly moved from her face and to the back of her head, gently guiding her face to his. They both knew what was next, and they both desired it.

Their lips touched. It started with a soft brush of his mouth across hers. Their bodies embraced, and the kiss went deeper into the hearts of both. Deeper into the pent-up passions of both. Deeper into the very essence of both their souls. It was almost an electrifying feeling. Their eyes held on to each other, then closed.

A wave of increasing excitement roared through Jamie's trembling body. His fingers lightly caressed both of her breasts and touched her nipples, sending shocks of pleasure throughout her. Her head rolled backwards, and a moan somehow found its way out from her lips which were still locked on his. He finally pulled away and started to kiss down her neck, and across her shoulders, and finally to the tip of one breast, and then suddenly without warning, to the other. She arched her back with the kisses as he continued to tease her protruding nipples, first with his tongue and then with his mouth. Her mind seemed to spin out of control as if she were a young teenager enjoying an amusement park thrill ride, screaming from within, never wanting it to end. And then it was her turn. Her two hands slowly drifted down across his muscular chest and further past his stomach, feeling the hardness waiting for her. It was his turn to gasp, as her hands closed around him and made her moan more as her body reacted eagerly to what she touched.

They kissed deeper, faster, more, and more.

His one hand moved quickly to, and between her parting legs, creating a tingling sensation throughout her that made her want to shout with joy.

"Oh God," she breathed softly in response to her excitement and pleasure she felt throughout.

They embraced tighter. Each wanting the other. Each wanting to be "one" with the other. Each wanting to...

Suddenly and unexpectedly, the door to their bedroom flung open. Stepping quickly into the shadowed room light were two burly and menacing resort security guards, both pointing guns. Pointing directly at them.

"You two, come with us, now!"

CHAPTER 24

"Are you sure you're okay?" Tina asked, still confused and concerned at Jeff's reaction since he returned to the veranda where she was being comforted by Jamie. He seemed somewhat cold, distant, not his playful, sexually driven self.

"Yes, I already told you I'm okay. Don't ask me again," Jeff replied with a certain amount of gruffness in his voice. Tina looked away, apprehensive of how he responded, but still trying to recover from her own mini-emotional breakdown minutes ago.

As they re-entered the resort ballroom, the awards party was already underway. Jack Hammer stood at one end of the room with a bevy of buxom, naked female porn stars and a trophy of a giant, metal golden penis held high in one hand. He was in the middle of his speech while they stood in the back of the crowded room.

"And now, for the final award of the night, our industry's own version of the Oscar®—porn's most coveted award, 'The Dickie!' Given out once a year to the leading lady and leading man who not only deserved 'the Dickie,' but enjoyed all the dickies they each got, or gave, all year long."

The audience laughed at his sexual play on words, and a lone, long whistle from an unseen Bridgett the Midget was heard from somewhere below most everyone's eyesight.

"And, of course, the shape and size of the award was patterned after me," Hammer added with his own proud chuckle.

Jack Hammer loved the attention he received and flashed a big smile. This was the moment he looked forward to all year, it was his night to shine, it was his party, it was his life on stage. And as "icing on the cake," tonight, as most likely, if not assuredly, whichever winning female received the prestigious award, she was also certain to receive "an additional award," Jack's own "dickie," later that night.

As the convention fans and resort guests waited for the result, Jack dragged the moment on and on.

Bored by the lengthy speech, Jeff took Tina by the arm and looked for the nearest exit.

"Come on, let's get out of here. We've got better things to do. We're invited to a private party."

"Are you sure... you still want to go?" Tina questioned him, and maybe herself, too, especially after the way he had been acting.

"Of course. And you, my beautiful young lady, will be the hit of the party," he replied in the tone of the old Jeff, the one she was used to.

Tina took the compliment, feeling more relaxed from Jeff's "cute" comment. She eagerly grabbed both of his arms and hugged them in a way of believing that everything was alright again between them. But if she saw his eyes, which she didn't, she would have known that it was far, far from the truth.

They quickly left the ballroom as Jack Hammer continued his speech. The award presentations continued with more applause and laughter, and the guests still had a lot of drinking and partying to do that night. No one had really seen them there, or paid much attention to them. It was a perfect time to leave, unnoticed.

Away from the crowded ballroom and all of its noise, Tina was becoming more relaxed as she and Jeff walked by the pool area, past the ever-constant fake waterfall, and towards the walkway area that led to the nearby homes and condos that were built within the resort walls. As Jeff told her, it was "time to party," and in a place like this, there was always a party somewhere for the many discerning adult-minded couples. Whether in one of the few homes, or the new condos and apartments that surrounded the resort pool and main building, there was always a party. Just "not" the typical party one would think. Besides the "fun in the sun" relaxing during the daytime, the nighttime fun was filled with sex, sex, and more sex. Adult games without the shame. This is what they had come for. So did a lot of the other guests. Some were "watchers"; some liked being watched. Jeff and Tina were both. But at this very moment, before reaching the party in mind, someone was actually "watching" them.

Following behind, unseen in the surrounding darkness, was the tall man from the earlier altercation at the pool. He walked silently, and swiftly, closing the distance between himself and them. Each step brought him closer.

"What a beautiful night," Tina said out loud to no one in particular, happy again, putting aside everything that happened from the recent past. "I'm really looking forward to partying with you." She squeezed his hand romantically, several times, waiting for a similar response from Jeff.

But one never came. Nor would ever come. Instead, some other voice interrupted.

"You have done well."

There, in front of them, suddenly stepping out of the surrounding shrubbery and blocking their path was a naked woman. The same woman who was part of the couple they had met earlier. The same woman who appeared to bite Jeff on the neck during their passionate encounter. She was alone. Her naked body appeared more beautiful than before, as she stepped into the soft beaming rays of the now full moonlight. But it was her eyes that captivated Tina's attention the most. Her eyes seemed to glitter brightly like she hid whole worlds behind them. Alluring. Hypnotizing. Breathtaking. And then she smiled. A small smile, but a wicked smile, just enough for Tina to see. She had fangs.

"Yes, he has done well."

From behind Tina another voice suddenly interrupted her frightened and confused thoughts.

It was the tall man stepping from the shadows, voicing his satisfaction. He approached Tina from behind, fully dressed. Stunned from first facing the woman, Tina was now shocked by his sudden appearance. Whether it was because he was dressed and everyone else here wasn't, or because he looked so different. His skin was paler than pale, as if not belonging in a place like this where everyone was so suntanned from top to bottom. Or different, because he looked so ominous, as if not being the typical carousing-type resort guest. For Tina, the sudden and unexpected interruption by both the beautiful naked woman and the fully dressed, tall, and strange-looking man was a very unsettling and frightening moment. Like a deer frozen in a car's headlights, she just stood there as their eyes focused directly on her. Stood there, transfixed, as if unable to move.

Jeff let go of her hand and slowly backed away from her.

"What?" she softly exclaimed, confused, maybe fighting back tears, maybe fighting back fear, looking back to Jeff for some sort of answer as to what was going on, or at least some sort of security knowing he was there to protect her. But there was no immediate answer. Nor would there be. Nor would he protect her. Jeff just stood there, a few feet away, motionless, expressionless, eyes glazed, staring at her, not lustfully, not sexually, but almost pitifully.

And when Tina turned to look back at the unknown male intruder, the original distance between them was no more. They were face to face. His wide-open mouth and protruding long fangs sunk quickly into her exposed neck—deep into her flesh, very deep, and immediately piercing her jugular vein. Her head slumped backwards as her eyes expressed an unspeakable horror that words could not describe. A horror that lasted an eternity in her soul as he sucked the very essence of her very life. He drank all her blood, and her death became a pleasure.

As the tall man let her limp, nude body fall to the soft ground, he licked his blood-stained lips and turned to look directly at Jeff. So did the woman.

The feeding was not yet over.

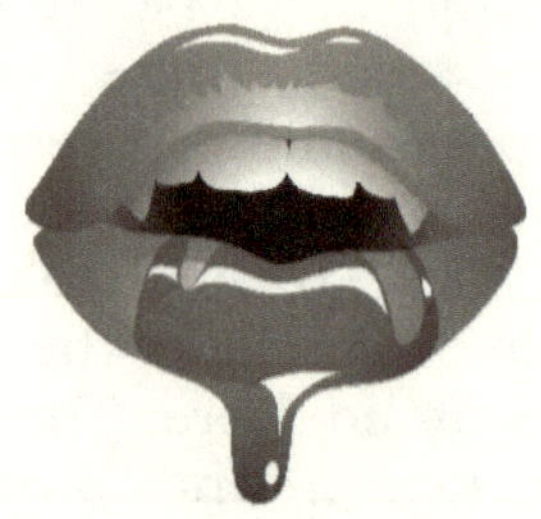

CHAPTER 25

"Who are you?" Winston demanded in a not-so-pleasant voice.

"At this moment, a very unhappy and disgruntled guest. Who are *you*?" McKenna shot back in an equally demanding and unpleasant tone, although he actually did know who he was, but couldn't reveal that.

"Who was the guy you wrestled with at the pool, and why?"

"I'm not answering any of your questions until you tell me why we were brought here at gunpoint and what this is all about," McKenna firmly replied.

"Are you a cop?" Winston pivoted away from McKenna's question with another question of his own.

"Do you see my badge? Am I carrying a gun?" McKenna responded with his anger now showing.

"Of course not, you're naked. That doesn't mean you're not a..." Winston tried to defuse the growing anger between them with a calmer response, but still an accusation.

"He's a cop," Jamie blurted out.

Both McKenna and Winston turned to look at her. She had been sitting calmly silent through their "macho" exchange, and her interrupting words seemed to shock both of them in different ways. "At least he thinks he is. He always gets involved trying to help people out. The woman at the pool was screaming for help," Jamie concluded.

"Are *you* a cop?" Winston now focused his attention and his eyes on her, mostly above her chin level...mostly.

"No. I'm a naked woman. A very angry naked woman. And at this moment a very cold and angry naked woman. You keep the air conditioning on pretty high in this room, don't you? Apparently, you must see my 'goosebumps' from the way you're looking at me."

Winston moved his head slightly back upwards as if to feign reaction to her accusation of where he was looking and why. There was a brief moment of awkward silence between all three of them. Winston's office was cold, very cold, and Jamie wasn't kidding about the goosebumps, especially as she sat fully naked in front of him. The air conditioning in his office had been set high to keep him cool from the constant hot weather. He really wasn't a fan of eternal sunshine; he actually liked and missed the four seasons. But this was his job, his life, and this office was his escape from the heat. In addition, his entire office was cold looking. The walls were painted in a dull gray color with darker gray swirled floor tiles. There were no colorful or fun and funky personal items on display that a typical business office might have. On the wall behind him were two large-sized framed color photographs—one of the resort under construction, and one with it finished, probably taken most recently. Two matching gray three-door filing cabinets hugged one wall with a gray metal table next to them, an assortment of neatly stacked paperwork, and a carefully placed stack of resort towels. Throughout their conversation

Winston had been facing them both as he leaned on a large expensive-looking walnut desk, while they sat in two fairly plush leather chairs directly in front of him. The two armed security guards remained silent and stood to one side, blocking the closed door to his office.

"Until you get something to cover my naked girlfriend and me, I have nothing to say other than I'm calling the 'cops.' As I said, who are you, and why are we here at gunpoint?"

Winston looked at McKenna briefly, then casually took his suit coat off and handed it to Jamie. He then moved behind the desk he had been leaning on and reached for a single resort towel that was part of a pile on a table next to it. He tossed it to McKenna.

"I'm Philip Winston, one of the owners of the resort. We have you on our surveillance camera tackling another guest and falling in the pool where you continued fighting. Not exactly the typical 'fun in the sun' activity we promote and condone here. I think I have every right to ask who you are and why you were fighting on resort property."

"Maybe you should focus on who the other guy was. For starters, how could he be a guest, fully dressed, walking around the resort? Maybe he was trying to kill someone!" McKenna answered, feeling more comfortable and in control of the conversation now that Jamie was somewhat covered up, and so was he.

"What makes you think he was trying to kill someone?" Winston asked, while keeping up his phony guard, which made it seem that he knew more than he let on.

"He was trying to kill Jim!" Jamie quickly added.

Winston took another moment, mulling over her words before continuing.

"Hmm. You two checked in this afternoon. We have no records of a prior stay here. We looked up your background and you're an out-of-town couple, checking in with a last-minute reservation, but something's not right in my mind about you two. Why are you here? For the convention? And who was the guy you wrestled with? Did you know him?"

"You're right, something's not right, like the two people who were killed here earlier today," McKenna replied by attempting to throw off Winston's train of thought.

"No one was killed here. One guy fell in the pool this morning and drowned. A drunken porn star. It was his own fault. There was no one else."

"What about the guy in the store window? He sure looked dead," Jamie added.

"That was a tipped-over store mannequin. Someone broke into the store and did a prank. And what do you mean he sure looked dead? You hadn't checked in yet," Winston replied with a concerned look as if he caught her in a lie.

It was McKenna's turn to give an answer while asking another question. It was a method of police questioning both he and Jamie were trained to use. "We heard from some of the guests at the pool that he was dead, and if he wasn't a 'real' person, why were the police here? There seems to be a lot of talk about two dead people and several missing people."

This caught Winston's attention. Obviously, they knew more than they let on, as he also knew the truth behind his own cover-up.

"Sometimes our guests complain about their significant others disappearing. Anyone missing is usually found drunk or recovering from some sex party on the grounds, in homes, or apartments. No one's been reported missing recently." Winston used another of his rehearsed and practiced storylines to cover up the mystery behind what occurred, whether he actually knew the truth or not.

"Why don't you let the police decide that?" Jamie inquired, trying to catch him in his lie.

"Police aren't allowed here. This resort is protected by state regulations. We have our own security."

"You mean the two 'goons' here?" Jamie nodded at them.

The word bounced off both of the guards. Either they had no idea what the word meant or thought it was a compliment.

Winston turned to the two security men who had stood silently through the entire conversation with their guns drawn. "Guys, put your guns away and wait outside the door. But if you hear me call you..."

Winston looked directly at McKenna and resumed his questioning. "Who was the guy you tussled with at the pool?"

"You mean the guy with the fangs?" McKenna stated as a matter of fact.

This really caught Winston by surprise, or maybe not.

"Well, he was probably part of tomorrow's masquerade party." Again, Winston looked for some type of an excuse.

"Yeah, nice costume. He tried to bite me," McKenna replied with a sly but serious tone.

"Maybe he tried to kiss you. We have some gay couples here," Winston shot back, more as a personal dig at McKenna.

"The people who died here had bite marks on their necks. Made by the same gay guy?" McKenna's reply made Winston pause, while he looked for an answer to this serious accusation.

Winston let out a deep breath, as he was tired of playing "cat and mouse" and wanted to find a common ground in their conversation.

"Listen, let me level with you both. This is an important time here at Paradise Lost. This convention is bringing in a lot of important guests, celebrities, and even some local and state big shots, if you know what I mean, and there is a lot of money at risk here if the guests believe the rumors you're spreading, or if they hear about the wrestling match you had with another guest with big teeth."

"Dracula," Jamie quipped.

"Is that the guest's name?" Winston asked, believing it was a real name.

"Just a hunch." Jamie smiled to herself, realizing Winston didn't get the "vampire" symbolism in her comment.

"All we know is that he was a tall, weird-looking guy with fangs. Not big teeth—fangs," McKenna calmly stated.

"Yeah, fangs, whatever," Winston replied, not believing his description, and also not liking what he heard, if it really were true.

McKenna again changed the direction of the conversation.

"Why did you bring us here by gunpoint? Why didn't you just knock on the door and ask us to come here on our own?"

"My guys didn't want to take any chances. You seemed to handle yourself pretty well in the pool fight. The guys overreacted."

"The goons," Jamie smugly corrected him.

Winston didn't respond to her comment. Jamie was definitely getting under his skin, but he was also liking the feisty dueling dialogue with her. She didn't come across as one of the typical swinger types looking for a good time and nothing but a good time. She actually was becoming his equal in their word battle.

"Like I said, this is an important time here. And we don't need any problems or situations to cause our guests any more concerns. Or anyone spreading rumors. I can ask you to leave the resort."

"And we'll go right to the police," McKenna politely replied, making the winning move in a game of chess.

It was obvious Winston didn't like McKenna's threat to go to the police. He started to frown, all the while controlling his temper, and then he let out a deep sigh, resuming a somewhat professional demeanor and continued.

"Or...I can ask you for your help, now that we know who you are, just guests, not troublemakers, and maybe even ask you to pass along anything that you might see or hear, you know, like these rumors, so we can get to the bottom of this."

"So, you want us to pretend we're detectives," Jamie replied slowly and with a bit of a caustic sarcasm in her voice.

"You already said he likes to pretend he's a cop. So maybe you can pretend you're a detective."

Jamie wanted to laugh out loud at his comment, little did he know how true his words were.

"How do we know you're really the resort owner, and not just posing as the owner?" Jamie quizzed, sensing that he may be involved in all of this.

It was becoming apparent to Winston that they weren't going to tell him any more details tonight, but now, at least, he was hoping they would play nice and be an extra set of eyes and ears for him.

"Listen, I want to apologize for any inconvenience, and maybe offer to buy you dinner in the resort restaurant, or if there's something else that..."

"Do you have embroidered 'his and her' resort bathrobes?" Jamie politely and somewhat coyly asked.

"I'd like my phone back." McKenna's request was more to the point.

"For the privacy and safety of our guests, we don't allow cell phones, especially those with picture-taking capabilities in our resort. This is a resort designed for a complete getaway from the stress of daily life. We don't allow phone calls unless there's an emergency. But if necessary, we allow calls at the front desk, or I can let you use my phone here. And no, we don't have embroidered resort bathrobes. People like going naked here." Winston's voice was definitely taking on a feeling of exhaustion.

"Then why are you dressed all the time?" Jamie playfully asked.

"In my position as the..."

"Maybe you're really afraid to show 'it'?" Jamie interrupted with a sly smile in her remark.

Here was an opening where she could get back at him, and maybe get under his skin for interrupting her and McKenna's "almost moment" in their room.

"Jim's proud to show 'his,' and so are the other male guests. Maybe you should consider that. Might make the whole environment here more natural and relaxing, and maybe guys in clothes like you wouldn't run around the resort trying to bite people."

Winston didn't know how to respond. Definitely, she was playing "cat and mouse" with him, trying to get the last remark in, or at least the last jab. Although this angered him, it also attracted him. He gave her a phony, yet intriguing, smile back.

"I'll be at the convention's final event, the masquerade party tomorrow night. Only masks are allowed."

"How will I recognize you?" Jamie asked with an equally phony, yet intriguing smile.

"With your boyfriend's permission," Winston nodded to McKenna, "I'll ask you for a dance."

"Fine with me. She'll add you to her dance card," McKenna answered his approval with a sarcastic statement that immediately went over Winston's head.

"Now I'd like to make a call," McKenna continued.

"To the police?"

"No, my mother. She's home watching my two dogs. She takes care of them while I'm away. And I always check in with her every night. She's getting on in her years."

"Yeah, of course, use my phone on my desk. And, no funny stuff. All outgoing calls are monitored." Winston raised an eyebrow with his remark.

"Actually, that's what I would call funny stuff." McKenna's look of disdain at Winston summed up how he felt about this guy. He didn't really like him, and he didn't really trust him. And most of all, he really didn't want him to be on Jamie's "dance card."

"No, that's what we call protecting our guests and their privacy." Winston's look back to McKenna was equally telling.

McKenna made no effort to cover up his call from Winston's attention. Punching in the numbers on the phone, which he knew would be recorded, McKenna pretended that this was just a "normal" call, although it wasn't. It was actually a secretly planned call.

"Hello, Mom? Jim. Yeah, we're having a good time. Just checking in. Dogs okay? They ate the new food I left. Yeah, the vet wants them to lose weight. So, easy on the treats. And you okay? Uh huh. We're just fine. No problems, just having a fun vacation at the resort. I'll call tomorrow night. Then off to Disney. Love you. Give Billy and Dozier a hug."

As McKenna returned the phone to the desk, Winston flashed him another of his fake smiles.

"Very nice. Your mother must appreciate hearing from a good son like you."

"In more ways than one." McKenna's smile matched Winston's.

Little did Winston know that the call McKenna made was to a prearranged phone number that a preassigned woman waited for. She was "a privately paid informant" who the police used to funnel messages when they worked undercover, and especially in situations like this where their personal phones weren't allowed. The message would go to their chief and he would know from the scripted words that they were both okay, as referenced with the two dogs being okay, and continuing to gather information.

Without any handshake goodbye, both McKenna and Jamie started to leave Winston's office.

"You can keep the coat on till you get back to your room. One of my security guards will accompany you to make sure you don't run into, or wrestle with any more guests tonight."

"Don't worry, I don't have an interest in wrestling with any resort guests. I have other more important and better things to do," McKenna replied.

He then looked at Jamie, and she looked back at him.

On the way out of Winston's office she stopped, turned back, and carefully took Winston's jacket off, leaving herself fully naked in his doorway. The hallway lighting seemed to put a sensual aura around her. Whether it was a tease, or to throw him off from wondering any more if they were cops, only she knew why she did this, if even she did. Without hesitation, Jamie tossed his sport coat to him and he caught it by surprise while looking at her totally nude body. Besides being a remarkable woman who held her own in a tough conversation like they just had, she was also quite beautiful.

McKenna followed her move and took the towel off his waist, also throwing it back at Winston, immediately breaking his fixation on Jamie.

Winston just stood there holding both his coat and the resort towel.

As Jamie and McKenna walked back towards their room, their hands automatically reached out and wrapped around each other.

Without looking directly at her, McKenna was the first to speak.

"You know, the way you're filling up your 'dance card,' I hope you saved some room on it for me."

Without looking back at McKenna, Jamie smiled, and with a tone of humor in her voice politely replied, "Why, Jim. There will always be room on my dance card for you. I plan to save the 'best' for last."

They squeezed hands and shared a quiet laugh between them.

The security goon trailed silently behind, trying to figure out what a "dance card" was.

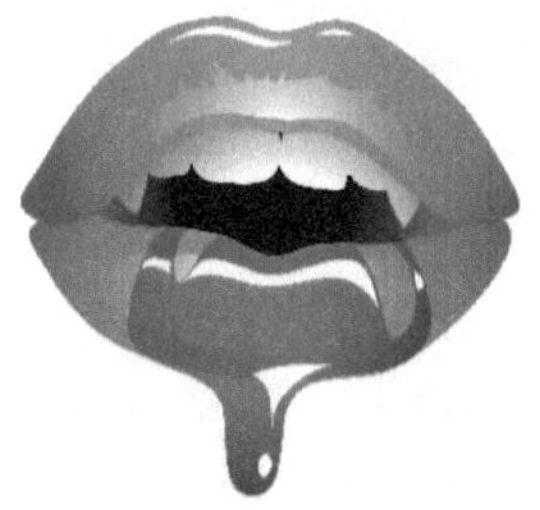

CHAPTER 26

When Jamie awakened in the morning her head was resting on McKenna's shoulder and one arm was across his naked chest. As they lay together in bed, the morning sunlight cast a long golden ray through the thin, sheer curtains of their large patio door and across both of their nude bodies. It was a blanket of warmth adding to the natural warmth of their touching bodies. She studied his face as he slept.

In the past 24 hours or less, she had looked at him many times—certainly at times to communicate in their assignment here, but at other times while just getting to know him and wanting to know more about him. After all, before yesterday, the most they ever said to each other was a friendly hello in the office and not much more, but today, they were naked and in bed together, and the once friendly hellos had certainly turned into something much more, and unexpected. Actually, something totally unexpected. Here she was waking up in the arms of an attractive nude man whom she hardly knew and was totally nude herself. And in that awakening, she wondered if she really knew herself. Jamie had never experienced a situation like this before, and here she was feeling very pleased and very comfortable with the moment. Very, very comfortable. A comfort she hadn't experienced in a long time. A comfort she was now allowing herself to enjoy. And she smiled not only at the moment and at him, but at herself as well.

Jamie cautiously took her one hand and gently pushed back some of his tussled hair from across the side of his sleeping face. He was handsome, there was no doubt about that. Very handsome, both awake and asleep. And she decided to let him sleep while she went out for her morning run. It was part of her daily routine and something she needed to do, especially today. Leaning softly, she kissed his cheek lightly with her warm lips. In doing so, one of her breasts lightly brushed across his muscular chest. It felt good, too good. And, although she paused to think about what she felt, she knew it would be best to wait. It was time to run—time for quiet moments to get her many personal thoughts organized as a detective and as a woman, who was facing both an unknown killer and an unknown adventure with a very handsome, naked partner.

Jamie had brought along her running sneakers and a pair of socks. That's all that was permitted by the resort rules regarding clothing, shoes, and socks. Sexy lingerie and adult toys were also allowed for the resort's specially themed parties, or for the guests' "in-room," personal activities. *"Actually,"* she thought to herself, *"packing light saved a lot of time and some of the stress associated with the proverbial 'what-to-wear' issue."*

Before leaving for her morning run, she took a brief moment and looked at herself in the full-length room mirror, just one of the many that were placed on the walls, and even the ceiling above for couples who liked to look, or watch each other, in whatever position they wanted. And as she looked at herself fully naked, except for the slightly worn sneakers and clean ankle socks, she could also see him in the mirror behind her, and she smiled again. A different smile from the previous one that she had when she woke up in bed next to him. This smile was just for him. She was becoming accustomed to being with him, and being without clothes around him, and she was beginning to like it—like it a lot.

Jamie left a note behind saying she'd be back shortly, and quietly left, but not before she glanced back at him one more time.

The resort had several walking and running trails that started behind the main pool area and went throughout the entire walled community, weaving their way between the custom-built homes, condos, and apartments that were specifically placed to give the entire resort its own "community" feeling. Although it was only 7 a.m., she passed a few of the early-bird nudists, referred to as "Jaybirds," a term she had heard, but really didn't understand, maybe referencing the "early bird gets the worm" saying, or in resort reality, the early nudist gets the better spot at the pool. They were already "lotioning" up and preparing for another day in the sun. Calm and relaxing "muzak" playing from the hidden garden speakers was the only early morning sound other than the ever-constant splashing of the pool waterfall. It was the start of what looked like another perfect Florida day. But looks can be deceiving sometimes, especially today.

After a few smiles to the guests she passed in the pool area, Jamie reached the start of the running trail. She realized that she had never run in the nude before, and that it might be a bit challenging. Just a bit. Fortunately for Jamie, her figure was tight and toned, and just the right proportions so that certain anatomical things wouldn't "bounce all over" during her naked run. That's what sports bras were designed for, to keep those "things" in place. But Jamie was blessed, both genetically and physically. Even though she always wore a sports bra when she ran in the park by her home, she didn't need one here. And inside the surrounding walls, this was a "bare-all world," and that's exactly what everyone did. Bared it all, and damned be the old phrase, "clothing makes the man," or in her case, the woman. It felt so right to be just as "bare" as the day you entered the world, and it felt satisfying on so many different levels.

As the warming morning sunshine and soft, summer Florida breeze caressed her body as she ran, it felt good, real good. And she remembered her recent thoughts while looking at herself and his reflection in the mirror in their room. She was really becoming comfortable to this "way of life," never, ever, imagining she would or could be nude like this in front of so many people. She was also beginning to like McKenna more than a "lot," never imagining that a feeling like this would or could happen so quickly. She suddenly felt "exposed" to her innermost feelings, which, of course, she was. She was, in reality, naked on all levels.

Running through the various gardens and strategically placed ponds, she recalled how a lot of Florida resorts were built in areas like this. Overgrown and heavily vegetated landscapes with lakes, streams, and ponds were often turned into theme parks and resorts to attract the "snowbirds" from up north. *"Snowbirds turned Jaybirds,"* she chuckled to herself as she ran, looking around at her pleasant and quiet surroundings, realizing that this was a perfect spot for a no-clothing resort like this. It was a private and serene landscaped world, surrounded by ten-foot concrete walls to keep the gawkers out, and hopefully any alligators, too. The only wildlife she had seen so far were the colorful tropical birds that flew in and out in the moss-filled trees, or a few spotted brown-and-green geckos and rabbits that scurried across the running path, as if playing a game of "catch me if you can." And that made Jamie think about this real-life game she was now a part of—"To Catch a Killer."

During her run, her thoughts drifted back to last night. Remembering the uneasy feeling she had of being watched in the ballroom. The scene of the woman struggling at the pool with a tall, mysterious assailant. The terror in Tina's eyes as she shakily told Jamie her story of a woman biting Jeff on the neck, even though it appeared he was okay, but not totally okay. The fight McKenna had at the pool, and how she saved him with their first kiss, if you can call a life-saving technique of "mouth to mouth" a first kiss. And she remembered the moments she had alone with McKenna in the room when they really did have that first real kiss, only to be interrupted by two goons with guns. And she recalled how she couldn't wait to get back to their room after the whole Winston interrogation thing. And when they did...

An unknown man's voice from behind, suddenly interrupted her thoughts.

"Morning," as a middle-aged, naked male runner passed her without saying another word.

Even though he didn't wear any clothing, just running shoes and socks like her, he could have used something extra to stop the "flapping." Some body parts weren't meant to be free in the breeze when running extra fast. She smiled to herself as she thought, *"What a place!"*

Quickening her own running pace, Jamie's thoughts again returned to last night when she and McKenna re-entered their room, how he held her in his arms, and how they gently kissed. It was a long kiss, a good kiss. Actually, a great kiss. She recalled how she decided that before things got any "hotter or heavier," she excused herself, wanting to take a quick shower to get the smell of Winston's perspiration-stained sport coat off her body and to freshen up. She wanted to make sure their "actual first" time was more of a special time, with only her and McKenna's combined sweat. He had politely told her to take her time, as he would pour some wine from the room's complimentary bar and relax, waiting for her. And he did. And when she came out feeling fresh as a daisy, he was very relaxed, too relaxed, actually. He was deep asleep on the bed with two waiting glasses of wine on the nightstand, just like a scene in some romance movie. We've all seen that scene before. But this wasn't a movie; it was real. And he was really asleep, as he let out some soft, deep snores. Although she wanted to wake him up and jump on top of him and smother him with her passion, she just shook her head and smiled. *"Probably best to take it a little slower, Jamie, to make certain that the moment is the right moment."*

Jamie thought more about that as she continued her run. As a detective, she always believed in finding the right moment, like finding the right clues. Being in the right place at the right time, or the wrong place at the wrong time. Everything was about "the moment." How one embraced it or wasted it. Moments were so important in one's life, especially in Jamie's life right now, with all the "unexpecteds" she had been recently faced with. And in her "next" moment, as the moment faded of her time with McKenna last night, she thought about the unknown killer and the possibility that it could be a vampire. She laughed to herself, *"Right. A blood-sucking vampire. Get a grip, girl! Vampires only exist in movies and books."* Perhaps; or perhaps not. For the next moment would be a defining moment, in both this case and her life. As the running path curved through some thick, colorful, flowery landscape, there, suddenly, just ahead, was another "unexpected." Jamie finally saw her.

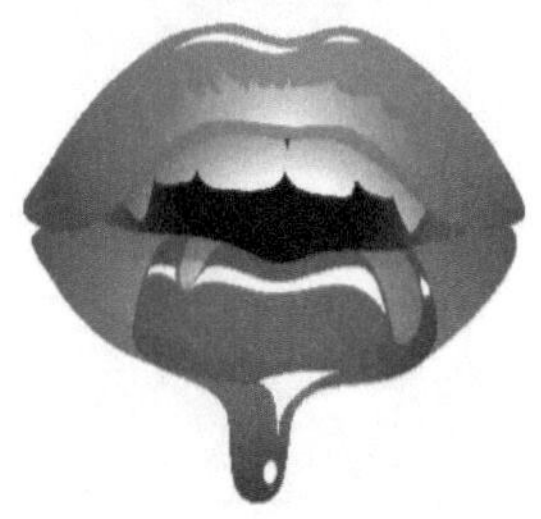

CHAPTER 27

When McKenna finally opened his eyes, he saw three things: a room full of sunshine, two untouched glasses of wine on the table next to him, and an empty side of the bed. He found the note and smiled. Jamie had signed it, "Back soon, can't wait. XOXO" He was feeling the same way, he looked forward to seeing her again, but he was also feeling something else. He was sore from last night's fight in the pool. It was certainly more difficult and exhausting to struggle under water than on the ground. As he stood staring out the room's patio door, he started to stretch; it was part of his morning exercise routine. But the stiffness remained, and he realized that the best thing for him would be a morning swim in the resort pool and a possible massage in the resort spa. It didn't take long to dress—he didn't—and he wrote a quick reply at the bottom of her note, "Ditto. At pool."

Leaving through the room's ground-floor patio door, McKenna was able to get to the pool area quickly. The morning sun was already making the outdoor temperature very comfortable for both relaxing or swimming in the nude. The Olympic-sized resort pool was also heated.

McKenna always enjoyed swimming since he was a young boy and, as he approached the resort pool, he remembered the time he and his brother had their clothes stolen while skinny dipping. Today there were no clothes to steal. He laughed to himself as the memory disappeared and he dove into the crystal blue water.

He did several laps in the deeper and wider section of the kidney-shaped pool as best as he could, as this pool was designed only partly for swimming, and mostly for playful conversations and drinking. The resort bar in the center of the water was also just opening, and a few of the resort guests already were having their morning tropical drinks as breakfast. Since there was no concern about "drinking and driving" here, all one had to do was drink and enjoy. The two-story waterfall was at one side of the pool within wading distance of the bar. Two early-morning risers—maybe newlyweds, maybe lovers, maybe just friends—were laughing and splashing each other as the waterfall splashed on them.

The refreshing water made McKenna feel better as he walked through the pool to the shallow area where the body of the porn star was supposedly found. He stopped and spent a moment in the area, recalling how he looked for any clues on the pool's edge yesterday to see if there were traces of blood, hair, or anything else that indicated possible foul play for the porn actor. There was none to be found then and, again, there was none to be found now. He then went to the area of the pool where he and the mysterious tall man fought. Again, nothing obvious to his discerning, trained eye. The resort had a good way of daily cleaning up, no matter what.

Satisfied with both the swim and his "look-see" of both areas, he left the water, picked up a resort towel and decided to take a moment standing in the sunshine to assess what he needed to do today and, of course, to think about Jamie. Just the thought of her made the warm morning breeze seem even warmer.

Then someone suddenly touched his ass.

Turning quickly, he did not see anyone there, at his eye level. But there, at waist level, stood Bridgett the Midget. And she didn't look happy.

"Jack Hammer wants to see you now. Follow me," she instructed him.

"Why would I want to see him?" McKenna asked, even though he was curious. Would Hammer provide him with any new clues?

Bridgett didn't answer and just nodded her head in the direction she wanted him to follow. And, he did.

At one end of the pool in a private roped-off cabana-styled enclosure, Jack Hammer was seated in a pool chair having his back massaged by one of the busty, naked Barbee Doll twins. He was turning his neck back and forth with a low moan while enjoying the moment. Hammer looked up when Bridgett and McKenna approached.

"Jim! Good morning. Thank you for seeing me. Hopefully you had a good night's rest?" Hammer gave him a friendly greeting.

"You're up early," McKenna replied, more as a statement than a question.

"Never went to sleep. So much to do to make the convention a success. Basically, I'm what they call a night owl. After all, work comes first before partying, wouldn't you agree?"

"Sure. Whatever you say."

"You're probably wondering why I asked to see you?" Hammer's tone became more serious.

"Crossed my mind," McKenna answered with a bit of sarcasm.

"Well, that was quite a scene you put on last night, so 'good a scene' that I might want to use it in my new movie."

"Not sure if I follow you," McKenna asked inquisitively, for the moment, not knowing what he meant by "so good a scene."

Hammer touched and patted one hand of the woman massaging him, indicating that she was done for now.

"Last night we were shooting a scene for my new movie, *Brides of the Vampire Lover,* a kinky X-rated parody of some of the old horror movies. Sex and horror all blended together. And our lead actor was attacking an actress playing an unsuspecting woman at the pool. That's where you come in. You suddenly entered the scene in progress and attacked my actor."

"Your actor?" McKenna replied with a very surprised look.

"Yes, the tall man attacking the woman was an actor, Jake Browning. Maybe you heard of him. Used to do some TV crime shows, then turned porn. They were both acting. He was playing a vampire, that's why he was fully dressed. Wouldn't want a naked vampire; the buying public want naked women. Lots of naked women. That's why we filmed the scene here, it's a perfect setting for a movie with a lot of nudity."

"I didn't see any cameras," McKenna's immediately questioned what he was just told.

"Of course not, they were hidden. There were two of them. Remote controlled by our technical crew working in the nearby bushes. We didn't want to cause too much attention to what we were doing at the time. Mostly everyone was in the ballroom for the awards presentation and it was a perfect night for us to do the scene, right then and there, with the full moon and all."

"You're telling me that this was all staged? An actor playing a vampire attacking an actress?" Again, McKenna's immediate response was one of doubt and disbelief.

"Yes, and then you suddenly and unexpectedly entered the movie scene...almost ruined it. Probably anyone else other than you would have ruined it. But with your physique..."

Hammer made an awkward-looking "muscle pose" complimenting, or maybe mocking McKenna.

"...and the way you fought with the actor, the resulting footage turned out so good that we want to use it. We actually want to include the whole scene in my movie. I'm offering you $500 to sign off as an actor in the scene and be part of my movie."

"Did the resort know about this?"

"Unfortunately, no. One of the owners here was too wrapped around making certain that the guests were enjoying the convention—so many activities, so much to do—that I didn't get a chance to tell him about this scene. It all happened so fast, as I said. The lighting from the moon helped me decide to shoot the scene last night. My intention was to tell him."

"Winston?"

"Yes, Winston. He was here last night. My plan was to tell him later. I knew he and the resort's other owners would be pleased with all the publicity the resort would get from this new Jack Hammer Production."

"So, they knew nothing about this?" McKenna questioned, still feeling disbelief with everything he was hearing, and trying to sort out fact from possible fiction.

"Well, thanks to you, they do now. Everything was captured on their security cameras and Winston even spoke to you about that last night. Actually, when he met with you and your girlfriend, what's her name?"

McKenna didn't reply with the information.

"Anyway, when he met with you, he still hadn't been told about the filming. He just thought you were an unruly guest fighting with another resort guest. Can you blame him with all the drinking here and womanizing? Sometimes things get out of hand. But once I told Winston about the 'movie scene' this morning, he was embarrassed that he accused you of being involved in a fight. Realizing it was all a misunderstanding, he has offered to match my $500 offer to you with comping your room and food during your stay. Of course, you just have to sign the model release made out for you, and everything is a win-win for all of us. Money, fame, glory. You get to be a star in my new film. Isn't that exciting?"

"I'm not so sure," McKenna replied hesitantly.

"Not sure about what?" Hammer narrowed his eyes with his spoken words.

"Not sure that the guy was an actor. He had fangs and tried to bite me. He even tried to kill me. This whole story seems made-up," McKenna answered with a controlled temper and not give himself away as an investigating cop.

"Ahh, the beauty of filmmaking—the pretend, the make-believe and always the unexpected. That's what made this scene look so real! You even believed he had fangs, just like these."

From the small bench table situated near his pool chair, next to an array of massage oils, Hammer picked up and showed McKenna a set of false, plastic fangs, similar to what the assailant, or possible actor, had in his mouth.

"Besides there's no such thing as a real vampire. Just folklore and legends which, of course, all come to life in Hollywood movies. It's all about making it seem real. And you did. You played your unexpected part so well that I may even want to audition you for some other movies I plan to make. Hey, with the stamina you had in the pool fight, you must have a lot of sexual stamina, too. And that's important in this business. So, I want you think about it. The paperwork is ready for your signature. You'll just have to keep it all secret until the movie is released, but just think, you'll be a star of a Jack Hammer movie. How incredible is that?"

"Yeah, that sounds real incredible. Too incredible. It all sounds make-believe." McKenna shook his head slightly trying to make sense of all this.

"Just like Hollywood, Jim, all make-believe."

With a sly grin on his face, proud that he made his "business" case well, Hammer handed the model release document to McKenna, who took it without even looking at it.

"So why don't you just sign this now and we can complete this business transaction and I can have a check cut for you immediately. We're planning to announce the movie at tonight's masquerade party," Hammer concluded.

"Well, it's an intriguing offer. But...let me talk to my agent," McKenna replied making up his own story in response.

This caught Hammer by surprise.

It was now McKenna's turn to flash a sly grin on his face.

"Jamie, my girlfriend. Let me read this offer over and talk to Jamie. We always discuss things together, and I wouldn't want to surprise her especially after what happened between me and your actor." McKenna was obviously trying to buy time on this before signing anything.

"Hmm. Yes, okay, but I need it signed before tonight's party. All a formality, you know. And by the way, where is she? I don't see that she joined you this morning for your swim."

"No. She's joining me shortly," McKenna answered as if it were planned that way.

"She seems like such a sweet girl. Winston said it's your first time here. Remind her to be careful of too much fun in the sun. We wouldn't want anything to happen to her."

"Thanks, I will."

"And do remind her to save me a dance tonight at the masquerade party."

"I'm sure she won't forget."

"I may even wear fangs."

Hammer inserted the plastic fangs in his mouth and made a growling sound. Taking them out he tossed them to Bridgett and laughingly added, "See how real they look? Almost scared you. You probably thought I was a real vampire."

"Yeah, almost."

Without any formal goodbye, Hammer ended the conversation, got up from the pool chair he had been sitting in and left with Bridgett and the one Barbee Doll twin. As McKenna watched them walk away, Bridgett turned back and blew him a puckered kiss.

McKenna remained by the pool, thinking about Hammer's last words, *"We wouldn't want anything to happen to her.' What did he mean by that? And, was everything that happened last night just a part of a movie? Or was it real? Did the one porn star actually drown accidentally? And was the dead guy in the store window really a mannequin? He did see the body. He was real. Real dead. What about him? Was this all a bunch of Hollywood make-believe or...? Two plus two didn't quite seem to add up, or did it?"*

And then he started to wonder where Jamie was. And if everything was alright.

Little did he know, it wasn't.

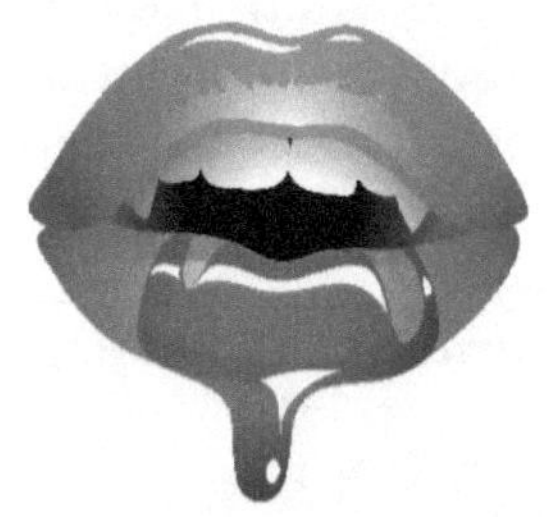

CHAPTER 28

Breathless. After a 30-minute morning run, Jamie was beginning to feel breathless. But when Jamie came around a bend on the resort's landscaped jogging trail, she saw *her* for the first time. Now, the remaining breath Jamie had was suddenly taken away.

Breathtaking. Coming out of the small pond next to the running trail, the mysterious naked woman was still waist deep in the water, but with each movement she took, and each corresponding ripple in the water she made, she was visibly breathtaking, and more.

Jamie slowed and stopped her run, shocked and mesmerized by what she saw. An apparition of goddess-like beauty, or an actual goddess come to life. Tall, with long, wet, jet-black hair that draped across her shoulders and back, and that partially covered the most beautifully shaped breasts imaginable. Drops of fresh pond water lightly flowed down and across her tight and toned skin. She had a curvaceous body that was "knock-dead gorgeous." Stunning. Magnificent. Unbelievable. As though she just stepped out of an adult magazine without the need for airbrushing, this woman was all natural, all perfection—and all mysterious.

Jamie was first to speak.

"Oh, hello. You surprised me, I didn't know people were allowed to swim in the ponds. Is the water cold?"

"The water is embracing. Relaxing. Inviting. You should join me. And let the water embrace you," the mysterious woman replied. Her words were very pronounced, spoken slowly, perhaps cautiously or intentionally. She even had a slight accent, perhaps European?

Not exactly the response Jamie expected but, out of curiosity, she moved off the jogging path and across some of the wet marshy-looking ground, stopping a few feet from the edge of the pond. The woman remained in the water, dipping both hands almost rhythmically, playfully in the pond, until finally cupping a handful of the water which she brought to the top of her chest and casually released across her perfect, large breasts.

Without moving her head, the woman's eyelids slowly raised to directly focus on Jamie. "Do you like to swim?"

"Actually, I'm more a runner, as you can see. Love pools, but not a big fan of lakes or oceans."

"One should not be afraid of water. It is important to living," the naked woman replied, with a slight welcoming smile.

"Yes. Well, maybe that's why you have such an amazing-looking figure. You must enjoy swimming?"

"I enjoy living." Her smile broadened even wider, as her eyes locked onto Jamie's.

"Well, forgive me for saying this, but I'm not used to looking at naked women, although I've seen my share here, but you are exceptional. Either you exercise a lot or must have good genetics."

"Genetics?"

"Yeah, good genes. You must be blessed with good genes."

"Hmmm. Perhaps. But I prefer to say I'm blessed with good blood."

"Well, yes, that's another way of looking at it. We all need good blood," Jamie said, agreeing with her comment, still thinking of bloodlines and genetics.

"Yes. I do. I need good, rich, fresh blood." The woman's eyes seemed to dance and change with colors as they held onto Jamie's eyes.

Her unusual remark about "fresh blood" startled Jamie and even caused her to pause for a moment. She knew that there must be more to this story than just a beautiful, naked woman in an off-the-beaten-path resort pond, especially with her investigative background and with two mysterious murders victims supposedly drained of all their blood.

She introduced herself to the woman. "I'm Jamie."

The woman merely nodded slowly and smiled politely.

"And I'm a guest—first time here," Jamie continued, expecting a supportive response from the woman in the water.

"A guest! How nice. I am Alexandria."

"Alexandria, such a beautiful name for a beautiful woman."

"And you are also beautiful...Jamie."

No woman had ever said that to her before. Over the years she had been called cute, attractive, nice looking, but beautiful? Jamie didn't quite know how to reply, but she did, with a warm smile first, then a continuing conversation.

"Things here are so different from the outside world."

"The outside world?" Alexandria turned her head slightly, mulling over the words that Jamie had spoken.

"Yes, on the other side of the walls. I mean, here we are all naked, and out there they're all dressed. How different and interesting is that?" Jamie replied with a slight shrug of her shoulders as if indicating a question and an answer altogether.

"Yes, it must be different, and interesting. How sad people must hide in their clothes. Maybe it's their way of hiding their secrets."

"Yeah, secrets. Interesting perspective. We all carry secrets." Jamie paused as if briefly thinking about her own, especially her secret feelings for McKenna. She then continued, "Where do you live?"

"Here," Alexandria replied without hesitation.

"Here?"

"Yes... here. Not in the outside world, as you call it," Alexandria said as though it were a known fact.

"Right." Jamie nodded, trying to understand what she really meant. "The outside world," she repeated.

Alexandria smiled her reply and turned her head slightly back and forth as if stretching or just enjoying the warm morning sun.

"It feels so good to be alive, doesn't it, Jamie?"

"In a place like this, in a time like now, clothing free, carefree, just the warmth of the sun. Yes, it does. It really does." Jamie expressed a feeling of ease and comfort in her answer.

"You said you live here? That must be interesting. Have you always lived here?" Jamie continued, intrigued by Alexandria and wanting to know more about her.

"A very long time." She paused. "You ask a lot of questions. Why don't you just join me here in the water, Jamie?" she said with an almost naughty or wicked-looking smile.

"Well... It does look inviting," Jamie honestly admitted.

"It is, and I am inviting you, too."

Jamie paused for a moment, almost being lulled into what Alexandria suggested, but fighting this strange feeling of temptation, she hesitantly replied, "Actually, I have a friend meeting me back at the resort. He may be wondering where I am."

"Your friend can wait. You seem like the type of person worth waiting for."

"Thanks, that's nice of you to say, but you really don't know me."

"I know that I like you." Alexandria smiled with the smile of a "Cheshire cat"—intriguing, but foreboding.

"Well, I like you, too," Jamie replied, this time without any hesitation. This time meaning it and maybe more, as if she was being lulled into a false sense of security with this mysterious and attractive woman.

For Jamie, a growing feeling of strange temptation and desire embraced her. She had never looked at a woman quite that way before. A sudden cool breeze or maybe her own words resonated and sent a slight chill through her.

"You look cold, Jamie. The water is warm. It will warm you up. And it will make you feel warm all over. It will make your blood warm, too." Alexandria spoke almost hypnotically, definitely enticing, definitely suggestive, and definitely disturbing.

Jamie fought whatever the temptation was that she felt and quickly changed the subject.

"Since you live here, will you be going to the masquerade dance tonight?"

"Tonight. Of course, I have been looking forward to the dance and meeting new people, just like I have met you."

Suddenly from behind Jamie came two couples, jogging slowly on the trail, chatting and laughing. Catching her attention, Jamie looked back at them and smiled to let them know everything they were seeing was alright.

"Morning," Jamie added, to be friendly, or just to explain this was just a "normal" morning conversation between two naked women, one on shore, and one in the pond.

"Morning," some of the joggers replied back, catching their breath, as they continued past her and down the trail towards some of the resort houses.

When Jamie turned back to her conversation with Alexandria, she was surprised and confused to see that the pond was empty. Alexandria wasn't there. And there were no ripples in the water, indicating that she had just gone underwater for a quick dip. But she had to! Where else could she have gone? Jamie waited, and went closer to the water, trying to decide whether to step in. Quickly taking off her running shoes and socks, she rushed into the pond. She had saved McKenna last night from drowning; was it her turn to play lifeguard again? She went waist deep, pushing the water all around and turning in a circle in the pond, calling out the woman's name.

"Alexandria! Alexandria!"

No response. No reply.

Jamie submerged herself, but the pond water had thick and long, wavy grasses and tall, swaying reeds which blocked her total underwater view. After a few more attempts of looking in the water, Jamie slowly came out and returned to the grassy pond edge. She stared, concerned for a long moment. *"Where is she? Where could she have gone so quickly?"* And suddenly Jamie felt a bit dizzy, perhaps from the heat, the run, no breakfast, or the frantic search in the dirty pond. She felt as though she were going to pass out. Exhausted, she shook her head, and took a deep breath, trying to regain her composure, reawakening herself, and fighting some unknown presence that was affecting her. Was she hallucinating? *"Come on, girl, get your head together. You were speaking with someone. Someone was really there, but where is she now?"*

"Alexandria!" Jamie shouted out in a final desperation.

No answer. If she had gone underwater, she had been underwater far too long.

"Alexandria!" A final call out.

Silence.

The pond water was motionless. It was like nothing or no one was ever in it.

"Was this all a dream? Or?" Jamie started to walk away from the water, and looked back one more time, confused, concerned, and shaken by what she just experienced.

The pond was still empty.

Above in the sky, a gull flew by looking downward probably for morning food, or maybe just looking at her. It made a cawing sound that sounded like laughter.

Unseen to Jamie, a few feet from where she had just stood talking to the mysterious woman, there, in the tall grassy area next to the water, was a hand. And a body. A dead body. Staring upward at the sky, pale as a ghost. Ashen white skin color. Two eyes frozen in horror. Two large bite marks next to a ripped-open throat. Drained of all blood.

Jeff.

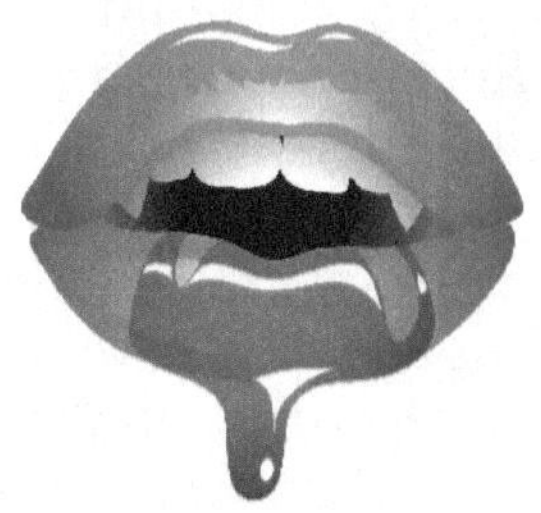

CHAPTER 29

When Jamie met up with McKenna at the resort's pool area, they both excitedly spoke at the same time, overlapping their words,

""I The met vampire the is real an vampire actor!""

Again, they both spoke together, but this time, they both said the same word.

""What?""

For a moment, they stared at each other trying to figure out what the other had just said.

"Okay, let's try this again, only you first." McKenna shook his head almost laughingly.

Smiling, Jamie answered hurriedly, "I met the real vampire."

"What?" McKenna exclaimed in total disbelief.

"And what about you?" Jamie crossed her arms in front of her and waited to see what could have been more important than what she just said.

"The vampire is an actor."

"What?" Jamie exclaimed in equal total disbelief.

For another moment, they stared at each other again, trying to understand what each other had just said. A long moment.

"I was jogging by a pond and she was there in the middle of the water and then she wasn't," Jamie started with a further explanation.

"What?" McKenna replied again in more disbelief, adding to the disbelief he already had with her first comment.

"And what about you?" Jamie put her hands on her hips and, again, waited to see what could have been more important than what she just said.

"I was told that they were filming a movie scene, with two actors. The tall guy used plastic teeth."

Again, they just stared at each other trying to figure out what the other had just said.

"I think we need breakfast, maybe a morning coffee, or maybe a tall mimosa, and we need to tell each other what we know—the facts, from the beginning." Jamie slowly replied, thinking about what he said, and what she was saying.

"A mimosa? For me a beer, and then the story, preferably in that order," McKenna nodded with a sigh.

And with that, they drew closer—close enough so that their bodies almost touched, and close enough to look at one another in the eyes. In that moment, their eyes said they wanted to embrace right now, right then, right there, in full public view, and, although they wanted to, they each realized that maybe they shouldn't, in case the resort's CCTV cameras were surveilling. For the moment, they both knew they had to wait; but, for the moment, they also knew that they could still hold hands and act as a couple, although it wouldn't take much acting on either's part. They each wrapped a hand around the other's. Softly. Gently. Tightly.

"Make that two beers," McKenna teased her.

While the early-rising guests lounged on poolside chairs or found a place in the water, Jamie and McKenna sat in a private section of the outdoor veranda restaurant overlooking the entire pool area. The sound of the nearby waterfalls helped to mask their conversation. Jamie and McKenna each told their complete story. And they each enjoyed a mimosa.

Jamie sat back in her wicker chair, shaking her head in disbelief while taking in everything he had just told her. McKenna did the same. After considering this new information, Jamie said, "If what you're telling me is true, it certainly puts a different perspective on everything. Actors in a movie? But that doesn't explain the woman I saw in the pond. A morning mirage? Or...?"

"Or maybe they weren't really actors and there isn't a movie. Maybe the mystery woman in the pond was real," McKenna suggested.

"Or, there is a cover-up here and someone is lying. Most likely, more than one person is lying," Jamie quickly interjected. "Could there be a connection to the convention or the masquerade party?"

They both thought about all the possibilities.

McKenna spoke first. "Okay, let's say the vampires are real. But, why here, why now, and what's possibly next?"

"We know the facts so far," Jamie began. "Two men were killed and drained of their blood before we arrived. Tina said Jeff was attacked by a woman with 'fangs.' Jeff had what appeared to be bite marks on his neck. A tall, fully-clothed man with fangs tried to bite you and kill you in the pool. Jack Hammer said that the man was an actor with fake teeth. I saw the mysterious woman in the pond who disappeared quickly." She paused. "We discussed any 'possible' coincidence, but don't have any evidence to back that up. However, the reality factor of what is or isn't possible is the wildcard. We know that you almost died in that pool. And we know someone can pretend to be or act as a vampire and use that as a mask to disguise the real reason for the killings, but what we don't know is if the killer is a real vampire," Jamie concluded.

"Well, that rules out the woman in the pond. You saw her in full sunlight. Aren't vampires supposed to be in their bed, or coffin, or whatever, before sunrise?" McKenna asked.

"Yeah, that's the way it is in all the horror movies I've seen, but this is the x-factor. If there isn't a 'made-up horror movie' being filmed here and someone is lying, and if the deaths we know of weren't coincidental or accidental, then the possibility..."

"Possibility, not probability," McKenna replied from a cop's perspective, not a detective's.

"Right, possibility, if such a person, a creature, or whatever it is, does exist, it may not play by the made-up Hollywood rules. The real question is, how do we stop it from killing again? We don't have weapons, and I'm not wearing any jewelry."

"Jewelry?" McKenna didn't understand her remark.

"Yeah, jewelry—a silver crucifix—like in the movies. So, what do we do if meet a vampire? Make a cross with our fingers?" Jamie asked with a bit of humor and sarcasm blended together.

"Well, that would be an interesting theory, stopping a killer by making a sign of the cross using fingers. That is one theory I don't want to try out if we run into such a creature. Especially one who may want to bite us on the neck and drain our blood."

"Yeah, the biting and draining... Sounds like an ad for someone's 'Happy Meal.' Maybe we should get some garlic," Jamie added.

"What?" McKenna said in a surprised tone.

"Vampires don't like garlic." Jamie half-smiled like a schoolgirl trying to give the right answer to a question she had no real answer for.

"Another movie thing?" McKenna tilted his head and looked at her like she was that schoolgirl.

"Right, no garlic. Smells anyway," Jamie replied with a slight "I-guess-you're-right" look and then continued. "So, we're working undercover to find a killer here, and to catch the killer, whether a man or woman, before he or she kills again, but not to catch a vampire. Obviously, we can't call in reinforcements because they'll think we're crazy." Jamie nodded to herself as she spoke with the realization of the dilemma they were in.

"Or had too much sun." McKenna also nodded in agreement.

"Right, or maybe both. So, as cops, we both know what we have to do. Separate facts from fiction, investigate and interview more guests, look for more clues and suspicious activity and, when sundown comes, be prepared to catch a killer, or killers, human or inhuman."

"Hopefully human." McKenna frowned with his reply to what she just said, and then continued, "And hopefully a beer drinker, not a blood guzzler."

"Besides, how do we arrest a vampire...?" she thought aloud.

Quietly, they both reflected on what they both had said, and what they both thought they knew.

"We probably should split up for a while. That way we can interview more people and cover more leads quickly. But let's make sure we don't go near any of the ponds alone, or wrestle with any more tall guys with fangs." Jamie seemed satisfied with her plan.

"Or put more names on your dance card," McKenna quickly added.

That made them both smile for a moment, but only a moment.

"I'll also talk more with Jeff and Tina. There might be more to that whole story from last night," Jamie stated, adding to her "detective-to-do" list.

"And I'll track down Hammer and ask to see the footage of the fight before I pretend to sign the model release. There may be a clue or something in the scene that could be helpful. And then I'll talk to Winston about Hammer to see if his story about making a movie is true or…"

From behind them, one of the restaurant personnel suddenly interrupted, and handed them an envelope. After the delivery person left, McKenna opened it and read the handwritten note inside. "Please accept my apologies for last night. Enjoy a complimentary couples' spa massage courtesy of Paradise Lost," signed Winston.

"Hmm. Sounds interesting." McKenna tapped the invitation card on the table while thinking out loud about it. "Well, maybe later. And the good thing is that it wouldn't show up on our expense report when we complete the assignment."

Jamie chuckled at the expense report comment.

"Yes, it does sound interesting," Jamie reflected on it for a long moment, thinking how wonderful it would be to put aside this whole job looking for a possible "bloodsucker" and just enjoy a nice full-body massage, naked together. And then she looked at McKenna and smiled, more than a smile. "Maybe we should save it and come back another time, when the assignment is over."

Jamie raised her tall, nearly empty mimosa glass, and clinked it with his.

* * * * *

Inside the resort's security center, Winston watched them intently from one of the many hidden CCTV cameras placed throughout the surrounding grounds and the restaurant they were seated in. Wearing headphones, he also could hear everything they said from a hidden microphone underneath the table. Everything.

Slowly taking the headphones off, he handed them to the technician who sat by the security monitor console. Winston gave him no indication of what he had just heard, or what he now knew from their conversation. He turned to the technician and stood silent for a moment, thinking something over in his mind.

"Keep an eye on them, especially the woman," he instructed the technician. It was the same man who had stood by McKenna at the pool yesterday and passed on a strange message before disappearing in the crowd of guests. Without a word, the man nodded his reply, stood up, and left the room, leaving Winston alone.

Winston turned his attention back to the security monitor and watched as Jamie and McKenna left the restaurant in separate directions. Satisfied as to what he now knew, he picked up his personal cell phone and punched in a number and waited while it connected. When it did, he spoke directly and to the point.

"It's Winston. You were right."

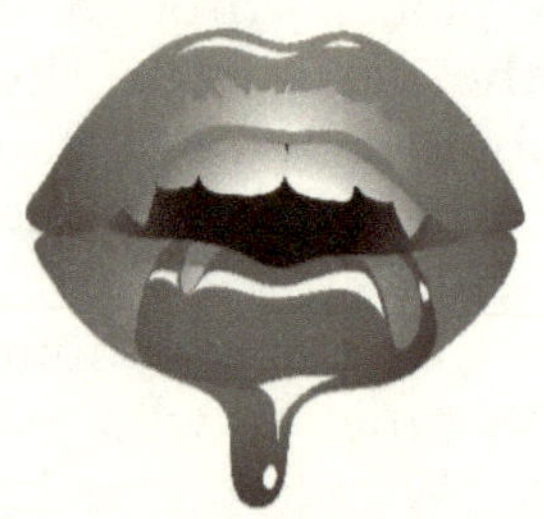

CHAPTER 30

When Alexandria surfaced from the water inside the dimly lit cavern, shadows seemed to dance and greet her from the flickering flames of the lit torches that were placed in the jagged rock walls. Water droplets fell rhythmically in a drip-drop pattern from the hanging stalactites. That was the only sound heard in the ancient cavern and it seemed to echo an ominous feeling throughout. As she slowly came out of the cavern pool, water gently rolled downward and off her magnificent naked figure. Having swam underwater from the connecting outside pond where she had met Jamie, she brought something with her. From underneath the water she dragged out, and upwards, a hand, followed by an arm, followed by a fully nude body of a dead woman. It was Tina.

Alexandria had no trouble dragging the body behind her and out of the water onto the large cave floor. When she let go of Tina's hand, it fell with an echoing water-logged thud as it struck the freshly made puddles on the stone floor surface. Taking a deep breath of the cool and humid cave air, Alexandria seemed relaxed and pleased that she was back here in this environment, her home. She paused, stretched, and turned her attention to the dark cavern tunnel at one end of the circular pool of water. Realizing that she was not alone, Alexandria stood quietly and looked at the person who stepped from the shadows. He, too, was naked and had the body of a male Adonis, chiseled with tight, toned skin, and muscles with striations that indicated he was more than just a fine-tuned athlete. Shoulder-length jet-black hair was the only hair on his perfect body. He was the same height as she was, and his eyes seemed to glow not only in the dark, but now in the light. He walked toward her with an assurance of knowing not only who she was, but why she was there.

Alexandria spoke first.

"I have left the other one for you, my dear Alexander. Father will be pleased," she spoke without feeling, just words, as a matter of fact.

"Because of who you killed?" His response had the same tone.

"That, and because I finally saw her." This time an emotion showed in her eyes.

"Then why didn't you bring her with you?" he immediately questioned.

"We were interrupted. Some others came together in a group, and I didn't want to be seen."

"But you did meet her?" He wanted to know more, not in an inquisitive sense, but in more of a voyeuristic one.

"Yes, and I will meet her again. Tonight."

"He will be pleased to know of this," Alexander replied, satisfied and content with the plan.

"Yes. He will. And you also, my brother. So will you." Her expression changed. A strange and haunting sardonic smile spread across her face. A look that would have sent a deep and dark chill through any innocent bystander watching her face.

"And what of the one with her? Does he know?" Alexander asked.

"Yes." Her response had no emotion, but definitely indicated something more.

"But he doesn't know why?" he continued with another important question.

"No, but he will." Alexandria seemed content in the secret that they both shared.

Without another word, he slowly walked over and faced her, putting his hands on her bare shoulders and softly moving his long fingers across her flawless neck. They slid easily across her skin, gently, passionately. They both stared at each other in silence, broken only by the constant water dripping from the ceiling onto the rock floor. The orangish-red, flickering cavern torch lights surrounded them, embracing them, creating shadows that seemed to have other forms than the images of themselves. Both she and her brother slowly brought their lips together tightly, kissing each other. When their lips finally released, a trickle of blood came from each other's mouths—a trickle of bright red blood which dripped from each other's fangs.

"It's time," he whispered in her closest ear.

And she responded with no words, nor any expression, just a demonic hissing sound, which grew with the widening of her mouth and the insertion of her long, sharp fangs into his exposed neck.

He stood there, motionless as she sucked his blood from him. Not killing him, but tasting him, enjoying him, and feeding from him.

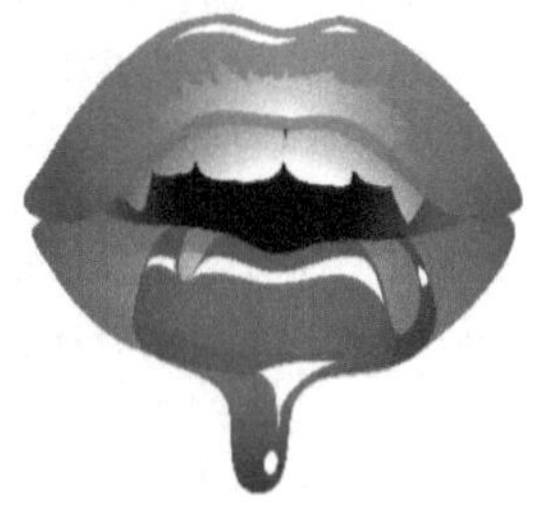

CHAPTER 31

Rock Hard was really not in a good mood. Hardly. Nor was he "hard" last night. Really. Expecting that he would receive two awards that night, both at the Resort Awards banquet and, later, in a planned after-awards celebration party in his private suite, he struck out both times, or, as they say in the porn industry, "He shot blanks." Rock had expected to receive a "Dickie"—the award of the night for "Best Male Performer in a Porn Movie." After all, it was only a choice between him and Johnny Rains, and Johnny was nowhere to be found, except in the city morgue, so it was only natural that Rock expected to get his due—and his Dickie. But the award went to a no-show, but "really dead," Johnny, and that resulted in a cringe-worthy moment where Rock threw a one-man temper tantrum and stormed out of the ballroom yelling, "I deserve a Dickie!" And he probably did, just for that memorable scene.

Sadly, Rock remained alone in his room the rest of the night, horribly disappointed, seething in anger, and hoping to calm down with his usual method of relieving himself of the pent-up stress. Unfortunately, after an hour of trying to get it up, it stayed down, and no matter how much he tried, it didn't "rise from the dead," and he finally went to bed with a tired hand and a sore dick.

Being an aging gay man in a mostly younger field of sexually active swingers and porn actors, Rock had seen his best days come and go. Now, mostly go. Years earlier he had been one of the top moneymakers in the industry, as he dared to act on both sides of the bed, being the first bisexual porn actor. Then he just stuck to one side; he liked men, lots of men, lots and lots of men. As the years passed and his sexual exploits took a toll on his body, he tried to retain his youthful look by doing the closest thing to having plastic surgery. Rock began to wear a strapped-on, flesh-colored prosthetic butt, to cover his saggy and fairly worn-out behind. He also began to lose his hair. Unfortunately, the cheaply made mail-order wig he wore, which he bought from some hard-to-pronounce foreign country, was a secret only he thought he knew, although everyone did. Sadly, Father Time was finally catching up to him in more ways than one.

As the industry changed and embraced more "amateur and fresh-face" actors, and as his hard-core fans were dwindling in numbers each year, some dying from too many sexual diseases, he himself was now engaged in a losing battle of an untreatable form of early dementia. Even though it mattered a lot to him that he didn't win the coveted "Dickie" last night, the actuality was that he probably wouldn't remember any of his "last nights" as his illness became progressively worse. But he did remember it this morning, and consequently, Rock Hard was not in a good mood.

When Rock went to the resort's pool area to drink his morning breakfast and have a planned, relaxing spa massage to forget last night, he unexpectedly encountered Jack Hammer. Jack was flanked on one side by one of the tall Barbee Doll twins and on the other side by a small, hardly noticed, Bridgett the Midget. They had just come from his earlier discussion with McKenna.

When they saw each other, their greetings were far from friendly and warm.

"Asshole!" Rock shouted first, from a distance of about fifteen feet away.

"Limp dick," Hammer immediately yelled back at him.

The few resort guests who happened to be within listening distance turned from their early morning sunning to watch their "war of words" escalate.

"That Dickie belonged to *me*," Rock proclaimed loudly while punctuating the word "me" by pointing at himself.

"Haven't you had enough dick–ies?" Jack responded smugly, as he paused on one specific word while pronouncing it louder than the others.

"I was robbed! You know it; my fans know it." Rock stepped closer to Jack with each word becoming more audible than the last.

"Whatever fans you have left know you're a has-been. The only reason you still get work is your name, and from your recent 'struggling' performances in my movies, your name should be changed to Rock 'no longer' Hard."

"I hate you. I hate you. I hate you," Rock stammered like a little girl yelling back at a scolding parent.

"Quiet, you old fool." Hammer brought his voice level down, his eyes darting from Rock to the nearby resort guests, noticing their reactions, and then back to Rock. Realizing that they had created a scene, he continued in a calmer tone.

"Your few fans, or, shall we say, the morning guests here are certainly enjoying your performance. One of your better ones, I must admit. So much passion, so endearing, but so phony, just like you.

Why don't you just walk away, take a cold shower, and find a nice group of young boy-toys to drool at, since that's all you can mostly do?" Hammer said as though putting closure to their argument.

"Phony! You call *me* a phony. You egotistical bastard! Have you forgotten that, without me, you'd still be a nobody like you were when I found you! It was *my* money that gave you your start in the industry and it was *my* dick that you enjoyed when you always asked for more money." Rock's words obviously revealed something that Hammer didn't want heard.

"Shut up!" Hammer exclaimed.

"Oh, truth hurts, huh, Mr. Big-Shot? Truth is, you have always been jealous of me; jealous because Johnny Rains wanted *me,* more than he wanted *you.*" Rock pointed a finger directly at Hammer's face, as his own face became even more flushed with his intense display of emotion and frustration.

"I said, shut up! You don't know what you're saying. You're only going to make things worse for yourself." Hammer tried to pivot from Rock's stinging accusation, turning the focus back on him.

"Yeah, like I don't know the real reason Johnny won the award last night! You wanted to get back at me for his leaving you, and his wanting to get back in bed with me. I bet the industry would like to know all about that!" Rock stated with a look of assurance to his spoken words.

"I said, shut up!" Hammer's anger grew. He had definitely heard enough.

"Yeah, what are you going to do to stop me from telling the truth, Hammer? You going to kill me?"

Hammer looked nervously around. By this point, everyone in the immediate pool area had stopped what they were doing and were looking at both of them. The words "kill me" seemed to get everyone's attention nearby. He then spoke out loud, saying his next words carefully and contrived to anyone who could hear their conversation.

"Don't worry folks, just a bit of play-acting for a scene in my new movie. Rock here is a great actor and is portraying a dramatic scene for my review. Just rehearsing it for your morning entertainment." Hammer threw in a fake smile as if trying to make everyone believe what he said, including himself.

Turning to the two girls who stood next to him, he quickly told them, "Leave me alone a minute with my friend here. Nothing of your concern. Go have a drink or talk to your fans. I'll meet you back in the suite later." It sounded awkward at best, but they knew well enough to leave without any reply, not that Hammer wanted or expected one.

Turning back to Rock, Hammer's anger grew in his eyes that narrowed as slits. "Listen to me," he snarled under his breath, "Watch what you say and don't screw up this convention. There's too much at stake, even your livelihood, if you know what I mean."

"Oh! Are you threatening me? Like you threatened Johnny? I heard the 'so-called' rumors about yesterday—someone found dead in the pool, some unidentified drunk patron. We both know why Johnny wasn't at the awards last night. Maybe that dead guy was actually Johnny. And maybe you killed him."

"If you don't shut the fuck up, maybe you'll end up dead, too!" Hammer's anger reached a boiling point and he started to spew words that shot out quickly and sharply.

"Or maybe *you* will," Rock shouted back at him, before abruptly turning away and strutting to the nearest poolside bar.

Hammer stood alone and stared at him, his eyes showing pent-up anger. Realizing that they had been watched, and he was now still being watched, he turned to the nearby guests and smiled again, while beckoning to a nearby pool-area waiter.

"A free drink for all these people here, on my tab." He pointed to the closest guests and continued to smile as though what they just witnessed had all been planned for everyone to see. He then unexpectedly gestured his two arms outward, in appreciation to an audience watching a live stage performance.

"Everyone, have a great morning! The preview of my new movie scene is over, but Rock certainly deserves a big hand for his acting."

Hammer started to clap, and so did a few of the naked guests who believed they had just witnessed live theater before their very sleepy, morning eyes.

Across the pool area, standing alone at the outdoor bar, Rock heard nothing but the clinking of ice in his nearly empty, tall, tropical drink glass as he drowned his sorrows. He was emotionally exhausted, deeply heartbroken, and he started to cry. His innermost feelings had been on display, yet no one paid attention to him. No one cared. No one.

He cried alone, until there were no more tears.

After a few long moments, Rock wiped his eyes with the back of his hand as the last tears turned to sniffles. He paused and looked at the deep wrinkles in his hand as he turned it back and forth. So many wrinkles. His youthful looks so long gone.

Rock composed himself with another drink, and then another. Having had too much alcohol and living with too much pain in his mixed-up life, he left the poolside bar and slowly walked toward the opulent-looking and very large resort spa. It was across from the pool's waterfall and was nestled with easy access underneath the resort's second-story veranda. It wasn't that far, but in his current inebriated state, he did zig zag quite a bit, and almost fell in the pool, twice.

The spa was a popular part of this hedonistic adult place. It was like part of a kid's giant outdoor playground, lots of things to do, with lots of ways to have fun. One could use the co-ed workout room with assorted cardio machines and light free weights, take a yoga or an aerobic class, use the co-ed showers, or the attached sauna or steam room. Of course, everything in the nude. And to top it all off, like a big cherry on a delicious whipped cream cake, there were the private massage rooms for the enjoyment of single people or couples. Each room had a different theme, different colors, different music, and different "sex toys" to use. Each with a reserved male or female licensed massage therapist, or basically just someone who knew how to use their trained hands to give very relaxing, and very erotic, sexual pleasure. The spa was a very popular part of the resort, and appropriately titled, "Heaven."

Unfortunately for Rock Hard, he was early for his scheduled appointment, and all the massage rooms were occupied. At his age, and his somewhat drunken state, he certainly wasn't going to spend his waiting time lifting weights while grunting and groaning or jumping up and down naked to pulsating aerobic music. He also never understood why people would twist themselves in uncomfortable yoga-like pretzel positions. All he was left with were two choices while he waited for his massage appointment. Sauna or Steam? He chose steam, so at least he could hide his unhappy life in the billowing clouds of extreme heat from other people's prying eyes.

Unfortunately, it was the wrong choice.

As he sat alone on one of the steam room's white ceramic-tiled bench seats, and the one-hundred-plus degrees of heat swirled around his naked and worn-out body, his mind wandered to other days gone by. He didn't even think of, or dwell on the words he and

Jack Hammer had just thrown at each other. Instead, he remembered how they were once lovers and how much he missed him now. Theirs had been a love-hate relationship for some time now, with Jack getting all the success as he rose in the porn industry, thanks to him, while he declined in popularity due to his age and the excitement over all the rising, new, young stars. And even though he was happy at first for Jack and did everything he could to help him get started in the industry, he came to eventually loathe him when he found out he was being dumped for another porn star, and that he was just being used. Used. So many times in his life, people had used him. On screen, he portrayed a strong character. In life, he was a weak and lonely man. And now at this moment in his unhappy life, his whole world seemed to have collapsed. Sighing to himself, he buried his head in his hands. Not to cry anymore, he had already done that, but just to seek a few moments of private solitude. Maybe that would help hide his conflicted pain and make the bad memories go away. Maybe.

Rock never heard the other person entering the steam room. The only discernible sound was the constant low pitch of steady hissing steam coming from the various wall openings. Nor was he aware that this person had just hung a resort sign, "Closed for Repairs," on the steam-room-entrance door. The steam room wasn't that big, nor that small, but it could fit a half dozen people at once who liked to sweat. Today, right now, it was just the two of them.

Shrouded in the white creamy-colored steam, the person sat across from Rock—just an outline of someone, unidentifiable, and quiet. The person just sat there. But Rock could feel his eyes, and it was that feeling that made him slowly take his head out of his hands and look. And when Rock looked up and towards the person, the only thing he saw through the thick hissing steam was two glowing red eyes. Two eyes that were fixed directly on him. Whether Rock was just too tired from a bad night's sleep, too drunk, too emotionally drained from his argument with Hammer, or too scared to even say what he really wanted to, Rock just sat in complete and utter surprise. All he could do was begin to mutter a few words, a few final words, not "acted" words, as he had said in so many scenes, in so many movies, over so many years. But a few "real" words, filled with real, and extreme, terror.

"No...you...you're..."

Rock never saw the attack coming. It just happened. Nor could he find enough last-moment strength to struggle or fight back. The ungodly creature was upon him in a split second. All he felt were two very sharp, very long fangs enter into his neck. Fangs that pierced his jugular vein and sucked on his blood while draining away his life.

As the steam continued to swirl around them, and in his final moment of life, Rock finally saw his attacker. It was Johnny Rains, back from the dead.

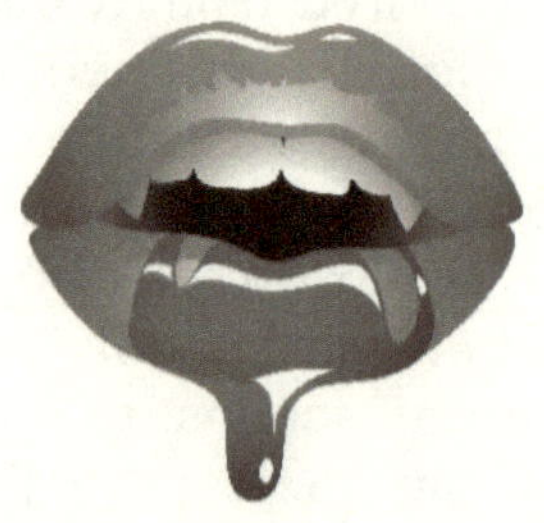

CHAPTER 32

Although McKenna couldn't meet with Winston, as Winston was busy in a meeting preparing for the arrival of some special guests for the convention's masquerade dance that evening, he decided to spend time in the resort's lobby area and the adjoining sports bar talking to random guests. Some of the conversations paid off, as he heard about some interesting occurrences that were going on at the resort. Some known; some in rumor stages. Apparently, the guests for the party included some well-connected government officials and a very popular Hollywood TV and motion picture star. Names were speculated, but no one knew who they were for sure.

McKenna also heard that the resort was having some financial problems. That piqued his interest.

When resort guests became members and paid exorbitant yearly fees to use the facility, they had been promised expansion improvements, shown in elaborate drawings and photo renderings. Included in the plans were an amazingly new, state-of-the-art, four-story clubhouse, a hotel with all of the latest sexual fantasy themes throughout, and a large-scale, onsite, members-only gambling casino. McKenna thought about that—gambling in the nude. Of course, with high-tech computer-programmed slot machines, winners didn't need clothing pockets to hold their cash. Everything was transferred electronically to a personalized computer chip card and transferred directly into a bank account. Easy way to avoid taxes, especially since this resort was built with a special grandfathered clause dating back years and allowing the naturist activities to go on and on, uninterrupted by any government regulations, including audits.

But even with that information, which could lend some suspicion to what was really going on there behind the scenes, McKenna's attention turned to something else. News quickly spread that another "dead body" was just discovered in the resort spa.

Without drawing any attention to himself, other than that of being just another nosey guest, he got as close to the crowd of gawkers outside of the spa as he could. The body of a man, wrapped partially in a black sheet, was being carried out of the building. The resort's security people were keeping the growing number of spectators back as the body was placed into a converted golf cart. From his position in the crowd, McKenna didn't recognize who it was, as the body was mostly covered up. He did overhear some of the onlookers say that it was an older porn star named Rock Hard. Not that the name mattered to him; what mattered was that it was another dead person. McKenna knew he had to get closer to inspect the body, but he also knew he had to be careful not to reveal himself as a cop and jeopardize the undercover assignment. However, realizing that the vehicle would be leaving at any moment, he knew that if he was going to do anything, this was his only chance to do it, right now. And he did.

"Coming through! Doctor! Coming through!" McKenna announced as the gathered crowd allowed him to pass and get close to the fully dressed security men, who were preparing to drive the golf cart away.

One of the security guards, who he recognized from the previous day's investigation of the pool area where Johnny Rains was found dead, tried to stop him. Fortunately, the guard did not recognize him.

"I'm a doctor, a registered guest, and a friend of Philip Winston. He asked me to look at the body," McKenna lied convincingly by using Winston's full name to bluff his way close to the body.

"Well, I don't know..." came the reply as the guard tried to figure out if this was okay to do or not, but it didn't matter as McKenna passed him and rapidly approached the dead body as it lay in the open back of the golf cart.

Before anyone could stop him, McKenna pulled back the sheet covering the dead man's face and had just enough time to see what he was looking for—two puncture wounds in the man's throat and a face that seemed ashen white, probably from having been drained of blood. McKenna immediately covered him back up.

"Hey, who are you?" shouted Davis, the resort's daytime manager who was just coming through another part of the crowd and toward the parked vehicle. Apparently, he had been talking with people in the spa as the body was being removed.

McKenna didn't answer or wait to have a conversation. He immediately slipped back into the crowd and easily disappeared. Hard to identify a man without any recognizable clothing on!

As McKenna continued to move further away from the scene, he could see Winston and two other men hastily coming down the veranda steps approaching the spa. McKenna turned his back as not to be recognized, and then decided to go up the same steps and to Winston's office. Maybe, just maybe, he could continue his ruse and find his way into the office somehow. *"A good cop always finds a way,"* he thought to himself, and he did.

The receptionists at the front lobby desk were busy checking people in and out for the day and he just walked by nonchalantly, not appearing out of place. Winston's office was just down the hallway next to a conference room, which he remembered passing with Jamie the previous night on the way to the involuntary meeting with Winston.

A young twenty-something female assistant sat at a desk in a smaller office adjacent to Winston's. She was talking to a woman who immediately looked up and spotted McKenna. It was Jamie. Without giving him away, Jamie returned to her conversation with Winston's assistant, whose back was to McKenna as she looked intently at her computer. It was immediately apparent to McKenna that Jamie must have come here to do some sleuthing, too, and now she was providing the perfect distraction for him. She knocked over a stack of papers on the assistant's desk.

"Oh, I'm sorry! How clumsy am I?" Jamie apologized in a fake, but seemingly honest voice.

Both the woman and Jamie reached to pick up the paperwork on the floor.

"Don't worry; happens all the time," the woman assured Jamie. "Now, let me see about that charity contribution you said you sent here from the mayor's office." The woman was totally unaware that a naked man, McKenna, was sneaking into Winston's office behind her.

McKenna smiled to himself while thinking how this was playing out. *"Good detective work! Use a known government official's name and a phony charity contribution. Gets their attention all the time."*

McKenna quickly slipped into Winston's open doorway and recalled his surroundings from the night before. He glanced at the papers on the desk. Nothing jumped out immediately until he saw a document entitled "Guest List." Scanning it, he saw that there were a lot of names that meant nothing but there were a few that began to catch his attention, especially the New Tampa Mayor, the Florida Governor, the Director of the Department of Defense, and the Vice President of the United States.

He would have whistled his surprise out loud to the last names he looked at, but instead kept himself as quiet as he could. Putting the guest list back down to where he found it, he hurriedly opened the top desk drawer. Nothing important. Just a lot of assorted desk stuff, pens, more paper, and more of the same.

He then opened the second drawer. It was then that he suddenly paused and stared at the item he found. A handgun. He recognized it as a FNX45, one of the most reliable semi-automatic pistols on the market today, especially because of its large-capacity magazines. Definitely a killing weapon, probably registered, and probably a security weapon. McKenna stored that in his mind and decided he didn't want to touch it and leave any of his prints on it. Then he spied something else. A set of assorted keys.

He picked them up and immediately recognized which keys fit filing cabinets. As a cop, he knew that this was an important find, and, of course, from his visual inspection of Winston's office during last night's interrogation, he remembered the two locked filing cabinets by the wall. He looked back out the office door and saw that Jamie was still leaning over the assistant's desk and pointing at the computer, keeping Winston's assistant busy.

Both filing cabinets had three drawers. Unlocking the first cabinet, he quickly went through the drawers, determining they held files marked taxes, property rentals, monthly reports, and other typical and expected resort day-to-day business transactions and communications.

But the second filing cabinet had something of interest. Placed on top of what looked like very old pieces of paper and similar old-looking documents was a folded map. The handwritten words, "Site Map 1931," were faded but still legible. Carefully opening it, McKenna recognized it as a map of the entire resort property and some of the adjacent areas. The map showed the grounds before all the buildings and resort amenities like the pool, volleyball courts, tennis courts, and houses were built, or even thought of. Lots of open land, mixed with trees and a layout for current and proposed future expansion. Obviously, it represented the beginning of the future naturist resort where he now stood today. But something unusual caught his attention. At the location of where Jamie had described as the area for her morning run, there were series of drawn ponds, and what looked like a small topographical drawing of a rocky area and an underground entrance, like a cave. She hadn't mentioned that, but maybe it was part of the overgrown, natural area for some of the wildlife living there. McKenna made a mental note and carefully folded the map back up. He then started to look at the other items underneath it. There were several old, original, and partly faded black-and-white photos of the resort dated the same time period of the map, 1931. Photographed were scattered campsites, several large and small canvas tents, a few medium-sized, shanty-like enclosures, some early small-vehicle trailers, and a bunch of older-looking nudists. There were also typical period photographs of people posing for the pictures, with hardly any expression. Just staring blankly at the camera. And then he saw it. And this time he had to stop himself from whistling out loud.

It was a group photo, all younger, attractive, naked people, all bathing and seeming to enjoy swimming and being together in a pond and, there, standing alone at the edge of the pond, fully dressed, was someone he recognized. The tall man he fought with last night. Or, at least it looked like him. McKenna had an ability to remember faces, especially when he was in a life-and-death struggle with someone. And last night wasn't that long ago; and this man in the picture sure looked like him. He was tall, same type of dark hair, same length, and he was dressed in the same clothing McKenna remembered the man wearing last night, a dark suit.

"The same clothing? But how could that be?" McKenna thought to himself, as this was not anything he would have ever expected. And it wasn't. The picture was almost 90 years old, according to the date on the back.

Adding to the mystery of this uncanny-looking picture, the man also appeared to be watching all the nude people in the pond, almost like a guard, or a parent would watch his children at play. And in the background, close to the man, was a pregnant woman. She was holding her stomach and looking very sad and out of place, as she stared at the people in the pond.

McKenna turned his attention back to look closer at the other people in the photo. There, in the middle of the scene, standing waist deep in the pond water, was a very beautiful woman, almost too beautiful. Alluring, seductive, and more. She had no expression on her face and was the only one in the picture staring directly at the camera. McKenna blinked his eyes in wonderment. She matched the description of the woman Jamie met earlier that morning. But she was so young looking! As young as Jamie had described to him. McKenna questioned whether or not she could be the one and the same, just as he questioned if that could be the same tall man. He turned the photo over again and rechecked the date on the back of the picture. It looked original, and it was dated 1931. It just didn't make sense.

McKenna thought about taking the picture with him to show Jamie, but he was completely naked and had no pockets or a way of hiding it. And if he was caught, he certainly didn't want to have it in his possession. He could be arrested for breaking and entering and now stealing. Even though he was a cop, and this could be some sort of evidence, he decided against it. McKenna took one more look at it, then put it back where he found it and started to close the drawer. Then, he saw something else.

In the very back of the drawer, tucked carefully and not in immediate view, was an old-looking, small-sized wooden box. It had the same engraved symbol that was on the man's shoulder who talked with him at the pool yesterday. McKenna picked it up and immediately turned it in his hand, examining it. The box was made of a heavy wood, square in dimension, about three inches by three inches, and it had an ornate gold latch on it. McKenna quickly opened it up and was shocked at what he saw—a perfect set of false teeth with two large fangs—vampire fangs. He carefully took them out of the box to examine. These were real; not like the fake plastic, fanged teeth Hammer put in his mouth earlier at the pool. These were very real. As he turned them back and forth in his hand, something odd caught his inspection. At the bottom tip of both fangs were very small holes that extended all the way through the teeth to the back of the set.

He decided that he had seen enough and had better leave while he could. From his police training and criminal investigations, McKenna knew that, in a situation like this, with Jamie as a diversion, he only had minutes. And the minutes were probably up.

McKenna put the box back, took one more look at the picture to make certain what he saw he really saw, relocked the cabinet, returned the keys to Winston's desk and ran to the doorway. Jamie had been watching for him to sneak out of Winston's office and he caught her attention. She knew she had to create another diversion to get him out of the office now, and she was about to, when Winston suddenly walked in.

CHAPTER 33

When Winston returned to his office, he was stunned to see a naked Jamie standing there and talking to his seated assistant while pointing at something on the computer.

McKenna, who stayed hidden close to the doorway leading from Winston's office, was now unable to leave unnoticed. It was all up to Jamie to try to create some sort of diversion so that McKenna could leave, but how? None of this had been planned out. It was all just unfolding as it was just happening. And there was no other way out of Winston's office except through his assistant's adjoining office.

Jamie looked quickly to catch a glimpse of McKenna, and then looked directly at Winston. And before Winston could ask her what she was doing there, she reacted.

"Oh, my God, I feel faint." And she started to sway slightly and grabbed onto the desk so as not to fall over from her fainting act.

"I need water. Please! Water!" Jamie said in a distraught voice while continuing her act.

Winston's assistant was halfway out of her desk chair to help her when she turned and looked to Winston.

"You heard her, get some water. She may be having heat stroke or something. Hurry," he barked at her.

"In the break room, or the bar?"

"Just get some water, now!"

She hurriedly left the office as Jamie continued to sway. Winston stepped closer to prevent her from falling and his arms reached out to stabilize her while brushing across her two naked breasts, either accidentally or purposely. He held onto both sides of her waist to keep her from falling as she reached out to stabilize herself by grabbing onto his shoulders.

"Perfect," Jamie thought to herself as she gave another quick glance to McKenna, followed with a short nod of her head. She wobbled purposely, continuing her act. Jamie immediately swung herself and Winston around, turning him so his back was now to his office door where McKenna remained in hiding. And with that sudden move, she quickly leaned in and kissed Winston.

McKenna was shocked. So was Winston. But it was a perfect diversion for McKenna to quickly leave. And he did. Without a sound he moved past them, but not before he nearly bumped into the desk. Stopping briefly, McKenna maneuvered himself to not touch a thing as he left the assistant's office and quietly entered the hallway. He looked back into the room, and what he saw didn't exactly please him.

Winston's two hands were now on Jamie's bare ass as he held her tightly to himself enjoying the moment. Jamie held the kiss just long enough for McKenna's escape, before pushing Winston's arms gently away and moving her face and lips to a safer distance.

"I just wanted to thank you for the complimentary gift massage," she smiled teasingly.

Winston was still stunned from her unexpected appearance in his office, her unexpected kiss, and now the unexpected thank you. Before he could reply, Jamie gave him a quick peck on the lips.

"I feel better. Thank you," Jamie continued as she started to leave, but decided to add one more remark.

"And don't forget tonight's event. You're on my dance card." Her acting was very convincing, so were her words. Winston completely forgot to ask her why she was there.

Still somewhere on Cloud 9 from what just happened between him and Jamie, he smiled back. "I'll be there, for sure." He touched his lips where hers had just been and added, "There's a private party after the masquerade dance if you can get away, if you know what I mean."

Jamie just coyly smiled her response and left. McKenna was long gone, but the assistant was hurrying back with a bottle of water. She was stunned to see Jamie in the hallway, completely well.

"I'll take that." Jamie suddenly reached out and without another word took the bottle of water and continued down the hallway back towards the lobby.

The assistant stared at her, perplexed for a moment, and then shrugged her shoulders and slowly walked back into her office.

Jamie opened the water bottle, took a swig of it, swished it around her mouth and walked to one of the large planters in the hallway. She immediately spit it out on a tropical-looking plant. Jamie then poured some water on her one hand and scrubbed her lips. Satisfied, she closed the bottle and walked into the lobby where McKenna stood near one of the huge center columns with his arms crossed. He didn't appear too happy.

"What else could I do?" Jamie raised her eyebrows and shrugged her shoulders as she tried to explain her previous actions.

"Fainted," McKenna replied with a tinge of anger in his tone.

"From his kiss?" Jamie tried to make light of what happened. After all, it did get him out of the office unnoticed.

McKenna shook his head and his moment of jealousy passed.

Jamie stepped closer and looked directly into his eyes. "You kiss a lot better." Her words were more than the assurance he needed.

He responded to her by touching her face with one hand, gently, as if agreeing that it was the right thing to do. After all they were on assignment. And maybe that kiss would help catch the killer.

McKenna let out a deep sigh. "I have a lot to tell you. Let's go for a walk."

Holding hands, they left the lobby and went through the open oversized glass doors that led to the veranda. The day was warming up and it felt good to be back outside and away from Winston's office.

Once outside on the veranda, they found a private area to have their discussion, nestled next to the concrete open-pillared railings overlooking the pool. A few naked resort guests passed by on their way to the pool area below. Some chatting, some laughing, not paying any attention to them. With enough surrounding sound from the splashing waterfall, Jamie and McKenna felt it was safe to talk without being overheard. And this time they weren't.

"You're probably wondering why I was in Winston's office when you got there?" Jamie began with a nice smile and a cute twinkle in her eye. She was glad to be back with McKenna.

"Crossed my mind," he replied with a smile of his own to let her know he felt the same way about her.

"I was in the lobby just talking with some guests, looking for any new information, when I saw Winston rushing through with two security men. Apparently, something was happening."

"Yes, another killing," McKenna replied as a matter of fact.

"What?" Jamie had not expected that. "What happened?"

"Well, first you."

"Another killing? Whoa!" Jamie processed and compartmentalized it, so she could continue her story. "Okay. When I saw him rush through the lobby, I decided to see if I could sneak into his office and do some snooping. I didn't expect to find that he had an assistant there, so I made up a story and told her I was there to see if a charity check had arrived on behalf of the mayor, you know the technique, 'phony name dropping, phony charity.' I watched as she looked through some e-mails in her computer. I wanted to see if there were any names I'd recognize or if something would jump out. That's when you came in."

"Okay. Well, I was leaving the veranda sports bar and on my way to the spa, after talking to some guests and hearing some rumors, when there was a nearby commotion which caught my attention. Apparently, someone was found dead in the spa. Don't know the specifics, but I played 'doctor' and got a close-up look of the body. Marks on the neck, drained of blood, like the others."

"The vampire killer?" Jamie exclaimed with a question.

"Well," he paused thinking over her last words, "there's actually more to the story than that."

McKenna told her the whole story of how he looked through Winston's desk and found a gun and some keys, and that one of the keys opened the filing cabinet where he discovered a topical map of the resort from 1931 and an assortment of old pictures. He explained that one strange picture, dated the same year, 1931, caught his attention. It showed a group of naked people in a pond, being watched by a sad-looking pregnant woman, standing next to a tall, dressed man who resembled the man he fought last night. And both were watching a nude young woman in the pond who matched the description of the woman she met earlier today. He concluded by telling her about the wooden box with the fake teeth and realistic-looking fangs.

Jamie stood in silence. It was a lot to take in, even with her investigative mind.

A sudden breeze blew across the veranda that gave her a slight chill. Some clouds were forming in the distance and indicated a possible storm was coming. But right now, from what he told her, she felt like "she" was in the middle of a storm. Like a lost Dorothy in fairytale Oz, looking for a yellow brick road to lead her to all the answers. But there was no yellow brick road to follow, just a body count that seemed to be increasing.

"You said the man in the picture was dressed and looked like the man you fought with."

"Yep."

"And the naked woman in the pond water looked like the woman I described to you?"

"Yep."

"How is that possible? If that wasn't a fake picture, they'd have to be..."

"...well over a hundred years old," McKenna interrupted. "Yes, if the people in the picture are the same people we saw, they would have to be a hundred-plus years old."

"That's impossible."

"And not probable."

"Maybe they're the parents of the ones we met?"

"Well…maybe? That's possible, I suppose."

"Or maybe they haven't aged."

"Not possible, and not probable."

"But maybe," Jamie concluded in her investigative manner.

McKenna took a deep breath, thought about the question he had to ask her, and did. "What else do you know about vampires? I mean…"

"They turn into bats," she answered like she almost believed it.

They both paused looking at each other seriously, then they laughed simultaneously.

"Yeah. Bats. We're the ones going 'batty.' We're in the middle of a nudist resort filled with wall-to-wall naked people, and a porn convention with more naked people, all here at the same time, all on display, including ourselves. And at least one killer who we believe is a possible vampire. Nothing unusual about that. But the bizarre killings. Why here, why now?" McKenna tried to summarize everything.

"Think about what you just said. This whole nudist resort is a perfect place to do some 'naked window shopping.' You know, like picking out the best-looking victims—everyone and everything is on display," Jamie remarked.

"Hmmm." McKenna thought about it.

"Or maybe this place is like a big bank, a 'blood' bank," Jamie quickly added as though piecing the bizarre clues together to find the right answer.

"You mean this is the perfect place to make blood withdrawals?" McKenna questioned, with a bit of hesitation in his voice, as if accepting the horrific idea.

"Yeah. Lots of blood withdrawals," Jamie agreed with a concerned look, a very concerned look.

And with those thoughts crossing their "cop and detective" minds, they both turned and looked down at the sprawling resort area now filled with hundreds of afternoon guests, swimming, drinking, exercising, partying. All totally naked. All in one place. All potential "next" victims. Including themselves.

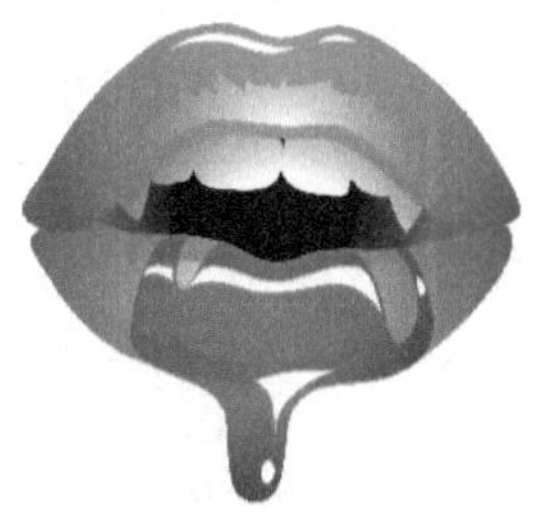

CHAPTER 34

Tina's and Jeff's lips were kissing, or so it seemed. Actually, their lips were just bumping into each other, brushing across each other's face, as their dead bodies swung upside down from the motion of the laboratory pulley system attached to the ceiling. Bright, but blinking fluorescent lighting illuminated them as they swayed back and forth and left grotesque dancing shadows on the nearby lab wall. Their necks were slashed open, apparently from a biting frenzy gone wild. If they were the main course on a dinner menu, they had been very well enjoyed.

With a rope tied to each of the bare legs of both bodies, a nearby lab technician used a turning wheel system to lower them from their hanging position. One body at a time was lowered to a shiny metal long table on wheels, which was placed strategically below them just for this purpose. A second technician stood by the descending body and, without much care, pulled the long IV needles with connecting clear plastic tubing out of their arms. The last remaining vestiges of their blood dripped into the silver metal bowls that were positioned on the floor beneath them. After each body was placed on its own table, the metal bowl with their blood was put on the table with them.

Without any conversation between them, the two male technicians wheeled Tina's and Jeff's bodies out of the room through a large metal sliding door that had been previously opened. Their bodies were brought into an adjoining laboratory room where Doctor Steffens was busy performing an autopsy examination with a large microscopic device. He was looking at human tissue samples pressed in between glass plates. Adjusting the nobs on the specialized microscope, he studied the samples intently, then sat back and let out a deep sigh. He moved his black-rimmed glasses off his forehead and back to their normal eye position and started to rub his chin with one hand. Paying no attention to the two technicians who had stood waiting until his analysis was done, he began to write some notes in a leather-bound diary.

Another person, a female technician in her early 30s, wearing a white lab coat, entered the room pushing a small metal four-wheeled cart. Atop the cart was a variety of surgical instruments and tools. After placing the cart between the two metal tables with the dead bodies, without a word, she turned and left as quickly as she had entered. Her job wasn't to ask questions, just to obey orders.

Doctor Steffens slowly got out of his chair and approached the naked bodies on the two tables. It was apparent from the look on his face that it had been a long day, or at least a long time focusing on what he had been doing, and, from the expression he wore, it didn't look like he had succeeded. He spoke to the nearest technician.

"Once I am done with my exam, take the ovarian tissues out of the girl first, do a DNA analysis, then remove the heart and determine its size during her death."

There was no emotion in what he said, or what he asked for. It was simply a medical procedure that he requested, which appeared to be one that had been done before, if not many times before.

"As for the male?" the shorter of the two technicians asked casually, as though this question was just routine in what they intended to do.

"Same as the others. Remove his sex organs and extract all of the sperm, and then extract the tissues connecting the penis and testicles. Leave all of the remaining blood here for me."

"And the bodies?" the other technician asked.

"The usual. The quicksand grave."

Holding a sharp, cutting instrument that he picked up from the cart, the doctor added a quick comment, "Looks like this one was the main course." He paused looking at Tina's ripped-open throat and poking at some of the extruding veins and flesh with the metal tool. "It is getting harder to control their hunger. Their thirst grows more each day. The deregulation of cell death mechanisms in the skin are leading to necrolysis at a faster rate. We are running out of time. Bring me the biometric results from what we discussed. I have to share it with him later."

"Morbius?" the first technician asked.

"Yes. He makes the final decision." The doctor stopped poking with the instrument in hand and paused a moment to exchange it with another on the cart. Now holding a sharp, curved, scissor-like tool, he began to cut the flesh off the neck area that had been ripped open and tossed pieces of it into a small empty silver bowl on the cart.

"The reversal process is happening much quicker and we need to continue the transfer before it is too late," Doctor Steffens continued.

Another male voice came from behind the doctor. "How exciting to know that it won't be much longer.

I've been told that they've met, and the plans are in place. Tonight."

Approaching from the open doorway was Alexander. He was wearing a long, flowing, black satin robe, open in the front to reveal his full nudity beneath it.

While holding a large piece of Tina's half cut-off and half still-attached neck flesh, the doctor looked up and his mood changed from one of previous disappointment to one of an upcoming celebration.

"Both of them?"

"Yes, both of them. We finally found her. The other will work also. They'll be the perfect match." Alexander lightly ran his fingers gently over Jeff's head on the table as he stood over the two dead bodies.

"Like a match made in heaven?" the doctor responded.

"No. More like a match made in Hell," Alexander replied with a wicked smile while licking his lips in anticipation. "For her to live, she must die."

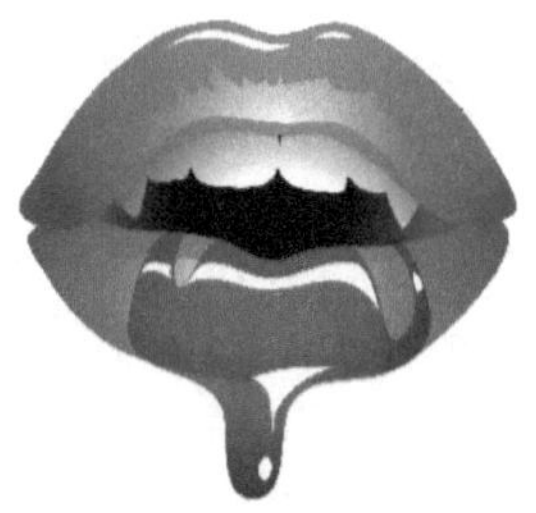

CHAPTER 35

As early evening approached, a long line of black stretch limousines stood waiting to drop off their occupants at the Paradise Lost Resort entrance. Winston, his security people, and the talkative parrot were all there to greet the arriving celebrities and distinguished government guests who were attending the resort's convention masquerade ball. Waiting behind the roped-off curbside barriers, a growing crowd of naked resort and convention onlookers jostled for a better viewing position.

The first to arrive was Hollywood and TV actress Savannah Strong, who got her start in porn at the age of sixteen before finally finding "God" and going mainstream in the politically correct and "accepting" modern era. The buzz at the convention was that she lost her way again and was returning to porn in a new Jack Hammer production to be announced at the convention finale. Stepping from the limo, she wore a long, flowing, bright red gown that was low cut to her waist. Her long legs were accentuated with her matching 6-inch, red high heels. Dyed red or maybe natural-colored curly hair fell across her face and onto her strapless bare shoulders. With each step she took, her large breasts were nearly exposed, most certainly planned that way for all the adoring fans' visual delight. However, it wouldn't be long before her breasts were in total full view at the evening's masquerade ball, as she was the honorary "Porn Queen" of the event. She was definitely the "definition" of the *Scarlet Letter* story come to life in today's world of "girls gone wild."

When one limo pulled away, another took its place. This time, two very tall NBA professional basketball star athletes emerged, one from either side of the extra-long stretch vehicle. In matching light blue custom-made jumpsuits, and bright yellow aviator sunglasses, they pretended to dunk imaginary basketballs with the movements of their long arms. Before entering the resort, they high-fived some sports fans and signed a few quick autographs while carefully checking out all the younger naked women.

The next vehicle to pull up to the entrance lobby had two sets of look-alike secret service men in dark black suits who quickly emerged with walkie-talkies. They each had short-cropped hair and black-as-night sunglasses. They each stood at their planned position waiting for the following limousine to arrive behind them. The Vice President of the United States, Stacey Adams, the Director of U.S. Department of Defense, General Richard Underwood, and Florida Governor, Richard Marino, along with their significant others, wives, boy toys, or hired evening escorts, exited, smiled to the crowd, and were escorted into the resort.

The final vehicle arrived, and everyone cheered in anticipation. This was the one that the crowd was waiting for. It was a completely gold-colored limousine with two rainbow-colored music speakers attached to its roof top. As its main door was opened by a resort staff greeter, a thick cloud of smoke from a large amount of still-being-consumed marijuana billowed out. Blaring hip hop music from inside the vehicle and from the rooftop speakers blended with the smoke, creating a very surreal scene. World-famous recording rap artist, Master XYZ stepped out of the limo, already completely naked except for a long, gold thong holding a long, thick dong and wearing an abundance of assorted gold chains covering his smooth, shaved bare chest. Waving a bottle of opened champagne in one hand, and a large burning joint in the other, he stood and turned his head upwards and shouted out loud, "Master XYZ is here to Par...Tee!"

The waiting crowd shouted back in a playful mood, apparently familiar with his widely recognized "party" pronouncement that he was here, he was ready, and he was the one to really get the party started. Flanked by two scantily clad, attractive white women in their early twenties, if even that, he staggered towards the resort lobby, wobbling and swaying with each step, apparently having already "started the partying" long before his arrival.

Mimicking the rap artist as he passed by, one of the colorful resort parrots danced excitedly atop its open cage. It flapped its wings and sang in a rapping chirping tune, "Par-tee time. Par-tee time. Par-tee time. Get down."

Either the parrot was an actual fan, or, it had just caught a deep whiff of the floating cloud of pot smoke that passed through its cage.

After all the new arrivals had entered the resort lobby, Winston turned his attention back to his staff who had stood with him during this parade of arriving celebrities.

"Keep them happy with free drinks. Keep them involved with the guests and fans. And for God's sake, keep them protected. Nothing, and I mean nothing, must go wrong tonight. Understood?"

They all nodded and quickly dispersed into the lobby to be the "extra" security for them, even though most had their own security. Once he was alone, Winston moved his handheld walkie-talkie close to his lips and made sure no one could hear.

"They're here. Everything is now in place."

Winston shut the communications device off and walked into the crowded resort lobby, all the while keeping his attention to the total surroundings. Savannah and the basketball stars were busy shaking hands and signing autographs. Master XYZ was doing an impromptu rap song in the middle of the lobby with some of the naked female guests dancing around him.

"Very nude, not too rude, lotta tittie, in naked city."

The government VIPs and their significant "whatevers" were all on their way to their suites to get naked and do "whatever." Satisfied with what he saw, Winston passed through the busy lobby and down the hallway to his office. His secretary was just leaving her office.

"I left the sealed envelope that came special delivery on your desk, as you asked."

Lost in his own thoughts, Winston just politely nodded and said nothing in return.

Once inside his office, he closed the door behind him. Picking up the delivered envelope, he used a letter opener from his desk to cut across its sealed flap. Taking out the contents, he looked at the document, turning the pages quickly, searching for something and then finding it. Reading it over, his expression changed to one of discovery or maybe surprise. Or maybe, something he expected all along. There was a photocopy of a New Tampa newspaper article from several months back with the headline *"Florida rapist case solved by local detective."* The photo showed the detective receiving commendations from the mayor. It was a picture of Jamie Parker with her name in the caption below.

Without any further expression, Winston put the paperwork back into the envelope and opened his desk drawer to put it away. He then opened his other desk drawer and took out his handgun. He checked to see if it was fully loaded. It was. He put the gun in his coat pocket and left his office.

CHAPTER 36

"So, what do you think I should wear to tonight's dance?" Jamie asked quizzically as she stood naked in front of McKenna by their room's open patio door overlooking the pool area.

McKenna's eyes gave her his response as he slowly looked at her nude figure from top to bottom and back up to her eyes.

"Well, right now, I'd say you're overdressed."

Jamie laughed and walked over to him putting her arms around his bare shoulders and responding with a short, but sweet kiss on his lips.

"You know, Mr. Stanton, or Mr. McKenna, or let me just say, Jim, I like what you're wearing, too."

And he smiled back and added to her reply with a deeper kiss as they embraced tightly, very tightly. Their eyes held on each other, then closed, as their touching flesh felt each other's warmth. Their passion was evident as the body heat between them far exceeded the late afternoon Florida hot temperature.

"This has become a very challenging case for me as a detective," she softly stated as they released their kiss but still held onto each other.

"And it has become equally 'harder' for me," McKenna replied as she felt his words come to life against her naked body.

"I really like you, Jim...a lot."

"My feelings are the same for you, Jamie, as you can see."

"Oh, I can more than 'see.' I 'feel' your feelings," Jamie said tenderly as she reached downwards to touch him.

And they kissed again. Deeply. Tasting each other and releasing pent-up emotions while caressing each other's inviting body. His gentle touch made her moan softly. Her gentle touch aroused him more. And then as quickly as they started, they suddenly stopped.

"Oh, my God!" she exclaimed. "We're by the patio door...in full view of..."

And there, in the outdoor garden pathway, two older couples stood and watched them, and when they knew they had been watched, the two couples started to applaud and jokingly yelled out.

"Get a room."

And McKenna jokingly replied, "Thanks, but we already have one!"

And with that, both Jamie and McKenna shared an intimate moment of embarrassed laughter adding to their awareness of falling in love. They both knew in their hearts that this was more than an assignment; this was a game changer, a life changer for both, in more ways than one. And the beginning of something more that they both wanted. Each other.

Jamie slowly ran her fingertips across his handsome face and lightly shook her head while letting out a long deep breath. Her hair moved slightly in the outdoor breeze. The setting sun illuminated her in a special glow of natural beauty.

She looked happy; she looked like a woman who "felt" like a woman for the first time in a long time.

Jamie shyly stumbled for words as she looked at him, and as he looked at her.

"Perhaps we should..."

"Yes. Perhaps." He let out a deep sigh, helping to get their thoughts back to what they were here to do, and what they had to do, even though they wanted to do something else. He half-heartedly smiled as his one hand gently touched the side of her blushing face. "The night is young. The dance starts soon. We probably should get back to work, and maybe I'd better..."

"...take a long, cold shower?" Jamie teasingly interrupted as she looked at him still in his fully aroused state.

And before he could answer, she quickly added, "Just save some cold water for me," although they both knew that no amount of cold water could ever "cool" their passion, now, later, or...

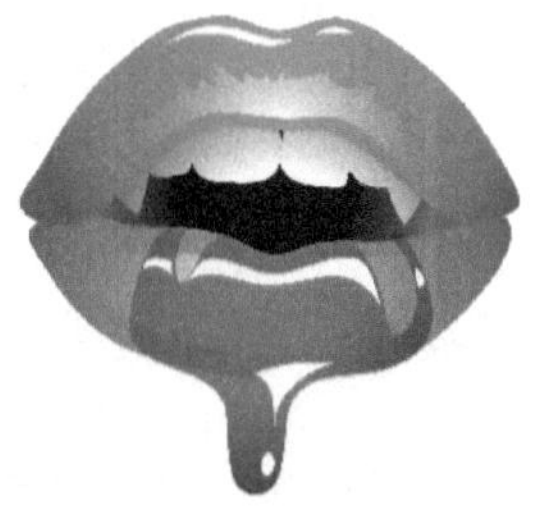

CHAPTER 37

The music was blaring from the resort ballroom as a line of naked guests made their way into the Paradise Lost Resort Nude-a-Rama Convention Masquerade Ball. Each guest was handed their own individual resort-approved and required eye mask. Each woman received a unique Venetian-style Mardi Gras lace masquerade mask. With bird-like feathers coming from above the eyes and a touch of sparkling rhinestones, the female masks were all very alluring and erotic looking, with a sense of forbidden mystery. Every man received the same type of masquerade eye mask—black, with a simple but elegant design shape. They all looked like a combination of the legendary and dashing "Zorro" mask and the mask of Batman's sidekick, Robin. It was mandatory for those who attended to wear a mask throughout the entire party. Maybe it was to protect the identities of some celebrity guests or rich patrons from being recognized, or maybe it just added to the mystique and kinky atmosphere expected at a porn convention party in a hedonistic place such as this.

Advertised to be the biggest swinger's event dance ever assembled, the resort ballroom held 500 people and it already looked quite full.

As they stood in line, Jamie and McKenna smiled in response to several of the passing guests who gave them more than just the "once-over look."

"Well, this will be interesting," McKenna leaned over and whispered into Jamie's ear.

"Ah, I'd say a bit 'more' than interesting. From some of the 'looks' we've been getting, I'd say people were undressing us with their eyes, but we're already undressed," Jamie replied apprehensively.

"Actually, you're wearing a gold necklace with a small cross."

"Hopefully to keep the vampires away," she flippantly remarked.

"Or maybe invite them in to play?"

Jamie shuddered slightly at his comment, but knew it was meant in jest.

"Did you get a chance to call your 'mother' today to let her know how things are going?" she inquired.

"Yes, the dogs are fine. Mom said to call again if we needed anything."

"Hmm. Good to know. Just in case," Jamie responded carefully, then sighed, thinking about how long it would take for backup to arrive if they really needed it.

She held his hand and continued.

"You know, Jim, it's quite amazing that this entire resort has its own rules and protection from the outside world. Other than the mysterious occurrences we've been following, it's actually a totally unique and fascinating place."

"To meet all the naked people?" McKenna asked teasingly.

"Or maybe to unexpectedly fall in love with one." Her reply contained a warm and sweet smile.

They squeezed each other's hand at the same time. It was obvious they both felt the same.

With their masks now on, they entered into the ballroom. Jamie's unique mask had red sequins, rimmed by rhinestones over the eyes, and big, black feathers. The party was in full swing and they had to take a moment to catch their breath.

Hundreds of dancing, naked, masked people. All shapes, all sizes. At the end of the ballroom on a large stage was a masked Master XYZ, standing nude behind a large mixing console, switching and blending song tracks. Creating his own music, he danced by himself and rapped out tunes for all the guests' dancing delight. On his shoulder was the resort parrot, swaying and bobbing, flapping and fluttering, and wearing a specially-made, very small eye mask, which matched the rapper's.

Throughout the large room were several elevated, round platforms, each with a ten-foot-high, thick-and-shiny golden metal pole protruding from it. Pole-dancing guests were taking turns gyrating, wiggling, and jiggling on the poles. And in the center of the room, high in the air for everyone to see, were Bridgett the Midget and Little Beaver. Even with masks, they were easily identifiable. Together they danced atop a giant eight-foot-wide and six-foot-high custom-made rubber dildo, which periodically sprayed steam and a little bit of water from its overly large penis-shaped head.

Flashing strobe lights surrounded the room and went off intermittently to the beat of the loud music. Female naked butts rubbed up against each other, as different-sized breasts bounced up and down, unless, of course, they were the implant kind that just stayed perfectly in place. As for the men and their naked anatomical wonders, different "directions" were easily understood from which way they pointed, depending on who was rubbing against whom. A day in the sun, followed by excessive drinking, and probably some drugs mixed in between, made the whole room a naked pleasure playground. And it was.

Jamie and McKenna finally turned to look at each other in awe.

"As you said, a totally unique and fascinating place," McKenna stated in a voice of uncharted amazement.

"For sure," Jamie agreed with a combination chuckle and fascination.

Suddenly and unexpectedly, a man's hand reached out and touched Jamie's shoulder, as another hand touched McKenna's. Standing behind them was Jack Hammer, with the widest of smiles, beaming like a kid in a candy store.

"Isn't this great? Paradise, baby! Paradise 'come to life'! And how's my new movie star, Jim?"

Squeezing Jim's bare shoulder as he spoke, Hammer then turned and looked at Jamie, feasting his eyes on her attractive nude figure.

"And I can make you a star, too, baby. Just tell me what you like, and where you like it, and I can make it all happen. Jack Hammer delivers anything and everything you could ever desire," he stated proudly.

"Maybe a glass of wine to begin with," Jamie answered somewhat sarcastically, but mostly unnoticed by the excited movie producer.

The Barbee Doll twins stood on either side of McKenna, lightly touching his chest and shoulders as they moved to the music, seemingly inviting him to join them without asking.

"You see, Jim, once you're a star in a Jack Hammer film, everyone wants a piece of you."

Hammer again turned his attention to Jamie.

"And as for you, Good Looking, I'm here to punch that dance card. What do you say?"

"Wouldn't you prefer to wait for a slow dance? You don't want to hurt anyone swinging that dancing..."

"Dong!" he interrupted, completing her sentence, while laughing out loud at his own joke. And from the look of "things," it wasn't a joke. "Why...Jack's legendary 'hammer' dances to every song!" he shouted over the blaring music.

He immediately grabbed her hand and pulled her into the nearby crowd of naked dancers. Jamie had never danced nude before, and although she was really shy about even attempting it, at this moment, in this fantasy world come to life, she had no choice but to be part of it.

Hammer seemed to be in his own world as he turned his bare body in a multitude of directions, creating his own dance moves with each beat of the blaring music. His hands sometimes touched her bare waist or shoulders, but he was mostly a gentleman, if one can call him that. It was just how he liked to dance, a little "touchy feely" with a lot of Hollywood showmanship, highlighting himself. He did give her the "Hammer look" a few times, and she responded by giving him her own look a few times back. Cat and mouse? Or maybe cat and dog? As an undercover uncovered detective, she just played along. Hammer probably held some answers to everything and anything at the resort, and she was determined to find out what those were.

As Hammer spun her around and quickly touched her tight and perfectly proportioned ass, she glanced over towards McKenna and saw the two statuesque Barbee Doll twins holding onto him very tightly, while thrusting their naked hips to the beat of the loud music, close to his nude body. Between the constantly moving dance crowd and flashing ballroom strobe lights, she couldn't really tell if McKenna was enjoying this, or just doing this as part of the job. She couldn't even tell herself what she was feeling. This was a whole new and totally different experience that no one would ever believe, if ever she shared it.

As the music continued and blended from one song into another, Jamie grabbed Hammer's hand and suddenly pulled him forward into her. His naked chest touched her naked breasts. She kissed him on the cheek and, as quickly as she pulled him in, she pushed him apart at a safer distance.

"Time for that wine," Jamie smiled.

"I'll be right back. Hammer-Man always delivers in more ways than one!" And with those words he leaned forward and kissed her quickly on the lips and danced away by himself into the crowd. Not that where she sent him really mattered to her, she just wanted to get away from him.

McKenna worked his way from between the two tall, dancing, naked Barbee twins and smiled his appreciation for their dance. They continued without him, now dancing together thrusting and humping their hips into each other. It was apparent that they weren't just putting on a show; they were the show. They were more than friends; they were lovers.

Without any words, he took Jamie by one hand and led her further into the crowded dance floor. She didn't resist. She felt comfortable with him and knew they needed to move away from Hammer and his dancing dolls.

He finally stopped, turned and took her into his arms, holding her tightly as they danced to the music. Without any wild dance steps, they just moved together, all the while looking at each other. After a few moments, Jamie turned her head slightly sideways giving him a friendly-like evil eye.

"So, I take it that's what was called a threesome?" Jamie asked politely.

"Actually, it felt more like a sandwich."

Jamie laughed.

McKenna moved his hands slowly up both sides of her body and touched her bare shoulders and continued. "Let's just say I prefer one at a time. And right now, my time is all about just that one—you."

His answer seemed to satisfy her question as she now took his hand from her shoulder and lightly kissed it before bringing it down to the side of her one breast where she let it stay and caress her. He kissed her passionately while they danced. It felt as though they were alone on the dance floor, and all that mattered at that very moment was the two of them.

With a change in the music, they broke their deep kiss and left the dance floor. Together they found a way through the many gyrating, naked bodies without touching them much, or just a few times being touched by someone else. At one of the many party bar stations, McKenna grabbed two free drinks that were placed on the bar. As they sipped their wine, they looked around at the enormous naked crowd, while they caught their breath from their passionate embrace earlier.

Jamie spoke first, but McKenna was ready to say the exact same words.

"That was the most incredible dance I ever had."

McKenna acknowledged her words with a special look that came from within his alluring blue eyes. She knew he felt the same.

"Ah, not really wanting to change the subject, but I haven't seen Jeff or Tina since last night, not that they'd stick out like a sore thumb," Jamie commented as both a question and a statement.

"Hmm, we'll probably run into them somewhere here. They always seem to have a way to find us. Besides, he was on your dance card, too."

"Okay. Enough with the dance card! I only want to dance with you, Mr. Naked Guy," Jamie answered with a cute laugh.

They toasted their glasses and took another moment or two while continuing to survey the crowded dance floor. It seemed like more people were there with each passing minute. Although they were enjoying the time being together, they both knew that they were also on assignment, watching for anything and everything that might offer some sense or clarity to the mysterious deaths over the past two days.

From out of the crowd, two naked, attractive young women accidentally, or on purpose, bumped into McKenna, one spilling her drink across her bare breasts. Without any apology or other words, she placed one hand on Jack's muscular chest and stood wobbling in a drunken state while her female friend licked the cascading alcohol off her nipples. Once done, she leaned forward and surprised him with a quick kiss before picking up another round of free drinks and staggering away.

Jamie crossed her arms in front of her and looked at him.

McKenna let out a deep sigh while shrugging his shoulders, begging for forgiveness for something he didn't do. "Well...This place is definitely a friendly 'meet market.'"

Jamie chuckled as she replied to his comment. "Let's hope not a 'meat market,' as in another definition of the word 'meet.'"

McKenna picked up on her choice of words.

He expressed his concern to the situation that was seemingly growing out of control from the excessive partying, "The perfect place is right here, right now, for the killer to choose a nighttime snack."

"In more ways than one." Jamie nodded agreeing with him.

"You know, Jim, from all the beautiful women I see all over the place, I'm still amazed at how you can..."

"Keep my composure?"

"Yeah, let's call it that."

"I keep biting my tongue."

"Oh, well, let me remind you to leave a little tongue for me to bite," Jamie said playfully.

"You're not a vampire, are you?" McKenna asked in a joking manner.

"I guess you'll have to wait and see."

She reached forward to kiss him, when out of the corner of her eye she suddenly saw *her*. Jamie stopped short of the kiss.

The mysterious woman from the pond was there, standing with a naked man. She was staring at Jamie. And so was the man.

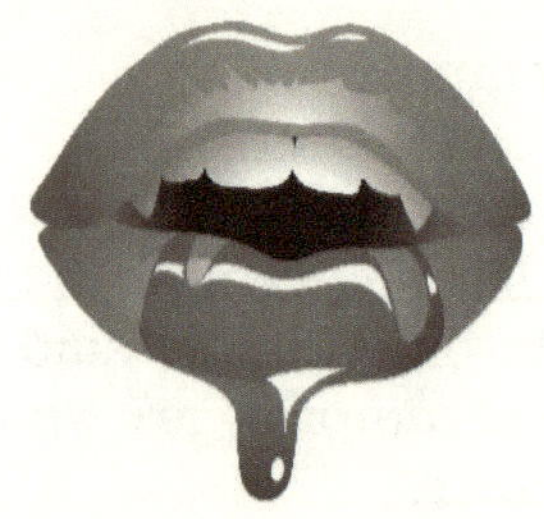

CHAPTER 38

"Jamie, I am pleased to see you here tonight."

"Hello, Alexandria. You are more stunning than I remembered," Jamie replied cordially, equally pleased to see the mysterious woman she had met at the pond earlier today.

"And this must be your friend, the one you said was waiting for you?" Alexandria asked politely.

"Yes, this is Jim, Jim Stanton."

"Your soulmate?"

As Jamie tried to find the right words to answer the question, McKenna jumped into the conversation.

"Well. Hi. Jamie told me all about meeting you this morning."

"Yes, this morning." She looked directly at McKenna, or maybe directly into him. "I remember at the pond, the water was so warm, so inviting," Alexandria replied. Her voice was soft, serene, and almost lyrical in tone. Every word seemed to hold its own special hidden meaning.

She then turned her attention directly back to Jamie as she continued.

"And this is Alexander," she stated without turning her eyes away from Jamie.

"Your soulmate?" Jamie decided to turn her question around and back to her.

Alexander spoke in response.

"You are more beautiful in person than my sister described."

"Your brother?" Jamie asked, somewhat surprised.

"Yes. We are family," Alexander replied while keeping his eyes also directly focused on Jamie.

It was McKenna's turn to ask a question, as if he and Jamie were playing the strategy of "good cop, bad cop" to get some clues. "So, are you both visiting here?"

"No, we are not visiting. We are enjoying. Aren't you?" Alexandria replied, again with a deep and yet haunting look at McKenna.

"Interesting answer," Jamie thought to herself, as it was now her turn to ask another question and put her investigative skills to work.

"How couldn't anyone not enjoy themselves here? This place has so many things to do. What do you enjoy doing most here?"

Alexandria remained focused on McKenna and slowly turned to Jamie with a pause before answering.

"Living."

Her single word comment gave Jamie and McKenna pause, as it sunk in.

Alexander continued, looking directly at Jamie.

"Life should be lived to the fullest. Time passes so quickly for so many, and time passes so slowly for so few. A shame there is no balance. You seem so full of life, young, beautiful, refreshing. How sad people must age and grow old and die. Wouldn't you like to live forever?"

The words seemed to have a chilling effect on Jamie as her one hand slowly and unknowingly reached upwards to touch the small gold cross she wore on a simple chain around her neck.

Without another word, Alexandria stepped closer to Jamie. Very close. Their naked bodies almost touching. She reached out and touched Jamie's hand that held the cross, and to also touch the cross.

"What a beautiful thing you wear! A symbol of life and death together in one simple piece. How interesting that some people hide behind fake truths that allege to protect them and are afraid to embrace the reality of death. Are you one of those people, Jamie?"

Both Jamie's hand and Alexandria's held the cross in their fingers. Their eyes were transfixed on each other. Neither blinking, just looking at, and within, each other.

McKenna finally broke the silence. It was his turn to play cop again.

"Speaking of life and death, have you heard about the resort murders?"

Alexandria carefully let go of the cross and now moved closer to McKenna. This time, their naked bodies almost touched. She didn't answer the question, but as the DJ's mixed music changed from loud to softer, she asked one of her own.

"Would you like to dance with me?"

Caught surprised by her request, McKenna looked towards Jamie, trying to find an excuse not to.

"Well, actually, I'm not the best dancer."

"And neither am I," Alexander stated as he stepped forward and suddenly touched Jamie's hand and brought it into his. "But it would be nice to dance with you."

Before either could say no, they were both led a few feet away from where they stood and onto the crowded dance floor.

It was a slow dance, and Alexander took Jamie into a proper dance position, holding her politely as a refined gentleman would, with just the right amount of distance between their naked bodies. He was extremely handsome, and very sensual in his look and voice. As they started to dance, he gently brought Jamie's body closer to his, while his eyes locked onto hers. He smiled slightly to change the mood and make her feel relaxed.

"Actually, my sister is the better dancer. I prefer to watch, but I have been interested in you from the moment I set eyes on you."

Jamie didn't know how to take this compliment, or if it were something other than a compliment.

She stumbled for the right words to answer as she looked at him.

"You are a fascinating man, Alexander. You must have plenty of women who would want to dance with you."

"It's not the dance that interests me," he said as he casually kissed her hand. "It's the feeling of the one I want to share the dance with that is more important."

He slowly brought her in closer to more than just a normal dancing embrace. Their bodies touched together for the first time. Her soft breasts felt his hard, muscular chest. Her nipples immediately became aroused.

He continued to look into her eyes. Deeply.

"Your eyes sparkle like the stars of night. I hear your heartbeat, Jamie, and I sense the warmth of your body." He drew her even tighter so that there wouldn't be any way to escape his hold, not that she wanted to. "I feel your blood flow. Do you not feel me as well, Jamie?"

Mesmerized by his demeanor, his handsome looks, the warmth of his flesh against hers, and his soft- spoken passionate words, yes, undeniably she began to feel a strange tingling throughout her body. A feeling of growing excitement, of wanting, and of fear. A feeling of needing more, right now, right then, as the unexpected anticipation of the "coming unknown" made her mind clouded, and her heart beat faster. She also felt every part of him as he tightly pressed his body into hers.

"My turn," a soft voice whispered in her ear and without warning. Alexander's arms let go of her as if on cue, and she was now in the arms of Alexandria. Surprised, but maybe pleased, she almost wanted to thank her for saving her, as if she were a white knight on a white horse sent to save the princess from doing something she didn't know if she should or shouldn't do. Saving her from the proverbial "frying pan," but not realizing she was about to enter the fire.

"My brother is such a romantic. It stirs his inner soul. Does it not stir you also, Jamie?"

Her words were most alluring, almost hypnotizing. Spoken with a woman's deep sensitivity but resonating with power and a hidden, unbridled passion. Their eyes locked together, Jamie was more than fascinated with her, more than mesmerized with her, if that could even be possible. But it was. Alexandria seemed to control her, and she was drawn to her, becoming a puppet in her arms.

"No need to answer, dear Jamie, I can feel your thoughts course through your body."

As Alexandria completed her words, she pressed her body tightly into Jamie's. Her breasts touched hers. Their nipples gently brushed across each other as they danced together, as if playing with each other in a life of their own. Jamie had never felt this sensation before, she had never experienced the sensual touch of a woman before, let alone the naked embrace of a beautiful body of a woman like Alexandria. Whether a fantasy or a reality, or an erotic moment somewhere in between, Jamie's body seemed to melt into hers. Jamie couldn't reply in real words. She could only let out a soft sounding moan, which spoke for itself. A soft, long moan, as Alexandria put her face next to Jamie's and moved her warm lips across Jamie's cheek and down towards her exposed neck. She kept her lips there momentarily, as she seemed content to smell her flesh as she licked Jamie's supple skin with her tongue.

Jamie wanted to stop, but couldn't. She wanted to tell her no, but knew she shouldn't. She wanted to run away and realized she wouldn't. Her world began to turn upside down and inside out as Alexandria's one hand slowly reached downwards across Jamie's warm, toned body and to the inside of her bare legs. Alexandria touched her. Lightly. Like a concert pianist touching the keys on a grand piano. And Jamie reacted, as she rolled her head backwards and moaned even more—a softer, yet deeper moan, that blended into the music which surrounded her and kept her a prisoner in Alexandria's embrace. Jamie felt her body heat rise. It seemed that her blood was at a boiling point as Alexandria's wandering fingers between Jamie's legs touched her, rubbed her, and entered her. And Jamie became wet, very wet, and she wanted to scream, but instead, she decided to enjoy. And she did. It was now her turn, as temptation took control of her feelings and her one hand reached downward to touch Alexandria, while her other hand caressed her own breast.

She had reached a point of no return, exploring her passion as never having been explored before by another woman. Jamie's and Alexandria's bodies now seemed attached at their naked hips, moving with the rhythm of the pulsating music and the sexual desires they each felt for each other, and for themselves. Was this shared lust or feelings of forbidden love?

It was Alexandria's turn to let out a silent moan, a silent scream, as they shared each other's deepening touches. Their eyes opened and closed a thousand times, seemingly to beg each other for more, as they slowly bought their lips closer together, closer towards meeting each other, closer to tasting each other. So close, so very close when suddenly...suddenly, Jamie stopped.

Shaking her head as if breaking out of a trance, Jamie suddenly regained her senses. Suddenly she knew something was wrong, not only in this very moment that seemed like a web of cascading lust, but something else. Something in her heart told her something was very wrong. McKenna.

Jamie broke the embrace with Alexandria and turned her head away and looked for Jim. He had been standing next to her with Alexander as they danced, but now they were no longer there. She turned to look in the crowd, and they were not nearby. They were nowhere to be seen. They were gone. Gone. But there, somehow, somewhere, suddenly, there, amongst the room filled with dancing, touching, mingling, naked bodies, she caught a glimpse of them. Just a glimpse. It was them. It had to be them. And it was. They were leaving the ballroom towards the outside veranda. Alexander's arm was tightly around Jim's shoulders, as if he was being guided or led away. But to where? Knowing that Jamie was watching at that exact moment, Alexander turned his head and looked back at her. He smiled wickedly. He showed his fangs.

And then they were gone.

Jamie shook her head, stunned, trying to compose herself from the dizzying passion she had experienced and what she had just witnessed. Trying to figure out what to do next.

Alexandria reached out and grabbed her gently by the arm and smiled wickedly matching her brother's. "Don't be afraid; he's waiting for you."

The words crashed through her mind like a hammer smashing an egg. *"What did she mean? Dear God, what is going on?"*

Jamie broke free of Alexandria's grip, and started to push her way through the thick crowd of dancers. It wasn't easy. There were so many people dancing now, as the music changed back to a wild tempo and brought even more people onto the dance floor. As she struggled her way toward the open ballroom doors, she was touched in a hundred places and asked a hundred times by a hundred different people to join in. The dance had become a "free-for-all" of sexual touching, grabbing, and inviting. She passed by Jack Hammer who wandered drunkenly on the dance floor. He held two glasses of wine in his hand and yelled to her.

"Hey, Doll Face, I got your wine."

She paid no attention, nor gave pause. She had to find McKenna. Something was wrong. She had almost lost him once and she told herself that she would never lose him again. Something was very wrong. She knew it; she felt it.

On the veranda, she stopped to catch her breath. It, too, was crowded with a spillover of guests from the dance. Many stood talking, laughing, drinking, kissing, groping, and more. Everything was a dizzying cacophony of sounds and sex.

Nearby, a hot and horny couple who had hands all over each other came up for air and beckoned her to join them.

"Where is he?" her thoughts screamed out loud in her mind as she turned one direction, then another, and back again. And then...

By the pool, there, in the mixture of the outdoor pool lighting and the shadows of the surrounding palm trees and exotic shrubbery, McKenna stood with Alexander, silent, facing each other. McKenna seemed motionless, emotionless, and not himself. The late-night Florida breeze moved through his hair as he stood there, like a deer in headlights waiting for it to happen. And it did.

Alexander turned again to look at Jamie, knowing where she was, as if waiting for her to watch, to witness, and this time, he didn't smile. This time his look sent a deep chill through her. This time she saw what she didn't want to see and couldn't ever imagine seeing. And she couldn't believe what she saw. Neither did she want to believe that this could really be happening. This time it wasn't Alexander who showed his fangs. This time it was McKenna.

Jamie had been running all this time down the resort steps and towards the pool when she suddenly stopped, horrified, terrified, as she watched McKenna slowly sink his fangs into Alexander's waiting neck. McKenna's eyes remained on Jamie as his mouth became covered in blood.

She was too shocked to scream, but she had to, but she couldn't.

From behind her, a man's hand came quickly around her face and immediately covered her mouth. Jamie's eyes widened as she tried to struggle. His other hand wrapped around her shoulders to hold her. Jamie's hands frantically grabbed at the man's hands, but to no avail. He was too strong and his hand over her mouth also held a soft white cloth dampened with chloroform. Her eyes started to close, as her body lost its fight and she began to slump forward. Her vision blurred, but she briefly saw who her assailant was. It was the tall man in the suit. He grabbed her falling body and swept it into his arms. Now, completely unconscious, he carried Jamie past the empty pool area and down the path toward the pond. Alexander and McKenna followed behind.

They all disappeared into the darkness.

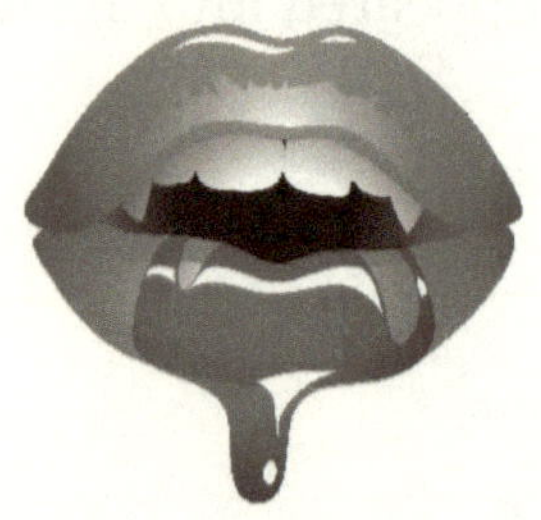

CHAPTER 39

"**I** know who the killer is," Jamie announced with an air of confidence. "And, I know how it was done," she added rather smugly.

The others seated around her just stared in shock at her sudden pronouncement.

"But how could you know so quickly?" one of the others asked.

"Actually, each of you helped. I listened to your questions. I watched where you went and I made mental notes crossing off all the possibilities. And then, when it was my turn to ask the questions, I already had more than half of the 'clues' already figured out," Jamie replied matter of factly, as if it was just that easy.

"Jamie, you always figure it out and win. I don't want to do this anymore. It's no fun."

"Aw, come on. It's just a game." Jamie tried to defend the situation.

"Not for Jamie; she plays it like it's real."

"That's why she's such a good detective at figuring things out. I mean, I never would have thought that Colonel Mustard was the killer, or that he used the knife and that it happened in the kitchen."

"He looks like the killer!"

"Well, the game of CLUE® is my favorite game. And sometimes, I'm just lucky in my guess," Jamie replied in her own self-defense.

"You have more than just luck, Jamie. You always have a way of finding things out. At 10 years old, you are my best friend, and I dub you the world's greatest junior detective."

"Who knows, maybe one day you will actually be a real detective," another of her girlfriends commented as if it were already a known fact.

"Me, a detective? Actually, I was thinking I'd like to be a female astronaut," Jamie sheepishly answered with a smile.

And they all laughed.

* * * * * *

When Jamie's eyes slowly opened, everything was blurry, and she could still hear the memory of that long-ago childhood laughter fading in her head. She had no idea how long she was unconscious, nor where she was. It felt as though she was trapped somewhere between a childhood memory and a living nightmare.

As her eyes cleared from whatever drug was used on her, her clarity started to return. Jamie's vision became clearer and things began to come in focus, she couldn't believe what she saw. It was more surreal than real to her. Her still somewhat distorted view of the room made her suddenly feel cold all over. And for good reason. Not only was she still completely naked, but she first felt, and then saw, the leather restraints attached to her hands and feet which bound her to the large operating table she was lying on.

"What the...?" Her mind was filled with dizzying thoughts as she tried to analyze her unexpected predicament.

The table was tilted at a 45-degree angle, so she had a good view of her surroundings. She could move her hands and feet and turn her head, but she did feel a slight unusual pain inside her female area. It was more of a discomfort, as she tried to free herself from the restraints. Looking around the rest of the room from where she was, what she saw was something she didn't really want to see, or believe. McKenna was also restrained to another operating table—this one was flat, not at an angle like hers. He was unconscious, or at least she hoped he was, as there was no movement from him. He just lay there, also naked, motionless. Just beyond him were two men in lab coats talking to each other. She couldn't fully hear what they were saying from where they stood, but she did catch the words, "It won't be much longer."

The room she was in looked similar to a hospital operating room, but smaller in scale, very sterile looking, lots of white walls and silver carts, and strange-looking medical implements and machinery. It was apparent she wasn't here for anything other than an operation. And from the looks of things, it would be an operation on both of them.

She tugged again at her wrist restraints, but to no avail. Her strength was returning slowly, but her vision and thoughts were now totally clear. She wanted to call out to McKenna. She wanted to know if he was okay, but she didn't want the nearby medical people know she was awake for fear that they might sedate her or put her back under to do God knows what. She again turned her hands back and forth in the wrist bindings, and the leather straps left red raw marks on her skin. Same with her feet. It was becoming obvious that there was no way to free herself.

A man's low moan broke the room silence and immediately grabbed her attention. McKenna was waking up. He was alive. But from what she thought about the situation they were in, she didn't know how long he, or she, would remain alive. And for the first time—in the entire time they were here on assignment—she felt helpless, and she felt frightened. But what she didn't know, things were about to get much worse.

From behind her, at an angle she could not turn to and see, a woman's hand suddenly and gently touched her bare shoulder, followed by a recognizable female voice.

"Ah, my dear Jamie, you are awakening. Perfect." It was Alexandria. She was wearing a long black satin see-through robe, open in the front to reveal her fully naked body beneath.

The way she spoke, so softly, so slowly, sent another chill through Jamie's body.

"Where am I? What's going on? Why am I tied up?" Jamie's voice was seething with anger.

"So many questions! All to be answered soon. So, try not to struggle. You need your rest. The operation went well."

Shocked by the word "operation," Jamie's expression and voice changed to immediate concern.

"What? What are you talking about? What operation? Untie me now! I'm a police officer," she ordered.

"Of course, you are. We know that, and we know all about your friend. He's one, too. We know all about you. That's how you were chosen," Alexandria answered calmly and punctuated it with a half-smile.

Jamie again struggled to free herself from the restraints. It was a futile attempt, but she knew she had to try.

Alexandria stood over her and softly rubbed the top of Jamie's head, as if soothing her, relaxing her.

Jamie stared back at her upside down in the position she was in on the table. Not cringing, but almost enjoying her touch. It was comforting, it was sensual, it was enjoyable. But she knew she had to fight the temptations racing through her mind, and she did, as she turned her face away from Alexandria and looked back toward McKenna. Alexandria's hand let go of Jamie's long hair in a long-lasting, slow movement, letting it fall gently back across her neck. Walking to the side of the table, she began to gently rub Jamie's bare stomach, not in a sexual way, but in a loving way.

"Shh, you must relax now. Everything will be okay," Alexandria stated in a chilling whisper as she left the room.

Exhausted from her struggles, Jamie let out a deep sigh. She knew she'd better relax to regain her full strength so that she could find a way to break free. But her relaxation was soon disturbed as she could hear the cold, echoing sound of approaching footsteps of several people on the concrete floor. A new voice came from in front of her.

"Ahh, our subject is awake. Hello, Jamie. I am Doctor Steffens, and there are some special guests who have been waiting to meet you."

Into Jamie's view came three people she recognized from the news programs she watched. All were dressed. One was the Vice President, Stacey Adams, another was the Director of Defense, General Richard Underwood. They were being escorted into the room by Florida Governor Richard Marino.

"Madam Vice President, General Underwood, Governor, here she is as promised." Steffens beamed with a sense of success, while he gestured with one hand which ended on Jamie's bare shoulder.

They stood next to the table Jamie was bound to, and all smiled silently, politely, indicating that they were pleased to meet her.

Vice President Adams also put her hand on Jamie in the same area of her stomach Alexandria had been rubbing.

"It went well?" She directed her question not at Jamie, but at the doctor.

"Very well," the doctor answered reassuringly. "And, with the expected results, Project Eve should be complete."

Jamie interrupted their conversation, talking directly to the woman standing before her.

"Listen, I'm a cop, tell them to let me go. Untie me now. I don't know what your plans are or what project you're talking about, but the police know I'm here on assignment and you better..."

"Better what, Jamie, free you, so you can call the police? No need to call, I'm already here," a recognized male voice interrupted with conviction.

It was New Tampa Police Chief Harold Johnson. He stepped out from behind the people who already surrounded her on the operating table.

Jamie was speechless upon seeing him. As her Chief looked at her lying naked on the table, she felt self-conscious without clothing for the first time since she disrobed in the room with McKenna, except that this was very disturbing and frightening.

"You're here because it was our plan to bring you here," Chief Johnson added smugly, also pleased with the success of his role he played in all of this.

Stunned and shock gave way to an enraged curiosity. "Your plan? To kill me? To kill McKenna? To turn us into some sort of vampires?" Jamie responded angrily as she again struggled against her restraints.

"And, what about all the coded messages for our safety?" she thought to herself, realizing another

option to be rescued was no more. Jamie envisioned the chief sitting in his office all the while with a smirk on his face, knowing he would not be sending anyone to their rescue.

Another older-looking man came into the lab walking slowly, limping with a cane. His footsteps were also heard on the concrete floor and echoed off the sterile lab walls.

"No, Jamie, you're not going to be turned into a vampire. Actually, there are no such things as vampires—just a lot of writers' imagination and a lot of Hollywood make-believe," he concluded as he stopped next to the operating table.

"Then you're going to kill me?" She tried to keep her emotions in check. If she was going to die, at least she wanted to die with answers.

"No, no, my dear girl. We're going to let you live. After all, you're pregnant!" he stated proudly.

With those words, Jamie's mind seemed to shatter into a million pieces like a broken mirror. The one word she heard and couldn't begin to even believe echoed deep into her heart. *"Pregnant?"*

"I see you're shocked. Yes. To be expected. Yes. You are pregnant. Let me explain, after all you are family," the older man continued.

Whatever pieces of Jamie's mind were still intact, they now fell completely apart. She wanted to cry, she wanted to scream, she wanted answers. *"Family? What does he mean? Pregnant how? She and McKenna...?"*

"And since you're one of us, you should know the truth, especially with your investigative curiosity."

Jamie just stared at him, speechless.

"You are beneath the resort in a specially built room funded by our guests and attached to a series of ancient tunnels made several hundred years ago by early Spanish explorers. I'm sure you studied in history about the Spanish explorer Ponce de León who came to Florida and supposedly found the Fountain of Youth. Just another legend, another tall tale, another imaginative writer made-up story? Actually, no. The Fountain of Youth is real, and it is here beneath the resort in a small pool of water at the far end of the connecting tunnel. It does exist, and it does have amazing powers. It stops people from aging. My family discovered it a hundred years ago, and we have protected it for as many years, as it remains protected today. This is an incredible discovery, Jamie, a miracle! The world would be stunned to know it exists, and so it must remain a secret."

"The Fountain of Youth? If this is true, this is a life-game changer. But why a secret?" Jamie asked, as she tried to put some rationale in her doubting questions, while adding time to her situation to try and figure a way to get out of it.

"If the world knew about this, there would be a stampede of people coming here." The older man continued, "Just think of the California gold rush. Everybody and everyone would be fighting and going crazy to have their youth restored. And it would put every pharmaceutical and beauty company out of business selling their useless lotions and potions. But even with this discovery, miracles such as this come with a price. You see, the water has a remarkable and unknown healing process to stop exposed skin from aging, but it does not stop the organs from aging inside the body. That has been a dilemma."

"The inside?" Jamie started to recover from her initial shock and began to seek more answers.

"Think of it this way. Our body is like a car. It is a special vehicle that allows us to move, to think, to do daily things. And like a car, as it gets old, we need to maintain it. So, with the water's remarkable and unexplainable powers to keep the skin young from aging, we need a way to keep the inside of the body young as well. Simply put, like a car, which requires its oil to be replaced after so many miles, we have discovered that we need to add new blood."

"So, you're blood suckers?"

The older man gave a slight smile while shaking his head back and forth.

"No, Jamie, we're more like blood feeders."

The thought of what that meant made Jamie shudder.

"So, if you're not vampires, why not have a blood transfusion?" Jamie questioned, trying to remain calm and not dwell on the sheer absurdity of what she was being told. Nor did she want to believe what she was being told.

Doctor Steffens stepped forward while answering her question.

"How simple that would be? And yes, it was tried and repeatedly failed. We couldn't just insert a needle and drain blood from someone. Our bodies crave and only accept the 'the donation,' as we refer to it, if we drink the blood. And here's the reason. Over a period of time, the water's unique properties have changed our internal DNA, mutating it, resulting in the rearrangement of our molecular and genetic structure. Because of the water's unique properties, although our skin doesn't age, our internal organs have evolved through the passing years. The water here stops our aging process but does not satisfy our appetite. We no longer require food, as does the normal person. All people need water to live, that's a basic law of nature. But the Fountain water here, which prevents our aging, is not part of that law of nature. Any drinking water, other than from the cavern pool, reverts our aging process and would make us dramatically old, and very quickly. And with that mutation, again simply put, to maintain our organs health, we discovered the way for us to live was to refresh ourselves with new blood. Our body now craves blood. We live on blood. The nourishment of fresh human blood allows us to live."

"Then you *are* vampires! I've seen your fangs and seen some blood sucking. Why haven't you or why *aren't* you draining my blood?"

The older man stepped forward as Dr. Steffens backed away. He showed no emotion as he answered her question. "Again, Jamie, there are no such things as vampires. We refer to ourselves as life feeders. And yes, we do feed and live on the blood of other people. Some we drain all at once; some we drain over a period of time."

"Like a tasty midnight snack?" Jamie added sarcastically.

"Well, that's a clever analogy. Your blood is important to us, but in another way. Remember, I said that you are one of us."

"What do you mean one of 'us.' I don't know any of you!" Jamie sighed impatiently.

The older man lightly put his hand on Jamie's shoulder as if to reassure her of what he was about to say.

"You may not know us, but we have been searching for you, and know who you really are. Let me introduce myself. My name is Morbius. Our family migrated from Germany in the 1920s to find work and we moved here. As in Germany, where nudism began, we came here to this part of the country to enjoy the sun. We are sun worshippers, and remember, vampires, if there were such things, don't live in the sun. We do."

"But how am I related? I know nothing about you or your family."

"Your great grandmother was my wife. And she was pregnant...with my child."

Another shock wave hit Jamie like a sudden slap to her face. Again, her world was turned upside down.

"Oh, my God, my great-grandmother?" Then, like in the game of CLUE, Jamie suddenly recalled McKenna telling her about the picture from 1931 with what may have been some of these very same people here in this room, all being the same ones in that picture, including a pregnant woman. *"And this man—this man is my great-grandfather?"* Her thoughts wanted to scream out loud.

Resigned to all this unbelievable, yet possible information, Jamie just stared in silence.

"Sadly, and without my knowledge, my wife left here because she feared what might be happening to our unborn child when she stopped the aging process by drinking the Fountain's water. We had no medical knowledge whether it would or wouldn't prevent her from continuing her pregnancy. She wanted to have a normal child, one who would live and grow old like everyone does, not remain forever young and healthy like we do. So, she ran away, went into hiding, disappearing, changing her name, giving birth to a girl, your grandmother, who grew up in the normal world and got married and gave birth to another girl, your mother, who grew up and gave birth to you. You are a descendent of me. You belong with us. You are family."

Shocked again by hearing this story, now knowing all these facts, Jamie stumbled for some words to reply. Words that might prove him wrong, or maybe right.

"But, but, I mean, how do you know all of this? How can you be sure I am your descendent? How did you find all this history out, especially if your wife disappeared?"

The police chief suddenly stepped back into the conversation.

"When you were hired by our police department you had to pass a standard blood test. There were some irregularities in your blood that were brought to my attention. I ran your blood through another police lab using one of those new ancestry programs and was able to discover your bloodline. Your irregularities came from your great-grandmother initially drinking the water just enough to affect her DNA, but not change it, and it is also inherent in you."

"But how are you involved? Are you a vampire, too? This is all so crazy."

Vice President Adams spoke next.

"Chief Johnson is one of many people we call 'helpers.' They have all been rewarded for their continuing help. There are no vampires, Jamie, just a network of important people with financial interests who became aware of you and needed to meet you."

"Like the government? And I'm here to be experimented on? Is that why I was brought here? Why didn't you just invite me to be a sunbather? Why all the killings, and involving the police, and why McKenna?"

Morbius looked gently upon her and replied to her question.

"Some deaths were situations that should have been avoided. My children, Alexander and Alexandria, have had problems with their appetites lately. That is why finding you has been so important. We are doing the most amazing experiment mankind could ever imagine and your role in the experiment is critical to all of us here."

"I don't understand, what makes me so important, besides my blood?"

Adams replied, "Our top government officials have decided that the Fountain's water here will enable a selected group of the world's most brilliant minds and powerful leaders a chance to live forever, but there is a problem that we are finally on the verge of solving."

Morbius continued, "Within the mutated evolutionary process, we have lost the ability to reproduce. Our own blood antibodies have made us all sterile. But with your bloodline, and body chemistry, we believe we can reproduce through you."

"What?" Jamie exclaimed. Shaken by the words she heard, she tried to understand what he said, but still couldn't believe what this meant.

"We have been analyzing several test subjects' reproductive organs and tissues and have determined that we can use the eggs of Alexandria, but they cannot grow successfully within her. Alexandria's organs aborted every attempt. But you are family, and you have not tasted the Fountain water. We need to breed my daughter, and we have already successfully implanted her eggs in you while you were under anesthesia. The sperm of Alexander, my son, was added to fertilize her egg and, to be cautious, the sperm of your friend was also provided to fertilize another egg. The evolutionary process works rather quickly, and we have determined that the operation was successful and that you are pregnant with Alexandria's child."

"Oh, my God!" The horror of what happened and what would be happening in the months to come was overwhelming in her head.

"Interesting choice of words, actually, as we are on the verge of becoming the new 'gods.' And if the baby is born without defects, then all of the people who have contributed to this program, which we call Project Eve, will have their fertilized eggs implanted in you, as well. You will become a breeding home for the next generation of mankind. A generation that will live forever. You are the world's...new Eve!" Morbius proclaimed.

He smiled with the words spoken and revealed a set of rotting, sharp-pointed teeth.

Her only thought from what she saw in his face, his eyes, and the darkness of his heart, was, *"If I'm the new Eve, then you must be Satan!"*

Jamie stared quietly at all of them, one person at a time, one face at a time. She fought back the shock of being told she was pregnant, and if so, she needed to know one more thing, one very important thing.

"Will I also become a blood-sucking vampire or whatever you want to name me?"

Morbius reached to the tray and held up a pair of false teeth with fangs—the exact same teeth McKenna described to her that he found in Winston's locked filing cabinet.

"If you were able to look at these teeth closely, you would see that they have holes at the bottom. We have no real fangs, but these are very sharp and when inserted into our mouths properly and when puncturing someone's neck at the proper spot, we can use the teeth like a straw to draw blood out."

Jamie tried not to think of what he said, nor how the blood sucking was done. All she knew was that it seemed vile and disgusting. It seemed so unbelievable, so beyond the norms of anything she ever imagined, yet she began to realize it wasn't.

After a brief pause, she had one more question to ask. "Is my partner going to live, and why did he have fangs?"

Morbius continued, "We needed to get you away from the dance. My younger brother, the tall man in the suit as you refer to him as, was waiting to take you the other night, but instead he fought with your friend. Tonight, when we prearranged that dance with Alexandria, my son used a special chemical, courtesy of the General here, to put into your friend's drink as he watched you dance with my daughter. The chemical took effect and made him follow my son's orders to leave the dance."

"But I saw him bite your son," Jamie spoke with conviction, still trying to find a way out of this crazy clue puzzle.

"Alexander put the false fanged teeth into your friend's mouth and a blood packet exploded upon contact with my son's neck. It was part of the plan to lure you quickly away from the dance and into our waiting arms. And in your shocked state of mind, it lessened your ability to fight back, as you also were drugged."

Again, Jamie was too shocked at what she heard to even contemplate a reply.

"We really didn't want any harm to come to you. As I said, you're family."

Jamie remained quiet. She had no more questions, nor did she want to hear any more answers. Her mind churned upside down and inside out. She was at a turning point, a tipping point. Was this all just a nightmare that she was going to suddenly wake up from, and, perhaps after a deep breath of reality, laugh at the bad dream? Or was this all real, and was she now in the depths of what she believed to be her own personal Hell?

"I think I've answered all of the questions, so it's important you get some rest," Morbius concluded.

He softly patted her naked stomach.

"And your baby should get some rest as well."

One by one they began to leave. One by one they each reached out and touched her stomach. One by one she felt their touch and wanted to cry out, scream out, but she was empty of screams and the one lone tear that came from her eye rolled slowly down her anguished face. It had all been too much for her. This wasn't a dream. This was real. Too horrifyingly real to believe, but slowly, and finally, she did.

As they all left the room, she lay alone on the operating table, as complete emptiness embraced her—a tragic emptiness. Resigning herself to nothing more than a long deep sigh, she closed her eyes and could no longer imagine all the what if's, only the what is. Her life as it was had now been changed, changed into who knows what.

"Jamie," a soft voice broke the room's silence, whispering to her. "Jamie." Again, it came.

Opening her eyes, she looked across to McKenna. He was awake, staring at her. He was as helpless as she was, restrained to the operating table he was on. He tried to struggle but to no avail. She stared hopelessly at his struggle, but happy knowing he was alive.

"Jamie. I heard everything. I promise I'll get you out of here. Jamie answer me."

She wanted to reply, but didn't know how, or what to say. She searched her mind, she searched her soul, she found the answer alone in her heart. It had been there all along during their adventures together. Three simple words. The most important words she wanted to say. The most important words she had to say. And she did, in a whispery tone meant only for him.

"I love you."

McKenna's body trembled as he struggled to free himself. Her words gave him a renewed meaning to break free and save her. And he was ready to say the same words to her when...

The echoing sound of hand clapping suddenly came from behind them, out of their view. It was Alexander, alone, walking toward them. Continuing to clap. Finally, pausing in between them. Finally, stopping his clapping.

"Ah, I love a good love story. It is so deliciously sweet."

Smiling like the Devil would smile upon hearing his favorite words. Smiling, knowing that her words and McKenna's words were hopeless and that they would never again hold each other in a loving embrace, or touch each other again. Smiling, knowing he had other plans for both of them. Knowing it was his time to make this love story into more of a horror story.

"Jamie, dear, dear, Jamie. The mother of my child to be, you look so beautiful." He caressed her tummy softly.

She cringed at his touch.

Bending downward with his eyes remaining on her, he kissed her belly, leaving his tongue out to lick across her naked skin for a long moment before standing back up.

"Mmmmm, you taste so sweet." Alexander smiled wickedly as he licked his lips.

He let his fingers drag slowly from her stomach, upwards across her naked body, between her breasts and across her face and hair as he walked away from her and over to McKenna, where he stood next to him as he struggled with his leather restraints. He put his two hands calmly on McKenna's head and let his long fingers run through his hair almost as if he were brushing it in place, to make him look better.

"Ah, Jim, my dear friend, Jim. The father of my sister's baby to be. Of course, through Jamie. How nice to think we will have a child. Yours. Mine. Hers. Ours. Now that's what I call a beautiful and true family love story."

"Let us go. Please let us go!" Jamie cried out, trying to get his attention to focus back on her and to leave McKenna alone.

"Let you go? How much fun would that be for me?" Alexander replied rudely.

"I'll do anything you want. Let us both go," Jamie pleaded.

"Hmmm. The offer is intriguing. Especially the 'anything.' And, since we do need a happy ending to this, our love story, let me think. Ahh. Of course. It's simple. Like in any love story, you will make a choice. A choice. Of course. One will live; one will die."

"No, please, don't do this!" Jamie pleaded again, trying to get Alexander's attention away from McKenna.

Alexander's fingers began to dig slightly into McKenna's head as he struggled to break free, while holding his anger inside.

"No, you're right, that's not fair. You don't have to make a choice. The choice has already been made. You have our child, my child, so, of course, you have to live, but as for our friend here, the one you say you love. Hmmm." Alexander let out a deep breath, as if thinking about the possibilities, but he already knew the planned outcome. "We have already taken his seed and he is basically empty and of no further use to us, except for..."

Alexander smiled and showed his fangs.

"...his blood."

And with those very words he quickly bent over McKenna's face and sunk his fangs into his exposed neck—deep into McKenna's jugular vein as his blood spurted out.

And Jamie screamed!

The scream was heard from heaven to hell and echoed across the room. It seemed to be an endless scream. A scream of "Please, God, no!" A scream of complete horror. A scream begging for one's life, not one's death. A scream that was suddenly cut short by the sudden and unexpected new sound of a gun's scream. The scream of a bullet that crossed the lab and went directly into the head of Alexander.

The force of the bullet made Alexander's head snap backwards, his fangs dislodging from McKenna's neck. It happened in a blink of an eye, and in between that blink, blood sprayed from Alexander's head as his body twisted and turned as he fell dead on the floor with a resounding thud.

A figure stepped out from of the shadows. It was Winston.

A fully dressed Winston, standing with a gun in his hand.

Both he and Jamie looked to McKenna strapped on the table. McKenna's neck covered with a deep, red-flowing blood. He was bleeding out.

"Save him!" Jamie yelled. "Save him!"

Winston rushed to McKenna's table and put his hands across McKenna's torn throat, as he was convulsing. Blood flowed from underneath Winston's hands and rapidly down McKenna's exposed neck and across his naked body.

"I need a compress to stop the bleeding. Do you see...?" Winston yelled out.

"Beneath the table. Towels," Jamie yelled, back as quickly as the words could be said.

Winston let go of McKenna's open and bloodied throat and grabbed a white surgical towel, as she instructed. He wrapped it around McKenna's neck like a newborn baby being swaddled. Then he knotted its two ends together to put pressure on the wound. But the blood started to seep through the towel, turning it a dark, beet-red color.

"Untie me quickly. I'll help," Jamie barked, knowing Winston needed her immediate help to stop the bleeding.

Winston ran over to her table and undid the leather restraints as quickly as he could. First her feet, and then her one hand, and then...

Fangs suddenly sunk deep into the back of his neck.

It was Alexandria.

Winston's hands frantically reached backwards as his body twisted to fight off this unexpected attack. Jamie watched in horror, but quickly used her free hand to continue to undo the remaining hand strap.

She was finally free.

She struggled to get off the table, as she sought to find her legs and strength to help Winston.

Alexandria was ripping a huge hole in his neck, as he fell to his knees still trying to get her off. He screamed in pain as he fought for his life but was losing.

A *"whooshing"* sound of air broke into Winston's scream as Jamie swung a metal surgical tray, which smashed into the side of Alexandria's face. The force of the blow knocked her backwards and completely off Winston.

He hurriedly placed a hand over his wound and started to crawl across the floor to get a towel to compress the bleeding.

Alexandria, hunched over on the floor from the sudden blow of the tray, turned to face Jamie and hissed, barring her blood-covered fangs and mouth.

Jamie stood with the pan in both hands ready to strike again, while still regaining her strength from being tied up for so long.

"Not so fast, bitch." A voice broke through the standoff.

They both looked at Winston. He had reached the gun that had been knocked out of his hand.

He turned and fired at Alexandria.

BAM! The gun sound echoed throughout the room.

But she moved too quickly, and his aim was far from steady, as his arm was weakened and unsteady from the loss of his blood. The bullet grazed her right shoulder, tearing across and through her skin. She clutched at the wound and smiled.

Before he could fire another shot, she turned and ran towards the lab's open doorway and out into the hallway leading to the tunnel.

Jamie immediately wrapped another towel around Winston's wound and he half-heartedly smiled with words filled with pain.

"Stop her!" were his only words as he looked directly into Jamie's eyes.

"Thank you," Jamie replied with a look of gratitude and of determination, and maybe something more. "Save Jim. Please."

He nodded his response.

Next to where Winston sat on the floor nursing his wound were the medical instruments Jamie had knocked from the metal-tray that she used to strike Alexandria. She picked up the longest and sharpest scalpel, holding it tightly in her clenched fist. She looked to McKenna for a brief moment; his eyes, barely opening, lovingly locked with hers. Without another word, she ran out the same door that Alexandria went through.

Finally getting most of her strength back, Jamie hurried down the hallway, which turned into the cavern tunnel. She could only run so fast as there still was some pain in her lower abdomen from whatever procedure they had performed on her. But the pain didn't matter, what mattered was ending this nightmare right now, and right then.

The tunnel became damp with the moisture from the walls. Tiki torches placed every few feet into crevices in the stone walls lit her way. Her shadow was distorted as she ran, but her mind became clearer. Alexandria had been hit by the bullet and was heading to where she knew she could be healed. The sound of a bubbling water flow loomed ahead.

With each step, Jamie drew closer to her destination, and finally...saw it.

From within a circular pool of water, a lone three-foot-tall geyser sprayed upwards, and after reaching a certain height in the air, came back down in a perfectly formed umbrella effect.

"The Fountain of Youth!" Jamie exclaimed to herself. It existed! And there in the center of it was Alexandria bathing in its bubbling warm water, carefully applying the water to the wound in her shoulder. Whatever blood she bled, whatever wound the bullet made in her shoulder, whatever pain she had endured, it was no more. She looked perfectly healed. She looked fully radiant and beautiful from the lighting in the cavern. She looked totally at ease and in control, and her eyes were focused sharply and directly on Jamie.

"The water is embracing. Relaxing. Inviting. You should join me, Jamie. And let the water embrace you."

Jamie recalled Alexandria saying the same words to her the first time they met at the outside pond. This time the words spoken weren't as hypnotizing. This time the words were filled with evil.

"I don't know what type of games you like to play, but this time I'm ending the game right now."

Jamie entered the circular water fountain and kept her large scalpel blade in her one hand in front of her, ready to use it as a weapon of death. The warm water churned and bubbled around both of them, embracing them in what would become a final struggle between good and evil.

"Ahh, sweet Jamie, you have come to kill me. To release me from my 100-year-old prison called life. I look forward to it. I have wanted it for a long time, and now I know that, even when I die, whatever place in hell there is for me, I will always live through you. Through the child you carry. My child, our child. A part of me, a part of you, a part of Alexander, and a part of your friend Jim. The beginning of a new world. Together we will live forever through you.”

“No, Alexandria, that's not what's going to happen,” Jamie replied with total conviction. “That's not why I chased you. No, I came to tell you, it's over. There will be no new world as you say. There will be no new breed of us. There will be only a loneliness that you will live with and regret. I didn't come here to kill you. I came here...to kill the baby.”

And, with those “unexpected” words, Alexandria's eyes registered in shock as Jamie plunged the scalpel deep into her own womb. Her stomach accepted the entire blade as deep as it would go. Not into her heart as she first intended when she ran after Alexandria, but into the heart of the baby.

“Nooooo!” Alexandria screamed as she came forward in the pool of water grasping at the extruding knife in Jamie's abdomen.

But Jamie wouldn't let go, no matter how much Alexandria tried to pull it out. Jamie held it and forced it deeper into herself as her blood flowed into the water of the Fountain of Youth, changing it from a bright aqua blue to a deep, dark red.

Both of their hands were on the bloodied knife, which was still protruding from Jamie's abdomen. Alexandria's screams echoed through the chamber, bouncing from rock wall to rock wall. Anguished screams. Horrific screams. Until...finally, her screams ended. Finally, the tug of war between the two of them was over. Finally.

Jamie closed her eyes, her strength gone, slowly letting go of her hold on the knife, and fell dead into the water.

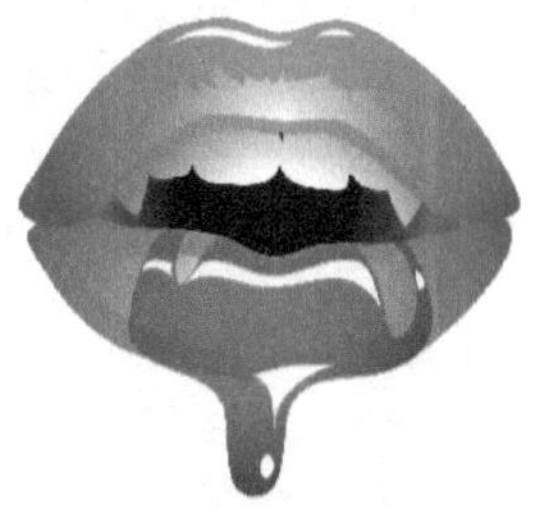

CHAPTER 40

"It's a boy!" the doctor announced. "A beautiful baby boy."

All Jamie could do was look on, exhausted from the ordeal of birth. Speechless, but filled with joy, as a lone tear came from one of her eyes.

Two of the attending nurses took the newborn boy to the waiting birthing table where they immediately cleaned the baby, treated his eyes, and swaddled him in a fluffy receiving blanket with blue and pink stripes before bringing him back to her.

Jamie sighed a deep breath as she held her son for the first time.

"Is he?"

"Perfect, Jamie. All of the advance testing showed no irregularities, and later today when we take a blood sample as you requested, we will confirm our findings," the hospital doctor concluded with a reassuring smile.

Jamie smiled back in relief, not only to the doctor, but to herself, as she looked at her child, bringing him close to her face, kissing him on the forehead.

"But you, young lady, had a rough labor and lost a lot of blood. You need to rest, to heal, to get well, and begin a new life with your son."

Jamie nodded, understanding the doctor's words and realizing the months of emotional anticipation had all come down to this moment. Yes, it was a difficult birth. A painful birth. A birth that she wasn't sure if she would live through. But she did. She had to. Not only for herself, but to be with him.

"Do you have a name?" one of the attending nurses asked.

"James. James McKenna Parker. It's a strong name. It's a good name. It's a promised name."

And with those words she thought of him. She thought fondly of him. And she missed him. Missed him greatly, as she had every day in the past nine months. They had a son. She knew it was his and her child, and everything appeared to be alright. She smiled to herself as she closed her eyes and remembered his gentle touch as they made love that late afternoon so long ago in their room at the resort. Although they discussed a cold shower to "cool" things off, their passion, their desire, their unbridled lust reached a boiling point so that no amount of cold water could stop them from wanting each other. Kissing led to touching. Touching led to... Their lovemaking was so passionate, so powerful, so sensual, so exciting! It lasted long and they climaxed together in each other's arms. And then they held each other, remaining coupled for a long time, knowing that they were meant to be, and would always be, one.

Neither wanted to leave their bed for the masquerade dance, but they had to; it was part of their assignment. Their one and only assignment together. It was their moment, their very special moment, and she had a feeling right then and right there, after their first and only lovemaking, that they would one day have a child. And so, they did.

They spent that beautiful late afternoon together in bed, holding each other, never wanting to let go. It was their memory to share; but now she had to remember it alone, just as she had to keep so many other things to herself.

They both died that night. He bled out, tied naked to an operating table from a vicious, horrible wound on his neck. She died as well, at her own hands. She wanted to be with him, and she wanted no part of a baby that would have been spawned in the depths of Hell. But the water brought her back to life. The miracle of the water in the Fountain of Youth. Winston had found her in it, and when he pulled her out of the water, there was no sign of any wound where she had plunged the scalpel into her own abdomen. Nor was there any sign of Alexandria. Jamie had healed. Physically. Miraculously. But would never heal emotionally.

She didn't remember much more of that night, as she probably wanted to mentally bury it along with McKenna, and she did. At his funeral, she stood by herself in the warm Tampa air next to his coffin. The gentle breeze of a morning wind seemed to caress her, just like he once had. Softly. Gently. Lovingly. As she said her goodbyes as he was placed into his grave, it was though he were still there with her and would always be. And now, he still was, and would always be, as the baby was pronounced "theirs."

Throughout her pregnancy, Winston was there with her for several long weeks as she drifted in and out of nightmares that she couldn't rid. He liked her—perhaps more than that—but she wanted him only to be a friend, and so he was. And he understood. But no matter what feelings they shared, he knew he needed to be with her as she healed. But she never healed. How could she, how could anyone, especially after all the horrors she lived through? He was also there to help fill in all the pieces of the puzzle that remained, although she had all the clues to solve the murders herself. She had been a chosen pawn in an experiment of evolution. Her bloodline, combined with the fountain's water, would carry the future children of all the rich and powerful who wanted to live forever. And it almost all came to be.

Winston was the wild card, the one person who held the final clue cards and figured it out the night of the convention masquerade dance. He really wasn't one of the owners of the resort, as the media declared. It was a pre-arranged story that the real resort owners agreed to. He, too, was on assignment. He was CIA special task force. He had been assigned to the resort under the pretext of suspicious activity, specifically the comings and goings of certain top government officials and some very rich, very powerful and politically minded business people. It was his role to find answers, just as Jamie was there with McKenna to find answers. Winston discovered the history of the resort from the paperwork and photos that had been secretly kept at the resort. He knew of the underground caves from the 1931 map and knew of the family who had once lived there. He was ready to report all of this when the first murder of Johnny Rains made him pause in the case. He was uncomfortable with the police arriving, especially because of the resort's grandfathered protections, and because of his own investigation. After he watched the security recording of the fight at the pool between McKenna and the tall man, he was intrigued and instructed by higher-ups in the CIA organization to learn more about McKenna and Jamie as they appeared to be more than "just naturists or swingers" at a nudist convention. After he interviewed them both, he returned to the pool area and searched for any clues from the fight. He found the vampire-like teeth, which the tall man must have dropped when he hurriedly left the pool area. He placed them in his locked cabinet and he pieced his own clues together. Alexandria was the same woman in the old photo, so was the tall man in the suit. He determined that they must still live secretly somewhere there on the resort property, and that the caves on the maps may have held that clue.

He searched for the caves using the old maps but so much had changed since the resort was built, altering much of the natural topography, covering up the caves. But one thing kept coming back to him— in order for them to disappear so quickly from the resort area, there had to be a long tunnel leaving from somewhere near the pool area connecting to the caves. He waited till the night of the big convention dance when the pool area was empty of guests to search for the entrance. He took his gun from his office and went directly to the pool's waterfall. After searching the immediate area around the pool, he finally had an idea. It was almost as if it were hiding in plain sight. The waterfall. There, he found it. Behind the waterfall, hidden from normal view, was a wall-like door, blending in color with the rocks. He entered through it just as this family must have used it for their comings and goings.

He was more than surprised when he discovered the tunnel led to a secret experimental lab, but his timing was impeccable as he hid outside the doorway in the shadows and heard the entire conversations between Jamie and the assembled people, including Morbius. When everyone left the lab, he hid against a shadowed wall so as not to be discovered. It was his intent to rescue Jamie and McKenna, but before he could enter the lab, Alexander came in. Winston's gun shot was well timed, killing Alexander, but it also brought Alexandria into the room. After his struggle with her and getting injured, he tried again to save McKenna as Jamie left the room, running after a fleeing Alexandria. He tried, he really tried. But he couldn't. McKenna was dead. And when he finally pulled Jamie from the fountain water, her first and only words were "McKenna...is? McKenna...?" But she knew from his eyes. She knew without being told. She already knew the answer in her feelings. After all, she was a detective. Although she had been brought back from the dead, she died again in that moment, in her heart.

After a brief hospital stay and check-up, Winston had Jamie fly to Washington to meet and discuss the entire events of that night with the special CIA task force team. Because of the sensitivity of the Fountain's discovery, she was informed and required to sign forms that prevented her from ever telling the story of what happened at the resort. No one ever mentioned anything about what happened to Alexandria, or Morbius, or the tall man in the suit, or any of the others she remembered from that night. It was as if they never existed. And maybe they didn't. Or at least she wished they never had. As for the Fountain of Youth, it, too, would be kept a secret. The world must never know it truly existed, or just like she had heard that one fateful night strapped to an operating table beneath the resort, if revealed, it could change the course of mankind. It became something like the classified UFO secrets of Area 51. And she was in the middle of all of this. She, too, became a secret.

When Jamie returned to work as part of the government deal, she was offered a promotion and a salary increase. She declined both. It wasn't what she was all about, and she didn't want it to be a part of her path forward. Chief Johnson was no longer there. The rumor was that he suddenly retired and moved out of state. Jamie didn't know for sure, but felt his sudden departure was all tied to his participation in Project Eve. Officer Dozier was promoted and took his place. He even brought several boxes of donuts in to work on his first day as Chief. And, he ate most of them. He was the last police officer Jamie would have guessed would get the position of Chief. Maybe he just was another puppet in the world where the higher command pulled the strings. It really didn't matter that much to her as she struggled to get her life back in order.

McKenna's death was reported as an act of heroic bravery. A made-up story was circulated that he fought and killed the resort murderer but was killed in the process. The footage from the security cameras at the pool, which Jack Hammer said was part of a movie being filmed, was used as a cover story with some careful editing, taking out the sequence of Jamie saving him. Jamie wanted the truth to come out, but after her meeting in Washington, she understood government protocol and the importance of keeping all of this a secret.

Jack Hammer was interrogated for his role in the convention and affiliation with the resort and was found to be innocent of any of the murders. He was just a carnival-type barker who used fraud and some untraceable money laundering to create the convention. He really knew nothing about the murders or the secrets behind them. Winston even used him to tell McKenna it was a movie scene he was in during the fight at the pool. It was an agreed-to "made-up" story to throw McKenna off and away from his investigation. Hammer was given community service and had to make a documentary movie on helping runaway girls. It changed his life and, rumor has it, he also changed his name. He is known now as Jackson S. Driver, a model citizen with the "S" never being revealed as to what it stood for, but it probably referred to "Screw." Appropriate. Once a carnival barker always a carnival barker.

Jamie did have a series of government-mandated tests performed on her to determine how she survived and healed from her wound. The results were kept secret with the rest of the classified information. All she was told and repeatedly assured was that the baby was hers, produced from the sperm of McKenna during their afternoon lovemaking. However, there was some underlying concern that her DNA was slightly altered by the water's property in healing her wound and saving her life as well as the baby's life. But again, she was assured, and reassured, that all of this change was minimal, and did not affect the baby or herself. In the back of her mind she tried to believe this, but a good detective as she was, she always considered the clues, the facts, and the possibilities.

As time passed, Winston had other out-of-the-area assignments, but he did show up about once a month to visit her. He continued to pop in and out of her life as things slowly returned to "something" she would consider normal. But it never really was. Although her grieving process for the loss of McKenna consumed her, she balanced it with the expected birth of a child.

Whenever Winston visited, they never talked about the experience at the resort; they just spent quiet evenings playing "her," and what became "his," favorite board game, CLUE. She always won, but she felt maybe he let her win at times. He was always a perfect gentleman, never asked her for that long-ago promised dance on her imaginary dance card, nor did she ever see him out of his clothes as she once dared him, and he once promised. They also spent time in her home watching detective and comedy movies while eating lots and lots of popcorn. She craved it during her pregnancy, not really knowing it was McKenna's special "cheat treat." They laughed a few times, especially when discussing a favorite horror movie they watched one night, both concluding there were no real vampires, nor could there ever be any vampires. It was just Hollywood make-believe, and some writer's fantasy. It was the only time they had a conversation that bordered on what they shared in a time gone by and now forever classified deep in both their minds. Maybe they wanted to talk more about it, but they didn't. They even cried one evening watching a romantic movie, maybe it was because of the movie, or maybe it was because of their hidden emotions. Their relationship was destined to always be just close friends. And it was.

As time passed, everything that happened at the resort seemed so long ago, and yet the memory remained fresh, but hidden, in between Jamie's dreams.

These thoughts drifted through her as she dozed in and out of sleep in the hospital room. She felt safe for the first time in a long time. Her son was safe in the nearby newborn nursery and she felt safe in the hospital. But "feeling" and "being" weren't always the same, especially to a detective. Her dreams held realities. Her realities held dreams.

It was shortly after midnight, a few short, yet seemingly long hours since giving birth, that a full moon from the outside hospital window cast a beam of bright light across her totally dark room. The hospital was quiet, and the few late-night, assigned staff members sat half asleep in their stations as they checked their Facebook pages or filled out patient reports. It was like that most nights. Most.

Without a whisper of sound, Jamie's partially closed room door slowly opened, and a mysterious figure stood backlit in the doorway. Silent. Standing.

Staring into the room. Staring towards the bed where she slept.

As the door quietly closed behind, the figure crossed into the path of bright light from the full moon. It was the figure of a man, a handsome man. A dead man. A dead man who had come back to life. Had come back to life to be with her. It was McKenna.

As he approached her bed, his attention suddenly turned as Jamie quietly stepped out of the shadows that filled the room. They both stood and looked at each other, and without another moment, or passage of a lifetime gone by, she crossed the moonlight and into his arms. It was as if this were planned. Without words, her hands reached slowly outward and gently touched his face. It was warm, it was welcoming, it was wonderful. His eyes seemed to glow with a beautiful fire within. Her eyes glowed equally in return. Slowly he took her in his arms and looked deep into her heart. The love between two was now one.

He smiled, as she smiled.

"I've come to see our son," he whispered softly. His words seemed to float across the space between them.

And she whispered back, "I knew you would. I've been waiting for you. I always knew you'd come."

As they drew their bodies closer together, and the space between disappeared, their heartbeats began to race with a passion that was once lost, but now reborn. A passion that only belonged to them, and would now belong to them forever. A passion that came back to life as their lips drew closer.

She smiled, as he smiled.

Jamie slowly opened her mouth and revealed her fangs.

Together, they danced in the moonlight.

Author's Notes and Acknowledgements

The answer is, "Yes." If you read this book first, before reading these notes, you probably have the "same question" I have already been asked by the people who knew I was writing this story. "Yes," adult naturist resorts, like the one I have created in this story, do exist worldwide. And yes, I have done my research with only a notepad and pen. The rest of your questions regarding this "lifestyle" and "my in-depth research" will be left up to your own imagination. Mystery authors want it that way— always leave the readers guessing and looking for clues. And besides, what better way to enjoy "fun in the sun"? But let me remind you, (clue #1) do bring plenty of suntan lotion, and (clue #2) be prepared to make up stories why you don't have visible tan lines!

THE NAKED DEAD is my second novel.

My first novel, *BANG-BANG YOU'RE DEAD,* was a horror/thriller murder mystery, set in a retirement home. In each chapter, the Killer goes from apartment to apartment on a cold, rainy night and has each elderly resident tell his or her life story before deciding whether they live or die. From the feedback I have received, every reader has been captivated by the characters in each chapter. And, as every character shares his or her story, you will learn how their lives were filled with happiness and sadness, joy and pain, the good moments, and the bad moments. You will laugh and may even cry as their stories touch upon your own lives and remind you of people you know and love. But, be prepared for a real roller-coaster ride. The murders are brutal, and the story is chilling. Several readers have told me that they now, because of this book, "double check their locked doors at night," and some even sleep with the lights on. It's exactly the reaction I wanted. However, not everyone may like the graphic killings, but I have described them exactly as I envisioned them. Although it is not intended to be a romance story, you will feel the love these characters have for life, and the love they leave behind as their stories unfold and as the body count grows. ***BANG-BANG YOU'RE DEAD***. As the tagline states, "It's Not a Game." Or is it?

This book, ***THE NAKED DEAD,*** is completely different and yet somewhat similar, all in one. The story also introduces interesting and fascinating characters. Again, an intriguing mystery. Again, a unique—make that, very unique—and unusual setting. Again, killings, but this time fewer killings. An actual romance, and, yes, a lot of nudity, a whole lot of nudity. Just remember, the visuals I leave you with are meant to be filled in with your own imagination. Mystery writers want it that way, after all, we all love a good mystery, especially one in a "bare-all" nudist resort.

Next up. Get ready for another and even more dramatic and chilling roller-coaster reading ride, combining everything I have included in my writing style before, and now adding the amazing talent of an award-winning author, Nathan Squiers, creator and author of best seller "vampire" novels, including the ***CRIMSON SHADOW*** series. I have the honor to announce my collaboration with him on what will be a very intriguing and controversial book.

Nathan and I met at a comic convention where he was a guest author, showcasing his works. I had just finished creating and writing a comic book entitled, ***BLACK MAN WHITE MAN,*** which was for sale at the convention and which Nathan had already bought and read. In my comic-book story, a black police detective goes to sleep at night and unknowingly transforms into a white serial killer who then goes out all night and kills family members and friends of the black police detective. In the morning, our hero, if we can call him that, wakes up to start another day and tries to catch the killer, not knowing he's one and the same. Or, is he? Well, that's part of the mystery, and if you like a good mystery, this story touches all the "hot buttons" in today's racially divided world and will have you asking yourself, "What is the real difference between good and evil?"

When Nathan and I discussed each other's works, we both realized that there was a destiny behind this unplanned meeting, and we decided to collaborate and write my comic book story together into a full-length novel. Like two song writers creating music and lyrics, we are creating words and descriptions and bringing the story to life in a way I cannot fully describe, but I guarantee, it will captivate you, frighten you, and keep you wanting to read more and more until...

The novel's release is planned for later this year. In the meantime, check out his books, as he is one of the most brilliant writers I have ever read. I am so fortunate to have the opportunity to work with him.

And finally, let me thank three very important people who have been with me on my book-writing journey.

First, my editor, Elly Stevens, who worked with me on my first novel, continued with me on this novel and recently completed her own first novel, ***DANGEROUS PASSION***, a contemporary crime thriller. Elly helped guide me through a maze of jumbled words and ideas which danced in my head and somehow came together in both books. Not only is she an amazing editor who knows where all the commas go (I should have paid more attention in English class), but she is a great writer herself adding elements which helped make both stories better. It has been a privilege to have her creatively involved with me, and this finished book is as much hers as it is mine.

Megan Parker is the book designer. Her vision is absolutely "perfect" in creating the cover image which brings the mysterious "killer" to life. She is also an established award-winning writer, creating the **SCARLET NIGHT** series. Megan also owns her own design company, Emcat Designs. She is currently developing the cover and design for the **BLACK MAN WHITE MAN** novel. Besides a good friend, I consider her my "personal guru" in helping me understand the book-writing business, in which she is very knowledgeable.

And finally, and of course, there is one person who I am so thankful to know and have as part of my life. Debbie has been by my side for 45 years of marriage, as not only my wife and best friend, but my confidant who encourages me to follow my dreams. And of all the dreams I ever had, Debbie is my most important dream come true. Together, we have raised a wonderful family and shared exciting adventures and vacations. I don't know where all the years have gone, but I am so happy to have shared them with her. I couldn't imagine anything but that. Describing my unique thinking, she tells everyone we meet and know, "When Joe was born, they threw away the mold." Maybe; hopefully. But I can honestly say that when she was born, she became a real live "angel" who has given me love and inspiration and has held my hand on this most amazing journey called life. Thank you, Hon, I wouldn't be the man I am, without you.

Joe Janowicz